BOUND BY SILENCE

Suzanne Cass

S C
STORM CLOUD
PRESS

To the courageous and selfless firefighters and volunteers who fought the devastating bushfires.

CHAPTER ONE

The wall of lava rolled toward her, a black unstoppable wave. Keira Puana stood, rooted to the spot, watching as her house was eaten alive. A bright-orange flame erupted where the molten rock seeped against one of the wooden pillars, flickering with astonishing speed up the pole and devouring the veranda.

She needed to move, to escape the lava engulfing everything in its path. But it was so surreal, so fascinating, a part of her wanted to stay and watch nature at her chaotic best. She was safe for a few minutes, at least, as she surveyed the scene of destruction from a grassy knoll a few hundred meters away.

Soon, the whole corner of her beautiful house was alive with flames shooting skyward. The large, wooden veranda where she liked to sit and watch the ocean change her moods every morning was now a smoking mess.

An explosion rocked the house, and Keira ducked. It was one of the large, floor-to-ceiling windows blowing out, sending millions of tiny glass daggers skywards. The fire really took hold then, turning the magnificent building into a blazing inferno, the high gabled roof collapsing inwards.

It was nearly dusk, and the flames from her burning house

mingled with the orange glow cast by the eruption, turning the sky a sickly burnt ochre. In the distance, Keira could see the yellow sparks of molten lava, so hot they almost burned her eyes, spewing into the heavens from one of the fissures that'd opened up after the earthquake, only a few hours ago.

It was time to go.

With one last glance backward at the place she'd called home for the last ten years, Keira hefted her backpack higher, and re-adjusted the heavy suitcase in her hand.

Higher ground, that's where she needed to be. Away from the fast-moving, deadly flows slowly filling up the valley. She'd lived on this island for a decade, and of course she knew about the volcanic activity—it was always there, hovering at the back of her mind; their house was built in an area of active lava flows. But the last big eruption had been sixty years ago, and it was easy for people to forget. Volcanoes were a part of everyday life for Hawaiians, but people still thought it would never happen to them.

Until today.

But the eruption wasn't the biggest thing to rock the foundations of her life today.

Her eyes were drawn back to the flaming building.

John was back there in the house.

She'd left him where he'd fallen. Halfway between the lounge room and dining area, in the doorway that adjoined the two rooms.

Her heart had been beating like a native tattoo on a drum as she'd stepped over his body to go out the back door. But she'd refused to look down. There was nothing she could do for her husband now.

Against her will, her mind replayed the past few hours, seeing the scene unfold in vivid Technicolor in her mind.

The scrunch of tires on the gravel driveway had made her look up from the bag she'd been packing. At first, she'd thought it might be the Fire Department coming to tell them to evacuate. She and John hadn't really believed the announcer on the radio earlier, telling everyone in Pahoa to get out while they could. There'd been eruptions before, and they had always been small, nothing to worry about. But today, as she stood next to John on the back step, beside the pristine, aqua pool, and watched in disbelief as lava began to spew into the sky, she knew the man on the radio was right; they needed to get out.

Keira had already started packing some of her belongings, throwing them haphazardly into the suitcase on the bed. She'd padded on bare feet into the kitchen to peer down to the driveway below to see who'd arrived.

Two men stepped out of the car, wearing flawless suits, with black hair slicked back, and quick, shrewd eyes that surveyed the front door of their house. Keira had no time to wonder what *they* were doing here, with lava flows threatening to cut the highway off at any moment, because John had come running from where he'd been watching from the lounge room.

"Hide," he'd grunted roughly, shoving her by the shoulders toward the linen cupboards. His large hands bit into the soft skin of her upper arms.

"What?" she squeaked. "Why?"

"Just do as I tell you."

Keira knew better than to ignore that tone. When John looked at her that way it meant she had to do exactly as he demanded. She scurried down the corridor and hunched into the small space beside the bathroom towels, pulling the door shut behind her just as the front door crashed open.

She'd peeked through the tiny gap between the doors of the linen cupboard but couldn't see anything, as the hallway hid the two men from view. But she could hear them. They were talking in low, unpleasant voices. She couldn't make out their exact words, but the sentiment was clear.

John's voice got louder as he led the men down the corridor, placating them with his normal charm, the way he always talked to these people. All cocky and blustering, but with a subservient edge to his tone. He knew exactly how far he could take it. Just how far he could push them. Usually.

John came into view as he continued toward the kitchen, waving his hands genially in the air. He was wearing board shorts and an old T-shirt boasting a guy surfing a huge wave, with the word Hawaii across the top. Gray hair slicked back, immaculate as always, his tanned arms and legs were impressively muscled. A supremely handsome man. Keira hardly noticed their age difference. Even though he was fourteen years her senior, John could pass for a man half his age.

She put a hand up over her heart, to try and still the erratic pounding. Everything would be all right. John would handle this. He looked at ease, like nothing bad was happening, and Keira wondered why he'd thought there was reason for her to hide. She almost convinced herself that everything was going to be okay, when one of the gang members sidled into view.

He had a gun in his hand, and it was pointed at John's back.

Keira covered her mouth to stop herself from screaming.

"Where's your wife?" the man asked, a cruel edge to his words. His accent unmistakable, the Japanese inflection making his vowels sharp. Keira didn't need to see his face to know those dark eyes would be narrowed and vicious. That his mouth would be curved into a smug half-smile. She knew his face so well. Intimately. Her legs turned to jelly at the very thought of him. And what he might do to her. Had done to her.

"She's in the bedroom," John waved a hand in the general direction, and then turned around. That's when he saw the gun and stopped in his tracks.

Raising his hands in the air, he said, "Now just calm down, Yoshio, we can talk it through. There's no need for this." John grinned, but the smile never made it to his eyes.

"Go find her," Yoshio said, jutting his chin in the direction of the bedroom. He had to be telling the other guy to go and get her, because she heard his footsteps disappearing. Keira's heart stopped. What would happen when they didn't find her in the bedroom? Would they start searching?

"I'm sure she'll be a lot more helpful than you've been." Yoshio waved the gun in John's direction. "Which makes you dispensable, my *friend*."

John's handsome face blanched, and he licked his lips. Then his features hardened. "I lied, Yoshio. She's not in the bedroom. I already sent her away, because of the lava. She's not here. So, it looks like you're stuck with me, after all."

Yoshio jerked his head around to look at the other man as he emerged from the main bedroom. The man nodded, confirming John's words, his narrow face pinched and thin, like a ferret.

"That's not good news, John. Not good at all. I don't like to be swindled." If Keira thought Yoshio's voice had a dangerous edge to it earlier, it was nothing compared to the icy tone he directed toward her husband now.

John twitched under the Japanese man's openly hostile gaze. Something flickered in John's eyes and then he was moving, running, like an arrow shot from a bow.

Yoshio lifted his gun and pointed—almost lazily—then fired. There was a loud bang. Louder than Keira thought should come from such a weapon, but then, she'd never heard a gun being fired before. John fell like a rag doll, limbs loose and flaccid, as if a switch had been suddenly turned off inside his body. The left side of his head was an odd shape, and the cream wall was splattered with bright red flecks. It took Keira a few seconds to realize the red was John's blood.

"What did you do that for?" the other man said, obviously startled.

"I couldn't have him running. I've had enough of his shit." Yoshio took a few steps in the direction of John's body and spat on him, a disgusting wet sound in the sudden silence.

Keira waited to feel something as she watched Yoshio lower his gun and stare down in contempt at the dead man. Waited for the raw anguish to flood her body. Waited for anger and despair to take over. She'd just watched her husband being murdered in cold blood.

But the only emotion that came was relief.

She was finally free.

It was quickly replaced by terror. Was she next?

"We need to find her. She's the only one who can get that money back. She must have access to his bank accounts. Otherwise we're fucked." Yoshio's dark gaze swept around the house. "Go look for her, turn this whole house upside down, if you have to."

"But boss, he said she was gone." The other man wasn't whining, not exactly, but he wasn't happy. "That lava is getting awful close." He indicated out the back window. Keira couldn't see that far, and she wondered exactly what *close* meant. "The road will be cut off if we don't go soon."

"*Baka yarou.*" Yoshio swore in Japanese at the other man.

They stood in a tableau for what seemed like an eon, while Keira held her breath. Yoshio craned his neck to see outside, up the gentle, grassed slope at the back of their house. Whatever he saw out there made him turn and give one final, disgusted look at John's body.

"Let's go." He marched down the corridor and out of Keira's limited gaze, Ferret Face trailing behind him. "Put the word out. Make sure everyone is searching for that bitch. We need to find her. Now," she heard him say as the door banged shut behind them.

Keira's mind returned to her present predicament. She'd thrown the two half-packed bags closed and gotten out of the house as quickly as she could after the men left. Now, she turned and forced first one foot and then the other to move. If she didn't go soon, it wouldn't be only the Yakuza she was fleeing. That lava flow would block off her escape, and she'd be swallowed up just like the house. The idea had a certain attraction. If she just lay down on the grass and let the lava roll over her, it'd be quick, the lava was moving at a fast pace. It would take only seconds for her to be consumed, never to be found. No one would ever know what'd happened to her. But would it be painless? What would it feel like to be swallowed up by one-thousand-degree molten rock?

Keira shivered. Nope, today was not the day to find out.

She headed up the hill and to the left, at an angle away from where the lava was flowing down the valley. There was a road at the top of this rise, and hopefully there might be other people fleeing, just like her. The open grassy areas around the small estate where she and John lived soon gave way to deep, green jungle, but she knew a small path that wound up the hill a little farther on. The other houses she passed were all deserted, most people had had enough sense to evacuate yesterday, after the first earthquake. John had been dismissive of those people, they were all chickenshit, scared of a little eruption. They lived on The Big Island for Christ's sake. Didn't people know that volcanic activity was a part of everyday life? Except this one was different.

Small twigs and leaves scraped the bare skin of her legs below her cut-off denim shorts. At least she'd stopped long enough to pull on a pair of sneakers, so she wasn't traipsing through the jungle barefoot. Keira stopped and rummaged around in her backpack, finally coming out with a black Yankees cap and a bottle of water. She swept a hand through her hair, pulling it back from her sweaty face, so she could put the cap on. Thankfully, she wore her auburn hair short now, bobbed just below her chin, to keep her cooler in the renowned Hawaiian humidity.

After a quick swig from the bottle, she picked up her suitcase and kept going up the hill, following the faint path. Fifteen minutes later, after a hard slog, sometimes dragging her suitcase up and over a fallen log, or swishing between close-growing bushes, she finally stumbled out onto the wide expanse of a bitumen road. Thank God.

Even better, not far away in the distance, was the sound of an approaching engine. Then a large, old, four-wheel-drive truck lumbered into view. As the truck came closer, she could see people squashed together in the front cab, and more people standing up in the box-tray behind.

The truck wheezed to a halt when she raised a hand.

"Jump in the back," the driver said without preamble. A large man, he waved a fleshy hand at the rear of the vehicle. "There's not much room, you'll have to squeeze in somewhere." She wasn't the first person to be caught out by the fast-moving lava, by the looks of it.

Hands came down from the back of the truck to take her suitcase and help her clamber up. She worked her way between the other bodies and found a small spot at the side near the front, where she sat down.

Her fingers grazed the brim of her cap, pulling it even lower over her forehead. She willed her hands to stop shaking, as she clasped them tightly in her lap. Keeping her head down, she curled up as small as she could, drawing her knees into her chest, with her back resting against the side of the truck. A large *haole* was crushed up against her left side. The white man's face was pale and pinched, sweat running freely down his temples. He kept muttering something that sounded like a prayer under his breath. And every time the truck went around a curve, his fleshy shoulder pressed into hers.

It wasn't hard to pretend to be scared. Because she was absolutely terrified. But not for the same reason as everyone else huddled in the back of this vehicle. Would anyone recognize her? Give her game away? She hoped they were all much too focused on saving their own asses. Hoped that no one gave a damn about her. To them, she was just one more woman fleeing this devastating natural disaster.

Still, it was better to play it safe. There were bound to be questions, once this all died down. About John and what happened to him. She needed to remain anonymous, blend in with the crowd. So no one remembered a dark-haired woman escaping on the back of a truck, when the cops finally started asking questions.

She needed to stay away from the cops. But that wasn't her biggest concern. She needed to stay out of the hands of the Yakuza. What had Yoshio said? He wanted her to get into John's bank accounts. What had John been up to? She had a sneaking suspicion she knew. But she was going to be of no help to Yoshio, because John had always kept that stuff to himself. She wouldn't know how to access his bank accounts if her life depended on it. Which was bloody ironic, really.

Where could she go? Her mind raced with possibilities, hopes and wishes. An idea flickered briefly in Keira's mind before she quashed it quickly. There was no way Eva would welcome her. Not when she found out what'd happened to John. There was no way she would allow such scandal to come into her house. Gianna, on the other hand, might offer her shelter, she would probably love the drama of it all. At first. But she couldn't be trusted not to turn Keira in. Just to see more of the drama. Keira nearly groaned out loud. What did they call those kinds of people again? Fair-weather friends? Yes, that was it. And now that she was in a dire predicament, she could see her two friends for exactly what they were. Not real friends at all. All of those girly lunches and dinner parties had only been because of John. Because of his wealth and influence, that drew people like Gianna and Eva and their husbands to him. The false people, who liked to revel in the money and the lifestyle.

Francesca would help her, no questions asked. Her oldest friend on the island lived in a run-down rental on the outskirts of Hilo, but she would stick by her, no matter what Keira revealed. Or would she? Even Fran didn't know her darkest secret. The one thing she never told anyone. Only John was complicit in that.

Keira had learned it was better to stay silent. Silence had become her friend these past years. If no one knew your secrets, then they couldn't hurt you. Not really, not down deep, where it mattered the most.

After nearly an hour in the back of the truck, she could no longer stand being cramped in amongst all the others and asked them to stop and let her off. She made up some vague story about having a friend who lived at the end of the road —even though she had no idea where she was—and no one questioned her. The rest of them were headed into the main township of Hilo, but Keira knew it would be suicide to show her face there. Not with Yoshio and his gang looking for her.

The road was dark and foreboding, but she stumbled along for over half an hour, hiding in the long *pilli* grass growing beside the road whenever a vehicle roared past, until she could go no farther, and picked a long, gravel driveway leading up towards the mountains. There were no lights on that she could see, but she shied away from the dark shape of the house at the end of the driveway. Instead, she followed a dilapidated wooden fence line until she found a huddle of sheds at the bottom of the hill, well away from the main building. A dog had barked in the distance, another reason to stay away from the house. The first shed had been small, and smelled as if animals were once housed in there, so she kept away from that one. But the second was larger and more open. Admittedly, it was filled with towering, metal monsters, but once Keira used the flashlight app on her phone to confirm it was indeed an old tractor and a few rusted car bodies, she found a spot behind an upturned boat where she could sink down onto the ground. Using her suitcase as a support, she leaned backward and finally let go of that steely metal gate she'd shut down over her emotions since she'd seen her husband murdered. The tears came like the breaking of a dam. Floods and floods of them. She held a hand over her mouth to keep her sobs from becoming too loud. If anyone was in the house up the hill, she couldn't take the chance they might hear her.

Some of the tears were for John. For the death of her husband. It was shocking and tragic. But most of the tears were for herself. For the loss of their beautiful house. For the loss of the life she once had. For the fact she had no idea what she was going to do next. Where she would go. How she would survive. She was forty-two years old, and suddenly had nothing or no one left in her life.

Finally, the tears dried up and she was left feeling empty and spent and very, very alone. Keira turned her phone off to save the battery, and drifted into a fitful, uncomfortable sleep.

CHAPTER TWO

Dalton Kealoha squinted against the mid-morning sun streaming through his windshield as he half-heartedly listened to the voice on the radio. He'd heard it all before. The news was broadcasting the eruption warnings over and over on repeat, telling people to evacuate the Pahoa area before it was too late.

He downshifted to take the left-hand turn into his long driveway and switched the radio off, giving an ironic grunt. If people hadn't left that area already, then they were pretty well screwed. For the hundredth time that day he thanked the powers that be his land was up in the hills, well away from the eruptions devastating the lower sections of the island. And he also thanked those same powers that he'd been able to persuade Flora not to take that rental house over near Orchidland Estates. It would've been right in the path of the biggest lava flow. Thankfully, she'd stayed in her little cottage in Hilo, where she and Tavi were safe. He'd had to help out with her rent. Again. To make sure she stayed, because her bastard of a landlord had upped the price. Again. But it was worth it for Dalton's piece of mind. To know Flora and his son were in a good neighborhood, near to friends and family.

The pickup grumbled to a halt as he switched off the

ignition. He ran a hand thorough his hair and blew out a breath. It'd been a long night, and now he was looking forward to a shower and food, then hopefully grab a few hours' sleep.

Bypassing the front steps up to the veranda, Dalton made his way around the side of the house and opened the gate to the backyard. Spike welcomed him home with an ecstatic dance and a grin from ear to ear. Thank God for dogs. They were the only creatures that truly loved unconditionally. He was too tired to take Spike for a run this morning. "I'll make it up to you, buddy," he promised, as he rubbed the dog's soft ears. "Maybe this afternoon. We can run over to Aunty Lei's. Whaddaya think?"

Spike pricked his rusty-colored ears and bashed his tail in response. Spike was a *poi* dog, a mongrel of indeterminate breed. But Dalton loved him as if he were a child. Spike's short fur was a red-ochre color, and he was fast and lean, loved to run nearly as much as Dalton did. He ruffled the dog's head and climbed the wooden steps to the back veranda. The dog wouldn't care where they went, as long as he was with Dalton, and as long as he was on the move, sniffing out an adventure.

That was a good plan; he'd run to Aunty Lei's this afternoon, it was past time he went to see her. And she'd love the treat he had for her. A large burlap bag of passionfruit lay in the backseat of Dalton's pickup. Cane had arrived at work yesterday evening, laden down with the huge stash of *liliko'i*, pushing the bag into Dalton's hands before he could argue. Cane said he and his wife were drowning in them; the vines in their backyard were producing fruit like there was no tomorrow. The passionfruit were a special favorite of his aunt's, so Dalton had accepted the bag, albeit with an ungracious grunt. The man was forever trying to offload fruit and vegetables onto him.

And Aunty Lei would repay the favor; she made the best *liliko'i* butter on the island. His mouth watered at the thought of hot toast with the gooey butter. Then his stomach rumbled loudly, reminding him he hadn't eaten since lunchtime yesterday. He could do with some of the *liliko'i* butter right now. But he'd settle for a couple of sausages fried up in a pan, because that was all he had in the refrigerator.

But first, a shower. He grabbed a clean pair of jeans and a T-shirt on his way through his bedroom and turned the shower on to heat while he stripped off his clothes. The bathroom had been the first thing he'd renovated when he moved into this place four years ago. His grandfather's old house had been practically unlivable back then, and Dalton wondered how he'd managed for those few months it'd taken to rip out the bathroom and refit it with new tiles, a claw foot bath, and a large, glassed-in shower, big enough for even him to fit into.

As he lifted his arm to pull his T-shirt over his head, he winced and let out a grunt of pain. The guy he and Cane had taken down last night had managed to get in a few good punches before Dalton was able to subdue him. He didn't think any ribs were broken. Dalton surveyed the bruising in the mirror. Dark-gray and purple blotches ran underneath his arm and down the left side of his chest. He lifted and lowered his arm experimentally. Nope, not broken, just soft-tissue damage. There was also a bruise darkening his chin, but at least the cut on his lip had stopped bleeding. He was getting too old for this. Today, he was feeling every single one of his forty-three years.

Sam had called him yesterday afternoon, the Hawaiian-Chinese man's lilting voice tight with excitement. "We've got a big'n, Dalton," Sam had exclaimed. "Paul Ohara skipped bail yesterday, the police think he's headed over here, to the Big Island. We need to get him before he hops a ride stateside."

A rush of adrenaline had Dalton out of his chair and pacing the kitchen floor as he listened to his boss.

"Get your butt in here, Dalton. I'm sending you and Cane after him. He's too big a fish for you to handle on your own." What Sam really meant was he wasn't taking any chances on Paul getting away. They needed this bounty; the company was struggling, what with the economic downturn. Even the druggies and the local gun-runners were feeling the pinch. Bail would've been set high for Paul Ohara, he was one of the top dogs in a Honolulu drug gang, which meant the bail company's cut of the bounty would also be high. They'd make more money from bringing this one guy in than they would in a month of bringing in the small-fry, bail-jumpers who were only up for possession, or domestic assault.

Dalton pulled the rest of his clothes off and dropped them in a pile on the floor. Then he stepped into the steaming shower, letting the hot water run over his shoulders as he closed his eyes.

Cane was one of Dalton's best buddies, as well as being Sam's son. It was Cane who'd got him the job as a part-time bounty hunter. Most of the time they worked on their own, but cases like these sometimes called for them to partner up. It'd taken them all night, but they'd finally tracked Ohara down in the small township of Honomu, a little farther up the coast from Hilo.

But he hadn't come easy. It'd been touch-and-go for a while. Dalton had even been tempted to draw his gun, but the asswipe was hiding out in a house full of women and children. Probably did it on purpose for just that exact reason, he knew anyone chasing him wouldn't put the innocents in harm's way. Cane—more prone to hot-headed acts—had drawn his gun and Dalton had to talk him down, before someone got hurt. Cane had a tendency to be a little cocky;

Dalton thought it came from being a *hapa*, or mixed blood, with a Chinese-Hawaiian father, and a Japanese-Caucasian mother. A lot of the older Hawaiians had no problem with being *hapa*, but secretly Cane saw himself as only part Hawaiian, and constantly had something to prove, which sometimes got him into trouble. In the end, Cane used his taser to subdue the wanted man, but not before Dalton crash-tackled him and the guy got a few heavy punches in, in return. Ohara was tough, a street fighter and brawler. Dalton was glad for his Navy training; it'd saved his life more than once, and it certainly helped tonight.

They'd transferred Ohara to the city lockup and checked in to the office early this morning. Sam had been ecstatic with their night's work and sent them both home for a well-earned rest with a slap on the back.

As they exited the office, Cane had asked Dalton, "Wanna go for a beer?" The younger man was clearly still high on adrenaline from the capture.

Dalton checked his watch. "It's only nine in the morning, man," Dalton had chided. "You should get home to your family."

"Yeah, I guess," Cane replied. "You going to stop in and see Flora and Tavi this morning?"

"I might go home and have a shower and catch some shuteye first." Flora probably wouldn't mind, he was always dropping around unannounced. She was used to it. Dalton smiled as he imagined his son's reaction when he saw him walking in through the front gate. His little face would light up like a beacon, and he would run down the path on his three-year-old, tubby legs, to be picked up by Dalton and whirled in the air, yelling, *Daddy, Daddy.*

"You and Flora ever going to get back together?" Cane asked, stopping at the door to his large, black pickup, juggling his keys to get it open.

Dalton forced a smile and replied, "Nah, we decided a long time ago that we were better off as friends." He and Flora had only dated for six months before they decided it wasn't working, but then Flora had announced she was pregnant. They resolved to do the co-parenting thing. And for the most part, it went well. Dalton saw his son nearly every other day, and made sure he was a big part of his life. Sometimes Flora and Tavi even came and stayed with him, after he'd completed the renovations.

"I might ask them to come and spend the weekend on the farm," Dalton mused. "Tavi loves running around with Spike in the backyard, and Flora and I can keep an eye on those pesky lava flows together."

Cane raised a suggestive eyebrow and said, "Sometimes I envy you, man. Maybe I've got it all wrong, living with a wife and kids. You've got the best of both worlds going there." With that, Cane hopped up into his truck and waved out the window as he roared past.

Cane's comment left Dalton wondering. Cane was wrong on one count, he and Flora were not sleeping together, as he'd implied. But was he missing out on something, by living like an eternal bachelor? Sometimes he wondered if his life could be different. If he'd ever meet that one special person he could share his world with.

Dalton shifted position in the shower and began soaping up, washing the sweat and grime and the slight aroma of discomfort from his body. It reminded him of the screams of the terrified kids watching as he took down Ohara. He never understood why these guys used their families as shields. Why didn't they just stand up and take it like a man? Admit they'd done wrong and take their punishment. It rankled Dalton that these men seemed to care so little for their kids, or their wives, or girlfriends, whatever they might be. Why would they put their stupid, pathetic drug habits, or their greedy need for power or money, before the people they professed to love?

He stepped out of the shower and toweled himself off, avoiding the bruised area along his ribs. Dressed in black T-shirt and dark jeans, he left his feet bare as he returned to the kitchen, and found the sausages at the back of the refrigerator. When the sizzle of meat frying in the pan filled the kitchen, he reached in and retrieved a beer from the fridge, leaning back against the counter and downing the cool liquid with a sigh. He closed his eyes and let the smell of the spicy sausages tickle his nose.

But when he closed his eyes, the spouts of gushing, red lava he'd seen on the news yesterday replayed across his mind. Those poor buggers whose homes had been destroyed. Should he be doing something to help? But what? The authorities had warned everyone to stay away from the area. Telling people not to go sightseeing, as they might very well pay with their lives. You couldn't stop a wall of lava in its tracks. The only thing to do was run away. They probably wouldn't be able to rebuild afterwards, either. The whole place would become a black field of barren nothingness. People would not only lose their houses, they might lose their livelihoods, too. He hoped everyone had got out safe, that no lives were lost.

The hairs on Dalton's neck rose up, and he knew Spike was looking at him without even opening his eyes. Sure enough, when he blinked a few times, there was Spike, sitting obediently at his feet on the linoleum floor, those patient, attentive, light-brown eyes staring up at him hopefully.

"Sorry, buddy, I was daydreaming," he apologized, and dumped two cupfuls of dry dog food into the bowl at the back door.

The sausages were nearly done, so Dalton pulled out a plate and cutlery for one. He cut up a whole tomato and half a cucumber, that would have to do for salad. Then he sat down on the top step of the back lanai, Spike lying by his side, and watched the mid-morning sun rise higher in the sky over the jagged mountains that were the backdrop to his little piece of paradise.

Maybe after he'd run the *liliko'i* over to Aunty, he'd take the pickup into town. It'd been a while since he'd been grocery shopping, and the cupboards were decidedly bare. And then he would go and visit Flora and Tavi.

Yes, that was a good plan. But only after he got some sleep.

CHAPTER THREE

Keira stretched out her legs, trying to find a more comfortable position amongst the jumble of old machinery. It stank of oil and grease and dust, and the heat was getting unbearable. The rays of sunshine slanting through the small, high window told her it was around midday. But she needed to stay in here until dark. She couldn't take the risk of being seen. She'd woken up with a crick in her neck and a pounding headache this morning. But at least the fear and exhaustion that'd gripped her last night was fading. Now, she needed to decide what to do next.

In a force of habit, the fingers of her right hand began to play with the silver ring she wore on her thumb. It was her favorite, one of her early designs, and she always wore it. Her finger traced over the intricate filigree and ran over the slight bump of the small topaz stone in the middle. Her birthstone, it was a beautiful, clear blue, like the color of the ocean off Pahoa on a balmy afternoon. She wore rings on some of her other fingers, all of which she'd made herself, but this was her most treasured.

She'd sat in this shed for most of the morning, the metal sides radiating more and more heat as the sun got farther overhead, until it felt like she was in an oven. As the day warmed, the humidity climbed as well, and soon her shirt was plastered to her back with sweat, as streaks of perspiration ran down between her breasts. She combed her fingers through her hair, to tame some of the tangles from sleeping rough last night. But it was no good and Keira gave up trying to smooth it down. Instead she lifted the auburn locks away from the back of her neck, letting the once-immaculate bob sit out in spikes and tufts from the side of her head. An hour or so ago, she'd finished the last drop in her bottle of water, and she wondered if she dared sneak out and try and find a tap. But just as she'd been contemplating her next move, she'd heard a car pull up at the main house and a dog give a few welcoming barks. The owners must've come home. Now she was stuck here until nightfall. Hopefully she didn't expire of heat exhaustion before then.

To pass the time, she began pacing across the small area. Four steps toward the door, then about-face, and four steps back again. She needed to think.

For the past decade, John had always been there. Her rock. Her anchor. He'd always handled the hard stuff. Like the finances, and all the paperwork. It never interested Keira, she was an artist and hated all those kinds of thing with a passion. She would much rather spend her time in her little studio out the back, designing her trademark jewelry. And John encouraged it, he liked the status quo. Liked to be the man of the house, to be the provider. Be in control. He'd often told her not to worry her pretty head about where the money was coming from. He just wanted her to be happy, creating her jewelry, and leave the rest up to him.

But it hadn't always been like that. Before she met John, she'd been more than able to take care of herself. Keira had traveled the world before she came to Hawaii. Had managed to scrape together a living from her jewelry and other ad-hoc jobs, like waitressing and administration. She'd lived in Italy and Scotland. Been to visit her grandparents in Israel, and spent time in Machu Picchu in Peru.

So why had she let John take over her life? It was a question she didn't dare ask herself these days. Because it wasn't going to change anything. He was certainly charismatic, had charmed the pants off her—literally—the first time they met. Handsome and rich, she'd been sucked into his persona like a leaf in a whirlpool.

Suddenly, her phone buzzed in her pocket. She'd turned it back on this morning, but had put it on silent.

It was a text. From her sister, Sierra.

Keira's eyebrows rose as she read the message.

Where are you? Are you okay? I'm in Hilo. Came to see you. But they're saying all of Pahoa has been destroyed by lava. Please let me know you're okay.

Shit, shit, and double shit. Of all the times for Sierra to decide to come to Hawaii. What should she say to her? Where did she even begin?

Keira picked up her pacing again. It'd been nearly four years since Keira visited Adelaide, where her mother still lived. At the same time, Sierra had come over from Kangaroo Island, an hour and a half drive away, to spend a few days with them as well. It was funny, they'd been so close when they were younger. Even though Keira was four years older, she'd taken to Sierra as soon as she was born, had kept her under her wing. Sierra had tagged along, like a little shadow, wherever Keira went. But now, Keira never really knew what to say to her sister, especially after she lost her baby daughter, Grace, in that terrible car accident.

Besides that, Keira had been gone so long, traveling the world for nearly ten years, before finally settling down with John in Hawaii. She missed her sister, and her younger brother, Logan, in an abstract way. Even though they grew up in the same house, it was obvious each sibling had a completely different view of their childhoods. It'd been a long time since she'd ever really thought of them as a family. She and Logan seemed to have been cut from a similar cloth, both feeling the wanderlust, the need to see new places, experience everything life had to offer. While Sierra had stayed at home, become a journalist, got married and settled down. Sierra had seemed like the perfect daughter, staying close by their parents, playing the doting child, unlike her other two siblings. Until her conventional life had been turned upside down by tragedy, and she'd retreated to hide out on Kangaroo Island. Divorced her husband and left reality behind, to go and live in solitude.

Last time Keira had seen Sierra she seemed like she might finally be coming out of her grief and loss, but because Keira didn't want to bring up the painful subject of Grace, there were often awkward silences, which she didn't know how to fill. There had been no new man in Sierra's life back then, and Keira wondered if her sister would ever find someone willing to take on the load of emotional baggage she carried around.

The phone began to vibrate in her back pocket. Shit, who was phoning her now?

Caller ID said it was Sierra.

Keira dithered. What should she do? If she answered, she'd have to make up some excuse not to see Sierra. But if she didn't answer, Sierra would just keep calling. Her sister was nothing, if not persistent. She hadn't become a journalist for no reason. She could just turn the phone off.

Shit.

Eventually the need to hear a friendly voice, to talk to someone and blurt out her problems overrode her urge not to answer.

"Sierra," she whispered into the phone. She had to keep her voice down, didn't want to make any noise.

"Keira?" Her sister's voice was high and laced with panic.

"Where the hell are you? What the hell is going on? Where's John?"

"I'm okay, Sierra. You need to calm down," Keira whispered, feeling her blood pressure rise at the irate tone in her sister's voice. Nice to hear from you, too, she thought sardonically.

"Don't tell me to calm down. We landed here last night and the first thing I see is your bloody face plastered all over the TV news. You need to tell me what's happening," Sierra demanded.

Keira drew in a sharp breath and her guts twisted painfully. "What do you mean, my face is all over the news? You're talking in riddles, Sierra. I have no idea why I'm on TV. I'm fine. You can hear I'm okay, you're talking to me." But her mind was racing. Had they found John's body already? Did the news reporters think she was dead, as well? Or did they think she was missing, perhaps? But no, that was stupid, John's body was covered by a deep layer of lava. No one was going to find him in a hurry. A million different scenarios rushed through her head. And then Sierra said the words that stole the breath from her lungs.

"You're wanted as a person of interest in a murder. They're saying you killed a young prostitute. A revenge attack because she was sleeping with your husband."

"What?" Keira almost screeched the word, then remembered she was trying to be quiet and her hand flew up to cover her mouth. This was insane. She hadn't killed anyone. If anything, she was the victim of a crime. "I didn't murder anyone. You have to believe me," she said in a hoarse whisper. And then it came to her in a moment of brilliant despair. Of course. It was Yoshio. He and his Yakuza mates had framed her, somehow. Blamed a murder on her. It was the perfect way to flush her out. Put her back in the spotlight, where they could get their hands on her.

She let out a little groan and sank to the floor in a limp heap. She could still hear Sierra talking loudly on the other end of the phone, but no longer had the energy or the will to lift it to her ear.

* * *

Spike gave a low growl, his ears pricked up and his nose pointed toward the back door.

"What's up, buddy?" Dalton asked with a yawn. "Don't tell me that pesky cat has dared to show his face again." He chuckled. Spike and the big, orange cat from the neighboring farm had an ongoing feud, where Spike tried to keep him out of the backyard, and the cat smugly wandered along the top of the fence, letting his tail dangle down temptingly, just out of Spike's reach.

Dalton rubbed a hand over his eyes and smothered another yawn. Sleep had been elusive today, even though he was exhausted. He'd tossed and turned for an hour or so, and then given up. A freshly brewed cup of coffee and a run over to Aunty's place might help clear his mind.

Dalton stopped midway through reaching for the coffee beans.

Spike growled again, low and menacing, his gaze trained out the screen door and on the huddle of farm sheds a few hundred meters away, at the bottom of the hill. Spike never made a fuss. Not unless there was something to be worried about.

Putting the beans carefully down on the counter, Dalton retrieved his gun from the special, locked, kitchen drawer, and tucked it into the waistband of his jeans. He slipped on his shoes and grabbed Spike by the collar.

"Easy, boy," he soothed. He didn't want the dog barking and giving him away. Spike was heading straight for the old sheds at the edge of the property. Probably some kid poking around, looking for something to steal. The pair skirted the back yard, hugging the fence line.

As they got closer, Dalton finally heard snatches of sound on the wind. This was what had been upsetting Spike. A woman's voice, holding what sounded like a one-sided conversation. Spike growled again, and Dalton tightened his grip on the dog's collar. The voice was coming from the big machinery shed, a dilapidated, metal building rusting away quietly in the long grass. It was filled with his grandfather's relics, a tractor and other farming equipment he'd used long ago, when this property had been a profitable one. Dalton still hadn't gotten around to clearing out the shed, it was one of the many things on his long to-do list.

Dalton rounded the edge of the shed. The door stood slightly ajar, and the sound of a conversation drifted through the opening. Whoever was in there might think they were being quiet, but they were failing miserably. He eased the gun out from behind him and pushed the door open with barrel of the Glock. Spike started up a mad barking, and Dalton struggled to hold on to him.

Someone screamed, but Dalton couldn't see who it was, the shed was so dark after the brightness of the day. All he could see was an outline of a woman, shadowy in the dimness. What was that in her hand? Was it a gun? He kept the door between him and them, just in case.

"Stop whatever you're doing, and make your way slowly out here, so I can see you. With your hands up," he added.

"Holy shit," came a tremulous woman's voice. "Please don't shoot me."

Spike was still barking madly, but Dalton didn't shush him. Let the woman think his dog was a vicious man-eater. The dim figure swayed towards him.

"Hands in the air," he growled, nearly as deeply as his dog.

She raised her hands slowly above her head, something still clasped tightly in one of them. Then she was coming through the doorway and Dalton backed up slightly so she could stand in the light before him.

"Please don't shoot me," she said again, naked fear on her face. Her gaze flickered between him and his dog, obviously not sure who to be more afraid of. A small pang of shame shot through his gut. He probably looked bloody scary, standing there with a gun pointed at her, and a rabid dog ready to tear her throat out. Her hands, still above her head, began to shake and he could see it was merely a phone held in her left hand. Not a gun after all.

He lowered his Glock slightly and told Spike to be quiet. The dog stopped barking but continued to growl deep in his throat. Dalton could feel the rumble through his hand on the collar.

"What the hell are you doing in my shed?"

"I was…Ah…" She stared at him, eyes wide and stark with terror, unable to form a coherent sentence. Dark-brown eyes, he noted. Striking, even when they were filled with unease. A curtain of auburn hair fell half-way across her face as she shook her head, still searching for an answer to his question.

His gaze took her in, this woman standing in the door of his tractor shed. Long legs were encased in cut-off jeans. Shapely, long legs, lightly tanned, but surprisingly, also covered in scratches, which got him wondering where they came from. Slim hips and waist gave way to a rather nice set of breasts, not at all hidden by the T-shirt that clung to her curves. She was dressed casually, as if she'd been out on a hike, brand new Nikes on her feet. That's when he noticed how disheveled she looked, as if she'd slept all night in his shed. Sweat stains marked her shirt, and her dark hair was rumpled and untidy.

"Shit," he swore softly under his breath. It couldn't be. He recognized this woman. Had seen her on Sam's list this morning when they'd returned to the office. She was wanted as a suspect in a murder case. What the hell was she doing in his backyard shed? His grip tightened again on the gun. If she was wanted for murder, she might be more dangerous than she looked.

A sound came from the phone still held above her head, and Dalton realized someone was still on the other end.

"Give me that," he demanded. "Slowly," he cautioned as she hurried to hand it over. The garbled voice of another woman, high-pitched and furious, was cut off mid-sentence as he pushed the End button. He turned the cell off and slipped the phone in his pocket. The woman's gaze followed his movements, as if she were desperate to get her phone back. Too bad, he thought.

"Well, come on then," he urged. "I haven't got all day." Even though he now knew who she was, he wanted to hear her story. How was she going to try and talk her way out of this predicament?

"Is your dog going to bite me?" she asked, her eyes fixated on Spike.

"Not if you answer my questions," he replied.

"Um…I got lost. I was out here last night looking for my friend's place and got lost in the dark. And next thing I knew, I was here. So, I thought it was prudent to stay put." Her voice still shook, but the fear in her eyes receded. Slowly, she lowered her hands as she spoke, and stood up a little straighter, seemed to gather herself, as if pushing the fear away.

"Mmhmm." Surely, she didn't think that explanation was going to fly? He wanted to ask her why she didn't just come straight to his house looking for salvation, but he kept his mouth shut.

"I didn't mean to intrude. But my house was destroyed in the eruption. You know, the lava flow over at Pahoa?"

Of course he did. Everyone on the island knew. He nodded

his head in reply, not giving away that this part of her story surprised him. If it were true. What was she doing? Playing the victim card? She suddenly went up in his estimation. He liked a woman who could think on her feet. Even if she had to lie through her teeth to do so.

"I was on my own, when the evacuation order came," she continued, her voice taking on a slight breathy quality. "I didn't know what to do. My husband, John, wasn't at home. So, I took what I could and hitched a lift up into the mountains." Dalton watched as she licked her lips, her tongue darting in and out. Something stirred in his groin. He had no idea if this story was the truth, or even a half-truth. It could be. Just because she murdered someone, didn't mean she also wasn't fleeing from the molten lava. He let her continue.

"I've got a friend who lives somewhere farther up this road, like I said before. I was on my way to their place, and I got lost in the dark. If you just point me in the right direction, then I'll be out of your way." She took a small step towards him.

Did she really think he'd believe her little story? But he'd play along for a while longer, to see where she was taking this. Catch her out in her lies. Call her bluff.

"Oh, I see. What's your friend's name? I know just about everyone who lives on Kilani Road. Maybe I can give you a ride up there." He lowered the Glock, so it was pointing at the ground, and told Spike to sit, hopefully putting her more at ease. Hoping she would let her guard down.

"Oh, there's no need to do that." She took another small step towards him, biting her bottom lip. Her teeth were straight and white against the plumpness of her mouth.

"I don't want to be any bother. I can see you're a busy man." Another step and she was within touching distance. The thing that'd stirred in his groin woke up and gave a growl at her proximity. She was a beautiful woman, he couldn't ignore that. Especially not when his body was reacting to her the way it was.

Another step and she was mere inches away, staring up into his face, lips slightly parted, desperation in her dark eyes that were fixed on his.

"What do you say? Point me towards the road. I'll take my stuff and go. Just let me go, and it'll be as if I was a dream. Like I was never here." Without him even realizing, one of her hands came up to rest lightly on his chest, just above his heart.

He could feel the heat of her through the palm of her hand. Dalton was frozen to the spot. There was something about her, something in him that responded to her. A subtle air of heartbreak surrounded her. A sudden deep yearning to lean in and taste this woman warred with the much more logical voice of reason, telling him she was treacherous.

Spike gave a whimper of unease. Dalton shook his head. What the hell was he thinking?

He was thinking with his dick, a small voice said in his head. And he'd almost let it win.

"Lady, I don't know what you're up to, but you're coming with me. We're going to have a little conversation with the local police."

"No." The cry of despair left her lips even as she turned to run.

Really? She was going to try and run away? From him? Again, that glimmer of respect ignited in his chest. It took some courage to run away from a menacing man all dressed in black with a gun in his hand. She must indeed be in trouble to attempt escape.

She was fast. It took him by surprise how quickly she sprinted up the grassy hill toward his house.

Shit. He tucked the gun back in his waistband and took off

after her. His running muscles took over as he pumped his legs, sprinting hard. Holy crap, it was taking longer than he thought to catch her, she was nearly halfway up the hill now. Spike was running by his side, thinking this had turned into a game. He gamboled after the woman, and then came back to him.

Dalton gained on her, but much more slowly than he would've liked. Now, he could hear her sucking in great breaths as the hill steepened, but she never broke stride. She must be a runner, as well. And a fit one, at that. The grass was long and lush here, and finally she half-stumbled, feet caught by the strands of *pilli* grass. Regaining her feet, she kept running, but the slight pause was all he needed. He dived and took her down in a tumble of arms and legs. The soft grass broke their fall, and she grunted as he landed on top of her. The bruises on his ribs sent sharp knives of pain through his side, and he let out a curse.

Breathing hard, he pinned her arms and lay on top of her, trying to get his breath under control. She squirmed beneath him, her hips and legs grinding into him. Suddenly, her breasts were pushed into his chest as he leaned on her hard to stop her escaping. A bolt of heat ignited in his stomach and he stilled. Her body was firm and taut as she fought him, but he could also feel every one of her luxurious curves beneath him.

And his body reacted, his cock hardening in an instant. Holy crap, this was *not* what he needed.

This is just like bringing any other felon down.

"Stop resisting," he grunted.

As if his words had pushed a button inside her, the woman suddenly went limp and stopped fighting. But that was almost worse, because now he could feel the soft mounds of her breasts as he crushed himself down on her, and the tops of her thighs, of those oh-so-long-legs settled against his.

She turned her face to look up at him. "Please don't," she said hoarsely.

Was that tears in her eyes? Shit.

"Please don't turn me over to the cops."

He hated it when women cried.

"Get up," he said, standing up over her and then hauling her up by her hands until she stood next to him, eyes red-rimmed and tears streaking down her face. But at least she remained compliant now. What the hell was he going to do with this woman?

Technically, she wasn't a bail jumper, so Dalton didn't have any jurisdiction to bring her in. But she didn't need to know that. Technically, he should call Joe Chin and get him out here in a squad car to come and arrest her. But there was nothing to stop him from making a citizen's arrest and taking her in to the Hilo police station himself. Which he might well do. But first of all, he was going to get to the bottom of her story.

CHAPTER FOUR

Keira swiped at her tears as she walked in front of the man with the gun toward his house. How humiliating. She hadn't meant to burst into tears like some weak, terrified, little girl. Usually, she was much stronger than that. Not allowing her emotions to show. John had taught her that. It went easier if you didn't show any fear or revulsion on your face. If you pretended nothing affected you. That way, they couldn't hurt you, because they never really knew what was going on inside your head.

Keira blamed the events of the past twenty-four hours for her breakdown. It'd all been too much, and this man pointing a gun at her and telling her he was going to hand her over to the cops was the absolute last straw.

Her mind tumbled, grasping for ideas on what to do now.

John.

Oh, Jesus.

John was dead. She had to keep reminding herself. It was so hard to believe he was no longer a controlling force in her life. She'd cried for him last night, but these tears weren't for him today, they were for her. What she was feeling now wasn't an ache for his absence. No, she didn't miss him at all. There was no love left inside her for that man. Instead, there was uncertainty and dread at how she was going to cope without him. How was she going to get out of this mess he'd dropped her in?

She sucked in some of the humid, mountain air, still recovering from her race to get away. At least the short walk up the hill was allowing her to regain her composure. Once they reached the back door, she would have her game face back on. Plus, these extra couple of minutes were giving her much-needed time to think. To find a way out of this predicament.

Chancing a quick glance backward, she caught the man's eye.

"Keep moving," he growled. "No funny business, either."

The guy was dressed in black. Keira nearly snorted at the ridiculous stereotype. But then again, she had to grudgingly admit, black suited him. Made him look dangerous and barely controlled. Even in her terrified state, while he'd pointed the gun at her as she stood outside the shed, she couldn't help but notice how his biceps bulged beneath the fabric of his T-shirt. He looked like he knew how to handle a weapon. And there was a newly healed cut on his lip, and a bruise on his chin, as if he'd been in some sort of fight. Just her luck to stumble into the backyard of the one man who looked like he belonged in an episode of *Criminal Minds*. He could pass as one of those sexy cops who liked to skate the fine line of not playing by the rules. The ones who would do anything to catch their man.

He could do with a haircut, she thought idly. His long, black hair hung down to the nape of his neck, surfer style, slicked back by a rough hand run through it every now and then. And those eyes, dark as coal, had burned right through her.

She'd noticed all of this at first glance, but then had been distracted by the gun. Now, with her quick look back, she discovered a rough, three-day growth covered his face, and there were tense, tired lines bracketing his eyes. Perhaps he wasn't quite as masterful as she first thought.

None of that mattered, anyway. What really mattered was finding out what this guy wanted from her. Finding a chink in his armor that she could exploit, so she could get away. If he turned her into the cops, she was as good as dead.

They reached the bottom of the back steps and the guy motioned for her to keep going.

"The back door's unlocked. Go in and turn to your left. Sit down at the table, with your hands spread out on top, so I can see them." His voice was gruff and held no softness, as if she were some kind of dirty delinquent, beneath his contempt.

Really? This was getting more and more like an episode of some crime show, with every word that came out of his mouth. She didn't want to go inside—it'd be harder to escape —but she didn't have any other options. So, she climbed the wooden steps up onto the small lanai, noting the two comfy-looking cane chairs and a small table. They were positioned to take in the amazing view out over the valley, and she could imagine sitting there, sipping a peppermint tea and appreciating the beautiful Hawaiian vista.

Inside, she turned left as she'd been told, to find a small dining room, with table and chairs, just as he said. But when she studied the furniture she was hit by a bolt of surprise. The room was tastefully decorated. Simple and functional in its style, but it was the gorgeous furniture that had her stopping in her tracks.

At first glance, the chairs looked to be made of simple, solid wood. But as she reached down to pull one out, she noted the fine scrollwork of leaves and vines carved into the back of each one. They looked old, too. Perhaps vintage, or even antique. The table was wood as well, smooth and highly polished. A chest of dresser drawers stood proudly up against one wall. The design looked to be of the popular *koa* leaf, which meant it was probably built of *koa* wood. All obviously Hawaiian, and all restored with a loving hand.

Keira glanced back at the tall man standing right behind her, waiting for her to sit down, a frown darkening his brows. Had he restored all this furniture? Now was not the time to wonder. She needed to figure out what he knew and get free of this mess.

The guy in black moved agitatedly behind her, so she pulled out a chair. How much did he know? Had he watched the news last night? Seen she was a wanted felon? Or did he believe her story, that she was a trespasser with a bad sense of direction? She'd have to play her cards close to her chest, not give anything away.

Sierra's phone call worried her. Apart from the fact her sister was now suddenly on the island—which was a whole other can of worms in itself—if what Sierra said was true, and Keira was now wanted for murder, then things had escalated wildly since the lava claimed her house last night. Not only was she being hunted by Yoshio, but it seemed the police wanted to talk to her, as well.

Sierra had also mentioned she was here with a man. A *friend*, she called him. Sierra was too agitated to give her much information, all Keira knew was that his name was Reed and he was a cop back in Australia. Had Sierra finally found someone? If it was true, it was a small ray of hope in her otherwise bleak world right now.

The man holding her captive now also sat down beside her at the table. "Why don't we start this off on the right foot? My name's Dalton Kealoha. I own this house and the sheds you were hiding in. This is Spike, and he's normally quite friendly." He let the unsaid sentiment hang in the air—*unless you're an uninvited stranger on my property.*

Keira decided to tell him as much of the truth as she was able. Her brother had always told her, if she was going to lie, stick as close to the truth as possible. "I'm Keira." She omitted her last name, because John Puana was well known. He owned the largest real estate company on the Big Island, patronized by many celebrities and rich moguls looking for luxury properties. Had his body been found yet? Or would it remain forever buried in the black lava? His disappearance might not have been noted yet. Which might give her the time she needed to get off this island. Somewhere she could never be found.

"And what I told you back there was true. I got lost last night and ended up in your shed." When he didn't answer, she was emboldened to add, "Actually, my bags and stuff are still down there. Do you think we can go and get them?" She went to stand up, but a large, strong hand on her shoulder prevented her.

"I don't think so." Those dark eyes bored into her, until she sat slowly back down. "So, you're sticking to that story, are you?"

She nodded, keeping her eyes wide and innocent. "Yes, my house was destroyed last night. Go check it out on the news, if you don't believe me."

"Mmhmm." He removed his hand from her shoulder and put it on the tabletop, but his penetrating gaze never left her. "You may well be telling the truth on that count. But why don't you tell me about the other things you've been up to recently? Like, oh, I don't know, perhaps killing some poor girl down in Hilo."

Keira sucked in a sharp breath. Shit. He knew.

Keep calm. It was the only way. She needed to convince this Dalton guy she wasn't a threat. "I didn't do that," she stated emphatically. "I couldn't do that. I mean…I would never kill anyone. It makes me sick just to think about it. I don't have it in me."

"Really?" His snort of contempt was loud. "They said you found out she was your husband's mistress and went down to have a *chat* with her. Perhaps it was a mistake. Perhaps you didn't mean it." His voice was low and calm, as if he were talking about an everyday event, something that might happen to anyone. "A little accident. A little slip of the hand. A push here, a shove there."

Who was this guy? If she didn't know better, she'd guess he was a cop.

"You'd be surprised what some people are capable of in the heat of the moment. I've seen it with my own eyes," he continued flatly.

And that confirmed it. He must be a cop to be talking like this. This was her first time on the wrong side of the law. She had no knowledge, no experience on how to cope with this new turn of events. She searched the recesses of her mind to come up with an answer. And came up with a blank.

He stared at her, those dark eyes glittering like obsidian glass.

By the look on his face, if she tried anything but the truth, it might be dangerous to her health. The only thing in her arsenal of ways to manipulate a man was the sex card. But this guy wasn't going to be swayed by that. It hadn't always been that way. It'd become her coping mechanism over the years, however, both with John and with the men he forced her to entertain. If she refused to do what John wanted, the consequences had often been violent and swift. She'd learnt that to keep him happy, she had to keep the men he hosted happy. Yoshio had been one of those men who'd taken what she'd offered.

A shudder ran through her at the thought of Yoshio.

Keira cast a glance up at Dalton's face. Was this man anything like Yoshio? Did he have depraved needs as well?

Did he view women as toys, something to be used at will?

There was no way of knowing; she'd only met the guy five minutes ago. Searching his eyes for the answer wasn't going to help, because she knew people could hide their demons deep. It was probably wishful thinking, but there was something different about him. An aura of integrity. He held himself still, watching her, waiting for her answer. Broad shoulders relaxed, one strong arm loosely draped over the chair back, the other resting lightly on the table. He exuded power, but his power was reined-in, controlled, like a lion on the prowl. Her gut told her she was safe with this man. Perhaps she'd have to trust her gut this once.

Perhaps it was time for the truth.

She met his eyes. "I didn't kill anyone. I promise."

One dark eyebrow twitched at her words, but he didn't say anything, waiting for her to continue.

"But I think I know who did."

Both eyebrows lifted at this comment.

"I think I've been framed," she continued in a hurry. "By the Yakuza."

Dalton let out a loud, sharp laugh. "Really?" His eyebrow still quirked upwards in amazement. "Well, of all the things you could've said, I have to admit I wasn't expecting that. Do go on." He didn't even try to hide the mirth in his tone and Keira twisted her fingers together. She was telling the truth. How dare he mock her?

"It's complicated," she said in a careful, measured tone. "But the Yakuza are after me. They think I can give them something my husband stole." She was suddenly glad she'd decided to leave her wedding band on. It'd help corroborate her story. She'd tossed up taking it off, to help her flee incognito. Thank Christ she hadn't thrown it into the long grass by the roadside, as she'd first thought.

"Oh, right." The smile still turned those serious lips up at the corners. "So, they what? They killed a girl just so they could frame you? And then? What's going to happen next? If the police think you killed her, you'll end up in a jail cell. How are the Yakuza going to get at you there? Are they going to bust into the Hilo courthouse and break you out?"

He was talking like she was some kind of simpleton. An amusing little distraction. She hated being underestimated. Hated that look in his eye. One that said she was just a stupid woman, and what would she know. Well, she knew plenty.

"Yes. No. I don't know. What I do know, is they're trying to flush me out. And this seems like a good way to do it." She sucked in a deep breath, wanting to calm her spiking heart rate. A sudden idea occurred to her. "Maybe they have a corrupt cop in their pocket."

His face hardened as she said this, obviously not liking what she was inferring.

She decided to drive the point home. "Who knows, maybe they're all corrupt. Are you one of them? Are you a corrupt cop, too?" She was sounding slightly hysterical now, she knew that. But couldn't seem to keep her voice down. In a fit of rage, she stood up, knocking the chair behind her over with a bang.

Faster than she thought possible, Dalton was also standing, towering over her, his face hard and ruthless, mere inches from hers. Now her racing heart rate was not only caused by her outrage. His presence, looming over her so solid and so… masculine, was doing all kinds of things to her stomach. Setting it aflame. She could see the cut on his lip, red and slightly bruised.

"I'm not a cop," he said steadily. "But the ones I know are all loyal and do a great job. They all put their lives on the line every day, for people like you."

He was mad and she suddenly felt contrite. "I didn't mean —"

"I'm sure you didn't," he growled. "Now, sit down."

Her remorse fled, replaced by more anger. Why should she do what he said? He didn't believe her. How else was she going to convince him? John was dead. Yoshio was after her. If this guy didn't believe her, then she didn't have a snowball's chance in hell with the police.

The prickle behind her eyelids was back. No, she wasn't going to cry. Not twice in one day. But a tear ignored her order and overflowed onto her cheek.

"Shit, not again," she heard him mutter.

CHAPTER FIVE

Was this woman for real? Did she somehow know that a crying female was his special kind of kryptonite? It took all his effort not to reach out and wipe that tear away. Not to take her into his arms and stop acting like an asswipe. He could've handled her a little more gently. But here he was, pretending to be the bad cop, with no good cop in sight. What'd got hold of him? She was affecting him, he could admit it now. And the tough-guy act was a form of protection. He couldn't let it show, how much he wanted to touch her silky, brown hair, to pull it away from her eyes, so he could see straight into them.

And right now, those pretty, brown eyes were looking up at him, emotions firing through them. Mostly there was outrage and resentment. She was angry at him. Fair enough. But there was something else as well. A question, a fragility that belied that scowl she was directing at him.

What the hell was he doing? She was a married woman—the wedding ring on her finger at least confirmed that part of her story—and here he was having lustful thoughts about another man's wife.

He also noticed she had many other rings adorning her fingers as well. Mostly silver, with intricate designs. They suited her long, slim fingers. There was more silver jewelry around her neck, too. A large circular mandala hung off a long chain, dangled over her collarbone, with what looked like one of the native plumeria flowers in the center.

He shook his head, wondering why he was noticing the woman's jewelry, then bent down and righted her toppled chair. Time to cut to the chase. "I'm not a cop. But I do work as a bounty hunter."

"Oh, shit," she said, and sat down heavily.

Shit exactly, he thought. He had to give her credit, that was some special story she'd spun for him. Of course, he didn't believe it. It was completely laughable. But he had to give her merit for coming up with such a far-fetched idea.

"I'm fucked then, aren't I?" Her shoulders slumped and she wouldn't look at him.

Captain Joe Chin wasn't corrupt, that much he was sure of. The man had been a cop for over thirty years, had an exemplary career. Joe wouldn't have issued a *person of interest* warrant for Keira if he wasn't damn sure it was correct.

Dalton was training to become a private detective. It was Sam's vision to branch out, make the company more versatile, and Dalton had jumped at the chance to add private detective to his resume. He was in the middle of a four-year criminal justice degree that would help him achieve the career milestone. So, he had a good handle on how the whole system worked. And he also had a good working relationship with most of the cops at the Hilo station.

"I wouldn't say fucked, exactly," he said gently. "But you have to admit, that was some pretty tall story you just fed me. I'm sure if you're as innocent as you say you are, then a quick trip to the station in Hilo will clear all this up. Won't it?"

"No, it won't," she replied. There was a heaviness in her voice, resignation. "Can I have a glass of water?" she asked. "My bottle ran out earlier this morning, and it was damn hot in that shed."

"Sure. As long as you stay right there." He stood up, but she made no move, just stared blankly out the window, hands folded in her lap. He noticed that her fingers were unconsciously playing with one of the many silver rings on her hands, almost as if it were a comfort to her. There was no way he should be feeling like a bad host. He'd caught this woman trespassing on his property. She had an arrest warrant out on her, and she was feeding him some dodgy, bullshit story. So, why was he feeling like he was the one in the wrong?

A memory sparked somewhere in the back of his brain. Of a girl with similar, dark-auburn, hair and soulful, brown eyes. Jaimie had been his best friend all through high school. They'd only ever been friends, had never taken it beyond that, but he'd loved her like a sister. Jaimie had the same air of sensuality mixed with vulnerability that Keira did. It'd attracted the guys like bees to honey. And Jaimie's problem had always been her inability to say no. Dalton had tried his best to protect her, but as they got older and graduated school, he saw less and less of her. He knew she'd gotten mixed up with a few shady characters, but he'd never guessed how deep she'd gotten into drugs and alcohol until she turned up on his doorstep one day, begging for somewhere to stay.

Of course, he took her in, and she went to rehab and got cleaned up, seemed to be on the right path again. So much so, she got a job and moved into a shared house he'd found, with two other girls. But two days after her twenty-first birthday, her roommate had called Dalton, frantic and crying down the phone. By the time he got there, it was too late. Jaimie was dead from an overdose.

Jaimie had been so beautiful, had so much to live for, it was such a waste. And Dalton had never forgiven her. Or himself.

If only he'd tried harder, kept more of an eye on her. Her death had driven him to join the Navy. He had to get out of LA, get away from his own dark thoughts, and do something useful with his life.

This woman had that same fragile beauty, with those dark demons swirling inside. Just like Jaimie.

He handed her the water silently and watched as she drank greedily. She certainly hadn't been lying about being thirsty. His gaze was drawn to her throat, long and graceful, as she tipped her head back to drink. His eyes followed the curve of her throat down over her collar bone, exposed by the low-necked T-shirt. Tempting, tanned skin disappeared beneath the fabric and then his eyes landed on the swell of her breasts, as they rose and fell with each swallow. Holy crap, he needed to look at something else. He quickly raised his gaze to where her short hair grazed the top of her shoulders as she stretched her head back, brushing against the back of her neck. It looked soft, and he wanted to reach out and touch it, to feel the silky strands between his fingers.

She put the empty glass on the table and turned to glare at him, and he knew he'd been caught staring.

"Come on, let's go," he said more gruffly than he intended. He'd made his decision, there was no point delaying it. And watching her doing something as simple as drink a glass of water was screwing with his head. He needed to get moving, get her out of his house. "My truck's out front." He indicated toward the door.

"What about my stuff? It's all still down in the shed."

He weighed that up for a couple of seconds before shaking his head. He wasn't taking the risk of her making another break for it on the way back down the hill. He might not catch her this time. "I'll bring that in later," he said.

His plans to go and visit Aunty were now in ruins. But maybe if he got this woman in to police lockup soon, he might have time to check in on his antique shop in town. It was a little side hobby of his, and his grandfather's money had helped him fund his passion. He hadn't been in for over a week. Sylvia was more than capable of running it without his input, she had a skillful knack of knowing just how to arrange each individual piece of furniture or artwork, so the shop looked elegant and uncluttered, to show everything off to the best advantage. But Dalton still liked to go in, run his hands over the aged wood, feel the history, each piece revealing little tidbits about the people and places it had inhabited before. The Hawaiian vintage pieces were fast becoming his favorite, and he loved to spend the hours he wasn't out hunting bail jumpers in the warehouse at the back of the shop, restoring the old, tired pieces, bringing them back to life.

Afterward, he would pop over and see Flora and Tavi before his son went to bed. That thought buoyed him and he became impatient to get going.

"Can I least have my phone back?" Keira was glaring at him accusingly. It was almost a relief to have some of her feistiness return. The quiet, defeated Keira had tugged at his heart strings. He'd almost forgotten about the cell, tucked in his back pocket. He could see no harm in giving it back to her.

"Leave it turned off," he said, handing it over. As he did so, their fingers brushed together. A sizzle of heat burned his hand and kept going up his arm. She snatched her own hand away and gave him an indecipherable look out of the corner of her eye. Had she felt it too? What was that?

"Move," he said brusquely to cover...whatever it was that'd just happened.

She stepped into the hallway and toward the front door. As Dalton followed, he had to mentally re-direct his gaze away from her swaying hips.

Mind on the job, Dalton. What was with him today? He'd

taken dozens of people into custody before—hundreds even —some of them women. He'd always remained cool and aloof. Professional. Treated them like any other felon. In all his four years of working as a bail bondsman, he'd never wanted to reach out and touch an offender's hair, for Christ's sake. And he'd never considered—not even once—they might be innocent. His job was to bring the person in. It was the cops' and the lawyers' job to prove whether they were guilty or not.

So why was he considering Keira's words? Worrying at her comments like they were a sore tooth?

He grabbed his shoulder holster from a hook near the front door and put it on as they walked toward his car, slipping the gun in so it sat snugly under his arm. He was licensed to carry at all times, so it wouldn't matter if his gun was on show for anyone to see. It might even be an added deterrent to keep Keira from trying to run again.

"Wait there," he said, as she stopped next to his pickup. He reached past her and unlocked the passenger door and then waited while she got in. His truck was high off the ground and she had to try twice before she managed to hoist herself into the seat. His hand was twitching, wanting to give her a boost, but he held it back. And then, all of a sudden, those long, golden, tanned legs were unfolded in front of him, as she stretched them out and got comfortable in the vehicle. He shut the door quickly, but it didn't help, the image was burned into his mind.

He stalked around to the driver's side, ready in case she made a break for it. But she sat there, docile as a mouse, which surprised him. She didn't look at him as he jumped in the other side, kept her gaze directed straight out the front windshield. He started the pickup and took off down the driveway. Even though it was just after mid-day, the day was gray and lifeless. Clouds of ash from the eruptions filled the sky. Up here on the mountain the air was clean and fresh, but Dalton knew the closer they got to town, they might be able to smell the putrid stench of sulphur and other noxious gasses that would be blown by the prevailing winds over the town.

"You're making a big mistake," Keira said quietly.

He didn't answer, just pushed his foot harder on the accelerator pedal. The faster he got this woman into the lockup, the sooner he'd be able to clear her from his mind.

It was a twenty-minute trip into Hilo, and the traffic should only be light at this time of the day. He could have her into the station and out of his life in less than half an hour. He turned out of his driveway, negotiating the familiar winding road with ease. A few minutes later he came upon a slow-moving car and had to slow right down himself. It was a large, dark sedan, driving slowly, cruising down the road. Probably a bunch of sightseers, tourists who'd gotten lost. Dalton's house was on the outskirts of Waiakea Forest Reserve, and some people thought they could get into the reserve this way, but the main entrance was clear around the other side of the park.

The car was still going slow, even as Dalton edged closer to it, impatient. He didn't want to get stuck behind this tourist all the way into town. But it was a winding road, and there weren't many passing opportunities. He clenched his fists on the wheel and settled in to wait. Keira said nothing, just continued to stare out the side window, watching the thick jungle flash past as they drove down the hill.

A few minutes later, Dalton's patience was wearing thin with the car doing about half the legal speed limit in front of him. He was thinking about flashing past this car, double lines be damned, when another big, black sedan barreled up the road going the other way. This one looked identical to the one in front, only it was doing double the speed limit, not half.

"What is it with crazy people driving black sedans today?" he muttered, half-under his breath.

"What did you say?" Keira's head snapped around.

He heard her sharp intake of breath and glanced her way. Her face had gone pale, as she leaned forward to peer through the windshield.

"It's them," she said, her words barely a whisper.

"What?" Had this woman gone as crazy as the slow driver in front of them? "Who do you mean by *them*?"

"It's them." This time her voice was more of a scream and she pointed at the car in front. "Yakuza."

Dalton looked to where she was pointing, and could see a man's face staring intently back at them from the backseat. Then the guy raised a weapon. Holy crap.

"Hang on," he yelled. He slammed on the brakes and Keira screamed in fright. The pickup slid to a screeching stop, smoke converging around the car as the brakes locked up. The sedan in front did the same, coming to rest sideways, across both lanes, blocking the road. A man dressed in a black suit got out of the car and swung toward them, the gun still held firmly in his hand.

"Get down," he commanded, and Keira ducked her head under the dash. At least she was good at following commands when they mattered. Dalton wrenched the wheel around and put the pickup into first gear, intending to swing the car back up the road and take off.

The other black sedan cruised over the low rise behind them and came to a scudding stop a few hundred meters away. Sideways across the road, same as the car in front. Effectively hemming him in. Trapping them. Another guy in a black suit—what was it with the guys and their black cars and black suits?—stood in the road, weapon trained on them.

What the fuck was going on here? It'd been five years since

he left the Navy. But working as a bounty hunter had kept his skills honed, his senses sharp. He knew he was going to need all that and more to get out of this predicament.

And the worst part. Keira had been right all along. He owed her an apology. But that would have to come later. When they were somewhere safe.

"What are we going to do?" Keira had popped her head up from under the dashboard. Her face was a mask of terror. That was a good question, and he mulled it over as he sat, letting the car idle quietly.

"Get out of the car with your hands up," a voice commanded. This was from a third man who'd slowly unfolded himself from the backseat of the car in front. He wasn't pointing a gun at them, he was leaving that to his associate. The new guy was wearing a gray suit—wonder of wonders—and was standing in the middle of the road, all arrogant, as if it were a foregone conclusion that Dalton and Keira would do whatever he told them to. As if no one ever dared to do anything else.

"I just want the woman. If you hand her over, you will be free to go."

Dalton snorted. He very much doubted that to be the truth. The man had a sharp, elongated face, with Asian eyes that narrowed even further as he stared at Dalton though the windshield. All three men were of Japanese descent. But were they actually part of the famed Yakuza? He glanced over at Keira and she shook her head wildly, eyes stark with fear.

"No. Please no," she pleaded. As if she really thought he might do it. Give her to them. Perhaps another man might, to save his own skin. But today was her lucky day, because he wasn't about to turn anyone—let alone her—over to these bastards.

"Hang on real tight," he said in a low voice. "This is going to get rough." Then he gunned the pickup, straight toward the edge of the road, into the thick jungle hemming them in on both sides.

A bullet slammed into the rear panel of the truck. And then another hit the rear tire. But it was too late, the pickup lurched over the edge of the road, down the sharp incline, and through the lush vegetation. Holy crap, please let him not hit a banyan tree, he would never be able to steer around the wide trunk. The front of the car crunched through the low-growing underbrush, bouncing and ricocheting off hidden rocks. Vines and large leaves smacked into the windscreen, so he had trouble seeing where they were going. But he kept his foot on the accelerator. They needed to get as far into the jungle as his car would take them. Then they'd have to do the rest on foot.

A large koa loomed in front and he swerved wildly, just missing the trunk by millimeters. Keira screamed. But he could see she was too busy holding onto the bar above her head to do much of anything else.

They careened down the steep slope, and Dalton tried to picture where they were in relation to his house. What the terrain might throw at them next. If he was right, a small creek ran though the bottom of this valley. If they could make it down to that, then maybe they could follow it, because trying to thrash through this jungle on foot would be hard work, to say the least.

The car had slowed, its momentum hampered by the ferns and vines and small shrubs, but the it came to a sudden, crunching halt, throwing both of them forward as the airbags deployed.

CHAPTER SIX

Keira groaned and lifted her head. What happened? She was dazed, and no matter how hard she blinked, everything was blurry. White puffs of powder drifted through the car from the exploded airbags. The windshield was a maze of cracks, and the only thing she could see was green. Jungle surrounded the car on all sides; large, iridescent leaves carpeted the hood, while branches and shrubs hemmed them in on both sides.

Keira searched her memory. She had vague recollections of a large boulder appearing directly in front of the pickup, coming too fast for Dalton to steer around.

They'd crashed.

She took an internal inventory. Was she hurt?

She didn't think so.

Gingerly, she moved her arms. There was a twinge in her right elbow, she must've hit it on the car door at some stage. But apart from that, her arms moved freely. Then she tried her legs, stretching each one in turn, cataloguing any injuries. They both seemed okay, although there was a dull ache in one knee. On the whole, she was unscathed, thanks to Dalton's sturdy pickup. Any lesser car would've been a complete write-off. She could see from her vantage point that the hood was buckled, and the dashboard was fractured in a few places. But otherwise the cab remained mostly intact.

Dalton! Her head snapped around.

How was Dalton?

He lay slumped over the steering wheel.

Was he hurt?

Shit. He'd actually plunged his car straight into the jungle to save her. He hadn't coolly handed her over to Yoshio as she'd half expected. Instead, he'd put his life on the line and driven the car down a steep embankment to escape.

To help her. A woman he'd known for less than an hour. Why had he done that?

Keira reached over and gently shook Dalton's shoulder, but got no response. *Oh shit, please don't let him be dead.* She shook him harder and gave a relieved gasp when he groaned. He was alive. But what state was he in? They needed to get out of the car and get moving. There was no doubt in Keira's mind Yoshio would follow her down here. Or at least send his men down to get her.

"Dalton, wake up," she implored.

He groaned again, a little louder this time and finally lifted his head, blinking groggily at her.

"Thank God," she said. "Come on, we need to get out of here." She took a visual inventory of the parts of him she could see. There was no blood or injuries on his face or upper torso, apart from the old bruises she'd noticed earlier today. Perhaps he'd received a knock to the head, and maybe even a concussion, but he should be able to walk. She needed to get around to the other side to make sure his legs were fine and help him out.

Lodging her shoulder against her door, she gave it a good shove. It opened, but only a few inches. Ferns and long grass crowded in around the car, blocking her way out. But the gap was just enough for her to squeeze her way through. The drop to the ground was farther than she anticipated, and she landed awkwardly, sending a shooting pain through her knee. She nearly fell, only just saving herself by grabbing onto the door. Maybe she'd twisted or wrenched it when they hit the boulder. Whatever, it was going to make walking—or running—difficult. Now she was on the ground, she could see the car was wedged on top of the boulder, its front wheels still spinning slowly a foot or so in the air. But that might be a good thing, if they'd smashed straight into the boulder, it would've crushed the hood completely, perhaps trapping them, or at the very least, injuring them severely.

The jungle closed in around her and she had to fight her way through as she limped around to the driver's side door. Wow, it was hot. Sweat was already breaking out on her forehead. The humidity was so high here in the jungle, it felt like she was taking great gulps of pure steam. The thought of all the things that could be slithering around nearby—snakes, and spiders, really big spiders—made her shiver, but she forced those thoughts away.

Reaching up, she hauled on the handle, prising the plants apart to get the door open. Dalton had collapsed back down onto the steering wheel and Keira felt a stab of terror. What if he was really hurt? What if he was too groggy to walk? For a fleeting second, she considered leaving him where he was, fleeing down the mountain on her own. But she needed him. Without him she'd be totally and irreversibly lost in this thick jungle. And even though he'd been about to turn her over to the police, she begrudgingly admitted that she owed him. He had crashed his car to save her and put his own life on the line.

"Dalton, wake up," she said, hauling herself up onto the sideboard, using her good leg. She reached in and shook him and was rewarded when he lifted his head. His side of the car was in worse condition; the steering wheel was pushed forward and up, and the dash was buckled. This side of the pickup must've taken the brunt of the impact. It was lucky Dalton hadn't been trapped by the caved-in metal.

"I'm awake," he groaned. "Everything's spinning, I need to clear my head. Give me a minute."

"Sorry, but we don't have a minute." Keira craned her neck, trying to see back up the mountainside. There was a clear path of destruction, where the pickup had plowed through the undergrowth, right back to the road, which rose a hundred or so meters above them. Keira thought she could see at least one dark, hazy figure standing up there, looking down.

They needed to move. "Come on. I'm going to help you out." She grabbed his arm and began pulling. The muscles of his forearm were solid and warm, rippling beneath her palm. She almost let go as a shock zapped across her skin, but she gritted her teeth and ignored the sensation. Now was definitely not the time to be noticing how his biceps bulged nicely as he grasped the doorjamb and lifted himself off the seat.

She jammed her shoulder under his armpit and waited as he swung his legs sideways, then she took some of his weight as they both landed heavily on the ground. Jesus, he was bigger than she thought, and her sore knee nearly collapsed beneath the load.

Dalton stumbled, and she only just caught him. He wasn't kidding when he said he was woozy, as he swayed on his feet. His breathing was labored, his hot breath coursing down the side of her cheek. His face so close to hers, the side of her chest jammed up against his. She could feel the flex of his pec muscles, and the lean length of his stomach. Heat flared deep in her gut. Why in hell was her body reacting to him now? She'd just lost her husband. She should be scared out of her wits—she was scared out of her wits. She should be concentrating on only one thing. Escape. This acute awareness of him was unwelcome and unwanted. Yes, he was a good-looking man. A bit too dark and brooding for her liking, but definitely handsome.

But just because he was good-looking, didn't mean a thing. Over the past few years she'd encountered many attractive men. John included. And all of them had only wanted one thing. Just because they *looked* good on the outside, didn't mean they *were* good on the inside. She'd become good at shutting down her own feelings, her own emotions. If anything, she found herself shying away from the handsome ones. It was easier to deal with the ugly ones. Most of them weren't quite so entitled. And they often treated her with more respect; she didn't have to put on such a show. Although, in the end, they all got what they came for.

"Which way do we go?" she asked, brusquely. Impatient to be on the move, and impatient to rid herself of these dark thoughts.

"Down. Keep heading down the hill," he croaked. "There should be a stream at the bottom. I hope."

"What do you mean, you hope?" she asked, but didn't wait for an answer. Her feet were already pointed downward, and she encouraged him to take a few steps beside her.

"I'm not completely sure where we are," he admitted. "But if my hunch is right, then the stream below us is the same one that flows through the bottom of my farm."

Keira was watching his face with incredulity as he spoke, wondering if she was crazy to be putting her life in the hands of a concussed man who may or may not know where he was going. And that's when she saw him wince and grit his teeth as he took another step.

"What's wrong?" She fired the words at him. "Are you hurt?"

She glanced down and saw blood streaking his pants.

Well that was just wonderful. They both had leg injuries. How in hell were they supposed to escape the Yakuza when they were both hobbling like geriatrics, and Dalton could hardly even remember his own name?

* * *

"I'm fine," Dalton said between gritted teeth. He didn't know how he'd hurt his leg, hadn't even felt it at first, because his head had been spinning like a top. Probably torn it on a bit of twisted metal when the car buckled beneath him. He'd look at it later. Right now, even though it was painful to walk, he could keep going, and that was all that mattered.

It took a second for the reality of the situation to sink in, then he reached around, desperately feeling for the cool metal of his gun handle. It was still there, and he let out a gust of relief.

"Let's go." He took another step, and thankfully, she stopped staring at him like a scared rabbit caught in a trap and moved with him. Which was good, because he needed her support. Otherwise, he might find himself sitting on his butt staring up at the trees. He didn't like having to rely on someone else for his safety. Of course, this wasn't the first time he'd been injured. His time spent in the Navy had scored him his fair share of cuts and bruises. One night, he'd beached his special operation river craft too fast and broken his wrist when he smashed up against the steering wheel. Then, there was the time a sniper's bullet had nicked his thigh as they'd approached a fishing boat suspected of smuggling drugs. But even then, he'd been able to calmly hand control over to his second in command, so he could staunch the wound. It hadn't impacted on the mission at all.

But never in his fifteen years in the Navy had he felt this kind of lack of control. His head was spinning, and it was a huge effort to corral his thoughts into any coherent form. If Keira decided to leave him here… He didn't want to finish that thought. His life had just become one complete clusterfuck. All because of this woman. What in holy crap had he been thinking? Going up against the Yakuza might just be the craziest thing he'd ever done in his entire life.

He sucked in a deep breath. And then another. Kept his feet moving, one step at a time. Keira's arm was around his back, her other hand pushed into his chest as she guided him down the treacherous slope.

"Are they coming?" There was no way he was going to swivel his head around to look back up the incline, he'd fall flat on his face. He needed all his concentration just to keep going forward. Her weight shifted slightly as she turned her head to check.

"I can't see anyone," she replied. "But that doesn't mean they're not coming. The jungle is so dense in here. They could be right behind me and I wouldn't know."

She was right, but that might also help them. If they couldn't see the Yakuza, then the reverse was also true.

They made their way slowly, but surely, down the mountain. Once they left the side of the pickup, the jungle became a tangle of vines and branches clawing at them, preventing them from getting through. His poor truck. It was probably a write off.

Keira kept her shoulder wedged up under his, her presence firm and reassuring, stopping him from toppling over. Lucky she was tall, she fitted almost perfectly under his arm. As his head began to clear, he noticed other things about her as well. Like her smell. She smelled warm and slightly musky. But even after a night spent in his shed, there was still a faint floral air around her. Was it her hair? Was that where the flowery smell was coming from? He had a sudden, mindless urge to turn and bury his nose in her dark locks.

And her long legs kept knocking into his, as they negotiated their way between the clinging vegetation. Long, slim legs. Every time he looked down to make sure of his footing, he was greeted with the view of her tanned thighs beneath those cut-offs, conditioned and shapely. A small butterfly tattoo peeked out the top of her left sock, just above her ankle. It was bright blue and pretty, and Dalton was mesmerized by the little thing. Until he stumbled, nearly pitching headfirst down the hill, Keira catching him just in time. He needed to stop looking at her legs and concentrate on where he was putting his feet.

To keep his mind off how good her shapely body felt pressed up against his, he said, "I owe you an apology." He gave a small cough as the words almost stuck in his throat. He wasn't used to apologizing. "I'm sorry I didn't believe you earlier."

Surprise lit up her features. "Oh…Well, yeah, you do." Surprise quickly turned to a scowl as she glared at him, before returning her gaze to the ground. "If you'd listened to me in the first place, we wouldn't be in this mess right now."

He couldn't argue with her. But there were great big holes in her story. She wasn't telling him the whole truth. He needed to know everything, now he was involved. If he was to help her—help himself—then he needed the whole story.

Now probably wasn't the time, however. First, they needed somewhere safe to hole up and go over their options.

Dalton suddenly stopped dead in his tracks.

Hang on. What was he thinking? He didn't owe this woman anything. Why had he suddenly decided to help her?

Keira let out a grunt at his sudden halt. "Are you okay? What's the matter?"

He stared down at her. Going up against the Yakuza wasn't only crazy, it would be suicide. If not figuratively, then at the very least, probably career suicide. Just because she was staring up at him with those chocolate-brown eyes, didn't mean he owed her anything. It was sheer coincidence she'd chosen his farm to hide out. He should just cut her loose and let her figure it out herself. Or turn her into the cops. She'd be safer in jail than she would with him. He needed to think this through properly before he made any hard decision.

But to do that he needed time and a place no one could find them. At least not until he was ready to be found.

"Yes, I was just thinking," he finally replied.

"Right. Well, can you think and walk at the same time? I know you're a man and all, and multitasking isn't something most of you are good at. But, you know… Scary guys with guns and all?" She nodded her head back up the hill, and he had to smile at her caustic tone. It was good, showed spirit and hinted at her toughness that showed up in times of stress. Which she'd need if she was going to get out of this alive.

He started walking downhill again. His head was clearing slowly. The blurry edges were receding and his vision was no longer swimming. He could probably walk unaided now, if he wanted to. Perhaps he'd give it a few more minutes, to be on the safe side. Which would give him a few more minutes to enjoy the feel of Keira under his arm. Her shoulders were slim beneath his bicep, but he wouldn't call her skinny. Rather, she was well-toned, trim, muscles firm and honed, as if she enjoyed an active lifestyle. You certainly didn't get those kinds of muscles from sitting still all day. And he was still getting wafts of that tempting scent from her hair, the one that made him want to bury his nose in it.

But the choice was made for him when the sound of bubbling water reached his ears, and flashes of blue through the green jungle announced they'd made it down to the stream.

"I think I can walk on my own now," he said, as they stopped to look down at the water.

"Okay, if you're sure." She gave him a sideways glance, full of uncertainty. But she didn't release her hold on him.

Almost as if she didn't believe him. Or didn't want to let him go, said a foolish voice in his head.

"I'm sure," he replied, gently lifting his arm from her shoulders. She hesitated for another second, before standing taller and pushing away. The gap between them widened even farther as she took a step back, but she watched him with narrowed eyes. Making sure he wasn't going to fall flat on his face.

He surveyed the creek below. The stream bed was rocky, and in some places the sides were steep and unmanageable. A short way up, he could even make out a few small waterfalls, where the water tumbled down in rivulets over the broken ground. They'd have to follow along at the edge, where the vegetation was sparser. It would also make them less of a target, if the Yakuza came down here after them.

"We're going to see if we can get back to my house," he said, eyes still searching the terrain upstream.

"What? Do you think that's wise?" she asked, putting her hands on her hips. "Surely, that's the first place the Yakuza are going to look for us?" Again, she narrowed her beautiful eyes at him. He could tell she was now worried he'd gone a little crazy. He liked the way her mind worked, because it was true, going back to his house was risky. But it was a risk he was prepared to take.

"Come on," he said, picking a path through the lush greenery, keeping the stream to his left. "I'll tell you my idea, but we should keep moving."

"Fine," she replied huffily, but she turned to follow him.

At first, he walked gingerly, choosing his footing carefully, not wanting to tumble headfirst into the small ravine. But his head was definitely clearing, and his legs were finally back under his full control, even though a dull headache had started at the base of his neck. His leg was now more of a bother, as pain shot up his shin and into his knee with every step. But he'd had worse, and if they had time when they reached his house, he'd take a look at it.

"I don't think they saw which driveway we came out of," he said. "It will take them time to find out where I live. They might be able to track my truck from the license plate, but even that will take time. If we can make it back to my place in the next fifteen to twenty minutes, then I think we'll be safe."

"Right," she said from behind him. He didn't need to turn and look to know she was close, he could hear her breathing getting heavier as they traversed the steep hill.

"There are a few items I need from the house, and then we're going to hotfoot it out of there. Because, you're right, they will find my place eventually." Dalton fervently hoped that they didn't trash the place. He'd only just finished the renovations. And he really liked his little farmhouse in the hills. Had become attached to it. Crap, why was he getting involved with this woman again?

Ignoring his headache, he pushed himself harder, taking longer steps through the jungle, then checked behind to make sure Keira was keeping up. If they were to survive the next few days—the next few hours, even—he needed that go-bag he kept hidden at his place. The rest of the climb was done without speaking, they both needed all the air in their lungs to keep going.

After one final, extra-steep incline, where he practically had to get down on his hands and knees, they made it to the top of the hill. Dalton stopped to get his bearings, and so they both could catch their breath. It seemed Keira was as fit as she looked. Although she was dragging in great gulps of air, she'd managed to keep up with him, her long legs eating up the ground as fast as his. Good. At least she wouldn't be too much of a hinderance. His plan might actually have a chance of working.

"Over there," he said finally, pointing through the trees. He could just make out the spot where his long driveway sliced through the jungle.

"What am I looking at?" she puffed.

"Never mind. But just so you know, we're almost there." He fought his way through the undergrowth toward the road. They would be taking a risk to walk down his drive, but it'd take much longer to try and beat their way through the heavy jungle. And they were running out of time.

He burst through a tangle of vines and nearly stumbled as his feet hit the gravel road. "Can you run?" he asked, as she emerged behind him.

"Yes, I can run," she replied, panting heavily. "But the question should be, do I *want* to run?"

He couldn't help the small smile that formed on his face. "Come on," he urged, breaking into a trot. She threw him a filthy look but started to jog alongside him. At least this was slightly easier than fighting their way through the labyrinth of plants. Pain shot through his leg with every step, and he noticed she was limping, too. Both of them were walking wounded.

"Do you want to tell me the rest of your plan?" she huffed. "I'm assuming you do have a rest of the plan."

"What, you mean apart from turning you over to the Yakuza and saving my own skin?"

Her feet faltered and she slowed to stare at him.

"Because that would be the most sensible thing for me to do right now."

Her eyes were as round as saucers. "But I thought—"

"Keep your panties on. I'm not going to do that. Although I'm not sure exactly why. And to answer your question, yes I do have a plan." Dalton stopped talking so he could suck some more air into his lungs. "I know of a place, high up in the mountains. We'll be safe there, for a while at least."

"Okay." She quickened her pace to run alongside him

again. "If you're sure."

"I'm sure," he growled. But he wasn't. He'd only been to the hut up on the mountain once before. And that'd been once too many. He'd vowed to never go back there again.

The only thing this place had going for it was that no one else knew it existed.

CHAPTER SEVEN

Keira watched Dalton's backside as he climbed up the tiny goat-track. It was a view she'd been happy to follow along behind, watching that jean-clad ass move in front of her. But she was beginning to wonder exactly where they were headed. She caught a glimpse of his gun, which sat snugly in a shoulder holster worn over his shirt. He seemed completely at ease with the weapon, which was equal parts comforting, and unnerving, to Keira. At least they had protection, but it meant she was putting all her trust in a man who used deadly force on a daily basis.

They'd been walking for over two hours, only stopping to gulp water from the bottles he'd retrieved from his house, before they continued. And he was setting a punishing pace. His dog, Spike, trotted happily along at his heels, enjoying the new adventure. Her knee was pounding with pain, but she knew she'd just have to suck it up. There was no point in acting like a princess, now. She'd either make it to this hut he'd mentioned, or she wouldn't. There was no other option. He was limping nearly as heavily as she was. Plus, he was carrying a large, heavy backpack. Much larger than her own small one. He'd allowed her to retrieve her pack from the machinery shed on their way out of the property, but not the large suitcase.

He called his backpack his go-bag. It was black and bulky, and she wondered exactly what he had in there. He'd retrieved it from his bedroom while she'd stood on guard, watching out the front window for any sign of the dreaded black sedans. Before she knew what he was up to, he shot past her into the kitchen and began shoveling bottles of water and dried foodstuffs into a plastic bag, handing it to her as he came back out of the kitchen. Then they'd hightailed it out of there like two jackrabbits. They were in and out in less than two minutes. She'd stuffed the food in on top of her clothes in her small backpack and followed him.

Finally, she couldn't help it. "How much farther?" she panted.

"Only another five minutes or so," he called back over his shoulder. "We're almost there." His glance told her he would be as pleased to stop walking as she was. One thing was for sure, no one would ever find them up here. It was in the middle of nowhere. Spike glanced back at her, long tongue lolling out of his mouth, but he didn't seem at all fazed by the climb.

Should she trust Dalton? It would be nice to know exactly where they were going. And how long were they supposed to hide out. But at the moment, he was her only chance. Surreptitiously, she pulled her cell out of her back pocket, and pressed the button to turn it on. She checked for reception. Surprisingly, there was a connection, albeit a weak one, but it was better than nothing. It made her feel better, knowing she had a line to the outside world. Although, who she was going to call was another question she had no answer to. Sierra was the only person she trusted at the moment, and while she might be on the island, there was no way Keira could even begin to tell her where she was. All she knew was they were traversing up the side of a very large mountain, somewhere in the Waiakea Reserve.

The trail stopped its upwards trajectory and the ground leveled off. Then the path ducked back down the other side of a little knoll into a dense patch of jungle. It was so overgrown, she had to push aside low hanging leaves and branches, and as she followed Dalton again, she muffled a heavy sigh. Would they ever get there? But all of a sudden, the jungle opened up and she emerged, as if out of long tunnel, into a small clearing with a jumble of untidy buildings scattered in front of her.

They were here. Wherever here was.

Dalton dumped the go-bag on the ground beside him with a grunt and ran the back of his hand across his brow. Keira studied the wooden hut in front of them. It was old, that much was obvious. No one had lived here for a long time. The wooden walls were coming apart at the seams, large gaps appearing in between some of the boards. And the tin roof sagged alarmingly in the middle. The jungle had encroached upon the building, so it almost looked as if it'd been born from the vines. Other small buildings bunched in close on each side of the main hut, but they were equally as run down and derelict. A large, rusted water tank huddled near the back corner, an accessory for a lot of Hawaiian houses and Keira sincerely hoped this one contained water.

"I haven't been here in a while," Dalton said, almost apologetically, interrupting her horrified study of the cottage. "I didn't realize it'd got this bad."

"Really?" she replied, still contemplating the building with undisguised dismay. He didn't expect her to stay in there, did he? There was no way she was going inside that building; it didn't look safe. An African tulip tree reared up, its long branches hanging over the roof. The tree was considered a weed in Hawaii, but Keira loved their bright-red blooms. Instead of cheering her up, like they normally did, the flowers reminded her of devil's horns today.

"Are you going to tell me where we are? Or are you just going to let me guess?"

He grunted in surprise at the acerbic tone in her voice. But she was in no mood to be polite. She'd followed meekly along behind him, trusting he was taking her somewhere safe. But this place…? This was the place of nightmares. This was the place where they shot movies, where the innocent young hiker, lost in the woods, goes inside seeking shelter, and meets an untimely and violent death. Keira shuddered as her imagination ran wild.

"Yeah, sorry. Perhaps I should've come out here a little more often." Dalton stared balefully at the cottage. "This place belonged to my father."

She waited for more information, but Dalton seemed to sink into a world of his own, his eyes glazing over as if he was lost in some kind of memory. Not good memories, if the deep frown lines on his forehead were anything to go by. He'd said *belonged to*, so did that mean his father was no longer around?

"And now?" she prompted. But this time she softened her voice, losing the caustic tone from before.

"Now it belongs to me. He died. A while ago."

"Oh. I'm sorry," she said.

"Don't be." He bent down and hoisted the bag back on to his shoulders. "He died in jail. He was a drug smuggler and an arsehole. This place used to be his hideout, when he was dodging the law." He strode towards the wreck of a house, leaving her standing in the same spot, staring after him. Spike followed him, tail high in the air, eager to explore.

Jesus. What did she say to that? There was so much backstory in those few short sentences she had no idea where to start to untangle all the information. Dalton couldn't hide the torment in his voice, though. There were all kinds of undertones of old, rotten emotions running through his words.

With a start, she lurched forward as Dalton reached the first of the antiquated set of steps leading up to a small lanai. She didn't really want to go inside this spooky-looking place, but neither did she want to be left out here on her own, with the jungle encroaching in on her, closing in, claustrophobic and steamy. She could almost imagine sets of beady eyes staring at her from between the trunks of the trees.

Why was she so spooked? And why was she being such a snob, all of a sudden? She'd stayed in some pretty bad places while she was traveling, before she came to Hawaii. None of them quite this bad, but she'd certainly stayed in some very basic accommodation, had slept on the floor, or on couches, or crammed in one room with four or five other people. So, she could handle this place. She'd make the most of it.

Straightening her shoulders, she hurried up the steps and nearly ran into Dalton's back when he stopped in front of the door, hand on the doorknob.

"Are we going in?" It was only after she uttered these words, she saw the look on his face, one of raw bitterness. Why couldn't she learn to hold her tongue? But as she stared, his face closed over, determination replacing revulsion and resentment.

"Yes, we are." His large hand tightened on the knob and he pushed the door open, striding through the doorway.

Keira stopped just inside and drew in a deep breath. The place wasn't nearly as bad on the inside as it'd been on the outside. It was dusty, and a few scattered leaves drifted around the floor, disturbed by their entrance. But otherwise it was fairly orderly, if very basic. There was a small kitchen in the far corner; she could see the worn Formica countertops, a sink and even a stovetop. A small, but functional, table, surrounded by four sturdy wooden chairs, stood in the other corner.

She'd half-expected the whole place to have been trashed. Looted by hooligans, or teenagers looking for a thrill. But it was as if this place had some invisible sign hung on the front door, warning of dire consequences if anyone dared to come inside. Either that, or the place was haunted.

Keira suppressed another shiver.

From inside, she could see all the windowpanes were still intact, and while the walls and windowsills were flaking paint like dandruff, they at least kept the jungle at bay, and were sturdier than they'd looked on first glance. A dark doorway led off to what Keira assumed to be a bedroom. Only one, by the looks of it.

"It's actually not that bad," she said, trying to sound helpful.

He grunted in reply.

Right, so he'd brought her to a place that obviously held memories and demons, and where he clearly didn't want to be. She wasn't sure whether to be thankful to him for having the strength to overcome his aversion to his father's hut, or mad at him for bringing her to somewhere he despised so much he had to physically force himself through the door. The man was a walking riddle, but she wasn't sure she had the strength at the moment to figure him out.

Keira pulled out the nearest chair at the small kitchen table and sagged into it. She was almost too tired to think anymore, and she was glad they were here, even if the place wasn't the Hilton, as she didn't think she could've gone on much longer. Spike came over and placed his head in her lap for a pat. She lay a hand on the soft, red fur. He was a cute dog, and clearly extremely loyal to the big man still standing in the middle of the room.

Dalton strode over and dumped his go-bag on the floor next to her.

"There's a first aid kit in there. Get it out. I'll go and see if I can get the stove going, so we can have some hot water." He turned his back. "And see if you can find some painkillers for this damn headache, will you?"

What, no please or thank you? She almost said the words out loud, but managed to hold her tongue. Instead, she leaned down slowly and opened the zip along the top. God, every muscle in her entire body hurt. Now she'd stopped moving, she wasn't sure she would ever get going again.

Rummaging through the bag, she was surprised at some of the contents. Apart from spare clothes, sweaters and lightweight long pants, a pair of leather gloves, and a hat, there was a flashlight, spare batteries—for what she had no idea—a wrench and a screwdriver, a compact bag that looked to contain some kind of tent, packets of freeze-dried food, even a spare cell phone. And many more items she couldn't be bothered sorting through. Eventually she found the first aid kit, tucked into one corner of the bag.

"Found it," she said, holding it up.

"Great," he said, coming back over to the table.

She could see a small gas burner set up on the kitchen counter, which must've been hidden in one of the cupboards when they first came in. It was flaming away, with a pot of water on top.

"Let's do you first." He sat heavily down in the chair next to her.

"I beg your pardon?"

He glanced up and must've seen the sheer astonishment in her face.

"Your leg." He raised one dark eyebrow at her. "I meant, let's look at your leg first."

"Oh, yeah, sure." She fumbled with the first aid kit, trying to hide the red flush of embarrassment rising up her neck. The zipper finally came undone and all kinds of bandages, tubes, and bottles of pills came tumbling out. "I think I've just twisted my knee, that's all. We'll have to strap it with—" She drew in a gasp as Dalton took hold of her knee, one hand on each side. His hands felt so... She couldn't explain the sensation. Strong. Warm. Capable. Nice. Her skin tingled where he touched her, and she became acutely aware of every nerve ending as his long fingers curved around behind her knee and lifted it slightly off the ground.

"What are you doing?" she asked, her voice coming out sounding like a strangled frog.

"Checking to make sure it's nothing more than a sprain."

She wanted to say, *can you do that without touching me?* But her tongue remained frozen in her mouth.

"Does this hurt?" His focus seemed to be solely fixed on Keira's leg. He was being totally professional. Cool and competent, like he'd done this before. Like being this close to her—touching her—wasn't affecting him in the slightest. But her mind wouldn't form an answer. It was lost in the sensations of his fingers on her skin. Wondering what they would feel like if he let them slide a little higher, up her thigh.

Keira felt a sudden stab of guilt. It was never like this with John. His touch had never elicited such a range of emotions, not even when she first met him. And more recently, in the past few years, Keira had almost been repulsed by any contact with him. But he'd still been her husband. And now he was dead. And here she was, fantasizing about some man she'd only met this morning. There must be something wrong with her, to let him affect her so strongly.

Then a sharp twinge brought her plummeting back to reality, as Dalton gently rotated her knee to the right, and she found her voice again.

"Ouch. Yes, that hurts." She pushed John out of her mind. There'd be plenty of time to think about him later.

"Sorry," he said, with a frown. What about if I do this?" He moved it straight up, then back down.

"No, not so much," she admitted.

He placed her foot gently back on the floor, and let go of her leg.

"Oh." The soft exclamation was out of her mouth before she knew it. She'd wanted him to hold on to her forever.

But he didn't seem to have heard, because he said, "Any other injuries I should know about?"

"Ah. No, I don't think so." Belatedly, she added. "I banged my elbow, must've been when we crashed, but I think it's only bruised."

"Let me look, just in case." His fingers picked up her arm by the wrist and were gently probing along her forearm, towards her damaged elbow.

Holy Mother of… Little sparks flew up her arm, like he was zapping her with tiny shots of adrenaline wherever his fingers landed on her skin.

"Does that hurt?"

Nope, she couldn't feel a thing. Her arm was completely numb to everything except the feel of his hand softly caressing it. She shook her head slowly, like a person in a daze.

"Good. That's good," he said, releasing her wrist. She sucked in a breath and gave her arm a surreptitious shake. "I've got bandages in the kit somewhere. We should really ice your knee, but, well…" His gaze roamed around the small room. "…there's no ice out here."

"I'll be fine," she replied.

"All right. I'll strap your knee in a minute. I'm just going to assess the damage to my leg first, if that's okay?"

The least she could do, was repay the favor. She wasn't good when it came to blood, but it couldn't be that bad, could it?

"Let me do it." Without waiting for an answer, she pushed

Spike out of the way, got down on the floor in front of Dalton and rolled up his pant leg. And quickly wished she hadn't.

"Oh, Jesus Christ," she swore, as she got a look at the wound.

CHAPTER EIGHT

All the blood drained from Keira's face. Dalton grabbed her shoulder with growing alarm as she swayed away from him. She wasn't going to faint, was she? Holy crap, maybe his leg was worse than he thought. But he'd made it all the way up here with the injury, surely it couldn't be that bad?

Still holding on to her shoulder with one hand, he bent down to view his lower leg. There was a deep gash on the outside of his calf, but it was only two inches long, it hadn't even gone down to the bone, and the bleeding had almost stopped. He knew all the running he and Spike did together had served him well today. He didn't think he would've made it up that hill with this injury if he hadn't been so fit. But still, he'd seen a lot worse, she seemed to be overreacting a little.

"Sorry, I'm not good with blood and stuff," she apologized. She took a deep breath. "But I'm okay now. Let me take another look."

He watched as she gritted her teeth and leaned in closer again. Her face remained pale, but her jaw was set at a determined angle. And he was impressed by her strength-of-mind, that she could overcome her aversion so quickly.

"It's not too bad," she said, her fingers hovering near the

wound as she inspected it. "Probably needs a few stitches, but I think we can get away with just bandaging it for now."

Not that they had any other choice, unless she had some hidden talents as a nurse she wasn't telling him about. But he didn't argue.

"Is that water hot yet?" She looked up at him, brown eyes questioning. It took him a second to understand what she meant, because he was suddenly ensnared in her gaze.

"What? Oh, yes. It should be good to go," he said abruptly, covering for his loss of attention.

She gave him a sideways glance, but got to her feet and went over to retrieve the saucepan of water. Spike followed her, and then went off to explore each corner of the hut, head down sniffing along the floorboards, tail up and wagging. His dog seemed to have taken to Keira rather well, which was unusual. He was normally wary around strangers. Dalton busied himself pulling a couple of large sterile swabs out of the first aid kit to clean the wound. He also rummaged around in his go-bag and produced a couple of large, old bandanas. They might just do the trick to wash away some of the blood. Then he found the small bottle of painkillers and swallowed a couple of them dry. His head was still pounding.

Handing the bandanas to her without comment, he watched as she gingerly lowered herself on to the floor again, beside him.

"Can I take your shoes off?" she asked. "This one is all covered in blood." She pointed at his left boot. "It'll be easier to see what's going on."

"Sure." He watched, a little self-consciously, as she undid the laces on each boot, and then helped her pull them off. It felt good to be out of the hot, heavy shoes. Then she dipped a bandana into the heated water and grasped the back of his leg as she gently dabbed at the dried blood on his shin. His skin flamed where her fingers pushed against the calf muscle.

He'd been hoping it might be different this time, with her touching him. But it was exactly the same as when he'd held her knee in his hands. An acute awareness of her had pulsed up his arm. And now his whole leg felt like it was on fire. And that fire was quickly spreading up his thigh, to the rest of his body.

"I hope I'm not hurting you," she said, not looking up from her task.

If only she knew. "No, not at all," he replied, his voice surprisingly even. Holy crap, he needed something, anything, to take his mind off her. Off the way he could almost see down the front of her T-shirt, as it gaped open when she leaned forward to get a better look at what she was doing. The front of his pants became uncomfortably tight. He was going to make a complete idiot of himself if he didn't do something to stop this exquisite pain soon.

Her voice suddenly broke through his spiraling thoughts. "So… You said this place belonged to your dad…?"

Of all the topics in the world, of course, she had to pick the one he really didn't want to talk about. But if it got his mind off what she was doing, then he'd play her game.

"Mmhmm," he replied noncommittally.

"So, I'm interested. I mean, you said your father spent time in jail? So, how did he come to own this hut?"

He grunted. If they were going to stay here for any length of time, then she probably deserved to know the details. But where to start?

"It's a long story."

She glanced up and shrugged. "I'm not going anywhere."

"No, I guess not," he agreed. Taking a deep breath, he started at the beginning. "My grandfather used to own a lot of land around here. My dad's side of the family are Chinese-Hawaiian, and they loved to be self-sufficient. You know how hard it can be to get fresh fruit and veggies in Hawaii?" Keira nodded and he continued, "My farmhouse, and all the land down to the stream, including the sheds you were hiding in, belonged to my grandfather." He thought she might've blushed slightly at the mention of hiding in his shed, but she didn't look up, just kept dabbing at his leg.

"Grandfather used to farm the land, grow pineapples and avocados. But I was never going to be a farmer. So, I sold most of it off, and just kept the little corner block with the farmhouse."

"Okay." She smiled at him and he kept going.

"But he also owned a few tracts of land up here, high on the mountain, as well. One of which he gave to my father."

"Wow. It sounds like you have a lot of history in this area. Have your family lived here for many generations?"

"Yes," he replied flatly. Was that condemnation in her tone? It wasn't his fault the farming heritage of his family had been broken. That mantle rested squarely on his father's shoulders. Dalton had been left to pick up the pieces afterwards.

"But let's not go down that rabbit hole today," he continued. "Suffice it to say, my father never wanted anything to do with the farm." Aunty Lei had filled Dalton in on all the intimate family details when he'd moved back to Hawaii. It was one of the many reasons Grandfather had left the farm to Dalton. Hoping he might return one day to find his roots again.

He winced as she got closer to the wound with her bandana but kept talking to keep his mind off the pain.

"Like I said earlier, my father was involved in the drug trade. He moved to LA in his early twenties, to try and make it big over there. That's where he met my mom."

"Oh, so you were born in LA, then?" She looked up at him for a second, surprise written in the lift of her eyebrows.

"Yes, I lived there most of my life. I was still quite young when my father returned to Hawaii. He said he was going back to fix things. And that he'd send us money." Dalton let out a snort. Like that'd ever happened. He and his mother had to survive on their own. Aunty Lei said his father, George, had got mixed up in the wrong crowd early on, and after a while had become so entrenched in the lifestyle and dependent on his drug habit, he couldn't ever see a way out. As far as Dalton was concerned, he was weak and corrupt. A no-hoper, who'd ended his days in jail. What the hell his mother had ever seen in the man, Dalton would never know. She told him back when she first met George, after he moved to LA, he was charming and easygoing. He always made her laugh. But Dalton never stopped hating his dad for leaving him and his mom destitute.

"This place was his hideout for many years. Until, eventually, the law caught up with him, and he was put in jail for life."

Dalton tried to keep the bitterness out of his voice, but he must've failed, because Keira said, "That's a sad story. I'm sorry you had a shitty childhood."

"No, no. Don't get me wrong, it wasn't all doom and misery. Yes, after George left, Mom and I spent quite a few years just living from day to day, trying to make ends meet. I was fifteen when she met Edward, a high-powered accountant. After they got married, we lived a more-than-decent life." His stepfather was everything George wasn't. And Dalton would be forever grateful to him for seeing through their poverty, to his mother's beauty and charm. Picking her up like a diamond from the dust. Pulling them both out of destitution and giving them an affluent life, full of everything they'd missed out on.

"I can see why this might not be your favorite place. It must hold some dark memories for you. I'm sorry you had to bring me here," she said, breaking into his reverie.

"Like I said, I don't like to be reminded of my father. But I never in a million years thought I'd be using his place as a hideout. It's a little ironic, don't you think?"

"A little." She dropped her head and continued to administer to his leg in silence. Dalton had seen a couple of different emotions flitter across her face before she looked away, but he couldn't pin them down. Did she regret him having to bring her here? Was she embarrassed, because she had to rely on him? Or was it that she felt responsible for him having to come face-to-face with his demons?

"Right. This might sting a bit," she said as she opened one of the alcohol swabs.

He grunted with the effort not to swear, as she wiped the swab over the wound. Even the magic of her touch wasn't enough to eradicate that kind of pain.

"It's all clean. Let's get it bandaged up," she said in an efficient, no-nonsense voice.

He watched as Keira wrapped up his leg, fascinated by her slim fingers. No one, apart from Aunty Lei and his mom, knew much of his father's history. He didn't like to talk about it. Both Sam and Cane knew his dad had spent time in jail; had died in jail. But they knew not to pry too deeply. Why was he spilling his entire life story to this woman?

Especially since he still wasn't convinced he was going to help her. He shook his head in wonder at his own stupidity. He had Tavi and Flora to consider. If he did help Keira, he might well be putting them in danger. The Yakuza were not to be messed with. They didn't have a problem targeting innocent family members if they thought it'd get them what they wanted. He had a lot of hard thinking to do before he made a decision. And he wasn't going to let some fleeting attraction, or chemistry, or whatever it was going on between them to make that decision for him. He was going to think with his head where Keira was concerned.

Keira rolled down his pant leg and got to her feet, leaving

the pot on the floor. "Before I throw this water out, I need to check you for any other injuries."

"I'm pretty sure the rest of me is unscathed," Dalton replied with a smile.

"Yeah, well, I'm not taking your word for it." She put her hands on her hips and stared down at him.

"Okay," he said with a shrug. He guessed there was no harm in letting her take a look, even though he was sure he carried no other injuries.

"Lift your shirt, so I can check your back and stomach," she demanded.

He stood and did what any male would do. Tugged at the hem of his shirt, then pulled it all the way over his head. It was the easiest way for her to check, then he'd put it back on again.

He heard her sharp intake of breath and looked up. "What? What's wrong?"

She was staring at him. Had he missed something? Was there a giant hole in his chest he hadn't noticed before?

She licked her lips. Opened her mouth and shut it again. Her eyes raked over his chest and then down to his stomach. Finally, when he was just about to ask her again what was wrong, she said, "Um…all those bruises on your chest. Did they come from the accident?"

"Oh, those. No, that happened yesterday, talking down a bail jumper."

"That's good." She nodded but seemed to be only half-focused on what she was saying. "Well, it's not good… But good you didn't get them today."

He wasn't fooled. It wasn't just the bruises she was staring at. He'd seen her eyes darken, her pupils dilate as her gaze roamed over his body. She liked what she saw.

And he liked that she liked what she saw. He could tell it also unsettled her, put her on edge. Suddenly he had a shameless urge to push it. To see how far this would go.

"What about my pants, shall I take them off, too?"

"Oh. Ah…" she mumbled, taking a step backward.

Ha, he'd left her speechless. It was somehow satisfying, that he had the power to render her without words.

"No… I don't think—"

But it was too late, he'd already undone his button and fly and dropped his pants to the ground, kicked them off so they skidded across the floor. She stood, her mouth slightly open, eyes large and mysterious. Standing there, practically naked, he did think perhaps he'd pushed it too far. But he wanted to know if she felt the same chemistry he was feeling.

CHAPTER NINE

"Now, it's your turn." His voice was low and husky and held a note of danger. Keira gave an involuntary shiver. How had it come to this? How had it happened that she was now staring at an almost naked Dalton, standing there as proud as a stallion, with all those lean muscles rippling in ways she never thought possible? He was glorious. He was tall, long legs with solid thighs and bulging biceps, all highlighted by his slight-olive complexion. The fact he was of Chinese-Hawaiian descent made him more beautiful, more attractive. And those bruises, while they looked painful, only added to his warrior-like appearance. She noticed a tattoo above his left pec. It said REBEL, which surprised her. What was he rebelling from? And there was another one of a skull above his ankle. That one looked older, faded, as if he got it back when he was younger. But these facts only registered vaguely, she was too busy devouring his body with her eyes.

"My turn to do what?" she asked, only half-listening for his answer.

"Your turn to take your shirt off." He took a step toward her, and her heat rate skyrocketed.

"What?" Her brain finally engaged, and she heard what he said. For one stupid second, she'd given in to an insane urge to see him shirtless, but this had spiraled out of control now.

He took another step toward her, and the hairs all over her body rose as awareness of him flooded through her.

"I don't think so," she said, more loudly than was necessary. He was standing less than a foot away from her.

"Fair's fair," he said. That serious mouth of his was pulled up into a half-smile. His almond-shaped eyes stared directly at her, boring through her. "You can see I have no more injuries. So, it's time we check you out."

She stared at him, speechless. What would happen if she got naked in front of him? The thought was inconceivable. But at the same time, it held a dangerous appeal. He took another step toward her, and now he was so close that if she breathed in deeply, her breasts would touch his chest.

Why was he doing this? It was like he was pushing her buttons, to see how far she'd really take this. And she didn't like it.

Because a part of her was screaming for her to get closer. That she wanted to feel his body against hers. But the other part was screaming it was all wrong. John was dead, for Christ's sake.

"I'm married," she said, waggling her ring finger at him.

"Mmhmm." His shrewd eyes never left her, waiting, like a cat outside a mouse hole, to see what she would do.

Her gaze drifted to his lips as if her eyes had a mind of their own. Firm and serious, the bottom lip slightly fuller than the top. A light stubble was beginning to form on his chin and around his mouth. Her fingers wanted to run over that dark stubble, feel the rough rasp against her skin. Time seemed to hang, suspended, as she stared at him, unable to move. Unable to pull away, but also unable to lean in and take his mouth as she wanted to do.

A shrill sound broke the tense silence. Dalton went into a half-crouch, eyes darting around the room, looking for the source of the noise.

Keira stepped back and took a deep breath. "It's my cell," she told him, reaching around to her back pocket to retrieve it.

He gave her an incredulous look and grabbed her wrist as she brought the phone out. His fingers were strong and immovable around her arm.

"What do you think you're doing?" he growled in a low voice.

"I was just going to check caller ID. I wasn't going to answer it," she added. "I'm not that stupid."

"I'll do it." He took the cell from her hand, even as she tried to snatch it back from him. What gave him the right to take control of her phone?

"Why is this even on? I told you to keep it turned off until we figured out our next move." He still had hold of her wrist and she wanted to shake his hand free. Instead, she met his steely gaze.

She didn't say the words that wanted to tumble out on her tongue. That she didn't completely trust him, and it was her damn phone anyway, so she'd do with it as she liked. She hoped her glare said everything her mouth wasn't prepared to.

He kept his gaze locked on her, even as he finally let go of her wrist. Then slowly, he looked down at her phone. "It says, *Sierra*. Who is that? Is that who I heard you talking to when I found you in my shed?"

"Yes," she said. If her tone was a tad sulky, then he'd just have to deal with it. "She's my sister, and she must be absolutely frantic. She's seen my face on the news and she has no idea where I am, or what's happening."

"Perhaps she is, but that isn't our problem." Dalton narrowed his eyes as he continued to stare at the buzzing screen. "What's the story with your sister? Is she trustworthy?"

Did he realize he was standing there, practically naked? Keira was still distracted by all the tanned flesh so close to her. "What do you mean?" she asked, sounding waspish and not caring.

"Well, I'm thinking that we have very few options open to us at the moment. And with both the police and the Yakuza out there looking for you, we have limited people we can trust. What does your sister do? Does she live on the island?"

Keira's head was whirling. "She's an investigative journalist. Or was a journalist, a while ago."

Dalton's sharp eyes found hers. Was that a good thing or a bad thing, that Sierra was a journalist?

"And no, she lives in Australia. She was phoning me this morning to let me know she arrived on the Big Island last night. I think her visit was meant to be a surprise. But she was the one who got the surprise," Keira added as she pursed her lips. She could just imagine the choice words her sister was calling her right about now. She would be beyond angry. Confused. And scared. Suddenly, Keira desperately wanted to talk to her sister. To hear her voice.

"At least now we know we can get a cell connection up here," he said wryly.

The phone finally stopped ringing and Dalton handed it back to her. "Do not answer that if she calls again," he warned. "I need time to think about this."

She took it from his hand meekly, but inside she was seething. How dare he order her around? She watched as he retrieved his pants and slipped them back on. Then his T-shirt went back over his head and the wonderful view of his fine back, with muscles in all the right places, was also covered up.

Keira let out a sigh but wasn't sure if it was one of relief or disappointment. Should she tell him the rest of it? That Sierra was possibly traveling with a police officer? This guy of Sierra's—Reed—might be able to help them.

"There's more," she said to his back, and watched as he slowly turned around to face her. "I don't know any more than what I'm about to tell you, because my conversation was cut off when someone pointed a gun at me and then proceeded to scare the shit out of me." She glowered at Dalton, so he knew exactly how she felt about his little reception at his shed this morning. "I believe my sister might be traveling with a male companion. I think he might be a cop, back on Kangaroo Island, where they live."

Dalton raised one dark eyebrow in her direction. "That's interesting." He ran a hand through his unruly hair as he considered her words. "It might be just what we need. Someone we know who isn't corrupt. Who isn't connected to anyone on this island."

Keira blinked. "Are you going to tell me what you're thinking?" The least he could do was to let her in on his ideas. Finally, he was listening to her now. Understanding that she wasn't safe anywhere. Certainly not in the lockup in Hilo. Not if the Yakuza had anything to do with it.

"Do you know if we can trust him? What's—"

She held up a hand and stopped him mid-sentence. "Like I said, this morning was the first time I've heard about him. I guess he was going to be a surprise, as well."

"So, let's give them a call. See what they have to say."

"Really?" Keira's heart lurched in her chest at the thought she might be able to talk to her sister after all.

"Yes, but we can't tell them anything. And we definitely can't tell them where we are." He must've seen her smile fall from her face, because he added, "Not just yet, anyway. We need a lot more info before we try anything. I'm hoping your sister and her friend can be our eyes and ears for us."

Comprehension began to dawn on Keira. "That might

work. She told me they were close to contacting the police, but thought they would give me a few more hours to explain myself. So, no one knows they are even on the island."

"Exactly." He smiled, and for a second Keira almost forgot what they were talking about. He had an amazing smile, when he chose to show it. Those serious lines around his eyes disappeared, and his whole face came alive. "Are you ready?" He held out his hand for her phone. "You introduce me, then let me do most of the talking. Okay?"

But before she could even nod her head yes, the cell trilled angrily. Sierra was calling again, and Keira could almost feel her impatience through the sharp ringing tones.

"Hi, Sierra," she said, as Dalton pushed the Answer button.

"What the hell is going on, Keira? Where are you?" Sierra was beyond mad, her voice had taken on an icy control. This didn't bode well. Even though Keira was the older, and supposedly wiser, sister, she knew she couldn't match her younger sister for temper, or for stubborn determination.

"Just settle down for a second, and listen to me," Keira implored. "I can't tell you where I am. I know this sounds bad, but I can explain everything, if you'll let me."

There was silence on the end of the line for two long seconds. Then Sierra said, "Go on."

Keira let out a long breath between pursed lips, silently thanking her sister for being prepared to listen. "I'm going to put you on speaker, sis." She hit the button and held the cell so both she and Dalton could hear it. "I've got someone here, who I want to introduce. His name is Dalton, and he's helping me."

"Hello," Dalton said into the phone. "Sorry we can't meet under better circumstances. But I'm going to cut to the chase, because we may not have a lot of time. Your sister seems to have gotten herself in to quite a bit of trouble. But you might be able to help her. Help us." Dalton glanced at Keira, an inscrutable look in his eyes. "Keira told me you have a, ah… friend with you, who's worked in the police force?"

"Yes, Reed. He's a cop on the island where we live. Do you want me to put him on?"

"Yes, please. Put the phone on speaker, it would be best if we can all hear each other."

A deep voice came over the line. "Hi. I'm Reed Kapua. Nice to talk to you, Keira. I've heard a lot about you."

They exchanged quick pleasantries. Then Sierra said, "Of course, Keira, you know we'll do whatever we can. But can I just ask, what about John? Where is he?"

Keira froze. She daren't look at Dalton. Sierra had just hit on the one problem she was hoping to avoid. Damnation, if only she'd had time to talk to Sierra alone, tell her not to bring up John. At least not until she could get her story straight.

Out of the corner of her eye, she could see Dalton staring at her, with that raised eyebrow she was coming to know meant he, too, was waiting for her answer.

"You told me your husband wasn't at home when the lava engulfed your house, but that's the only time you mentioned him. So, where is he?" asked Dalton, his glacial stare fixed on Keira's face.

CHAPTER TEN

Keira stared at him like he was a hawk and she was his prey. The question had obviously caught her off-guard. And he wondered why he hadn't asked it before. She'd mentioned she was married a few times now, but it was almost like he disregarded it, like he didn't want to hear.

She hadn't been telling him the whole truth. Even back when he'd interrogated her at his farm, he knew there were large holes in her story. But he hadn't had a chance to clarify any of that yet. They'd been too busy trying to stay alive and out of the clutches of the Yakuza.

Now he needed to know everything. If he was going to help her, he needed the whole truth.

"Oh, God," Keira whispered. She clasped her hands together and her fingers began the habitual turning of the ring on her finger he'd noticed earlier.

"What did you say?" Sierra asked over the phone.

"I...ah..." Keira still hesitated, and she glanced up at him, despair and something else hidden in the depths of those chocolate-brown eyes. The hairs on the back of Dalton's neck stood up. He wasn't going to like what she had to say.

"John's dead." Keira wouldn't meet his gaze.

There was complete silence as everyone digested this piece

of news.

"What do you mean, dead?" Sierra finally asked, taking the words out of Dalton's mouth.

"Yoshio killed him. I watched him shoot him. Then the lava came and covered the house." Keira's fingers began to tremble, and belatedly Dalton realized how much it'd cost her to say that. Leading her by the elbow over to the chair, he pushed her in to the seat. Her whole body was shaking now. Holy crap. Her husband was dead. She'd seen this Yakuza shoot her husband dead.

This was big. She'd lied to him. Well, a lie by omission, at the very least. But in a way, Dalton didn't blame her. She was running for her life. Desperate. And desperate people did foolish things.

This changed things, and he needed to think some more. Flora and Tavi were at the front of his mind. But there was also Sam and Cane to consider. His actions might also put them in danger. Anyone who was associated with him could now be affected.

Both Sierra and Reed were trying to talk over each other down the phone.

"Calm down everyone," Dalton commanded. He knelt down next to Keira and forced her chin up, so he could look her in the eyes. They were dry, and he was surprised. Her husband was dead, shouldn't she be grief stricken? Perhaps she was so scared by the Yakuza, she hadn't had time to process it all yet. "I'm so sorry you had to see that, Keira," he said gently.

"It was horrible," Keira admitted in a small voice. "But that's how I know they're after me. I overheard Yoshio talking to another man, telling him they needed to find me."

"Why do they want you, Keira?" It was Reed's voice. He'd obviously taken the phone from Sierra, as he was perhaps a little more collected than her. Sierra could be heard cursing in the background.

"They think I can help them access John's bank accounts." She seemed to shrink into the chair, as if she might become invisible. "But I can't. I don't know anything about it. He always did everything. Oh, God." Her last words were nearly a wail. "Why was I so stupid? Why did I let him control everything? Now they're going to kill me, because I can't give them what they want." Finally tears appeared in her eyes. But they were tears of terror, for her own life, not of sadness at the loss of her husband. What was going on here? It was almost as if her husband meant nothing to her. Dalton fumbled around in one of the pockets of his go-bag and came out with a clean bandana, which he handed to her to wipe her tears.

"Can you tell us why they want to get into John's accounts?" Reed asked, his voice cool and controlled, employing his cop persona.

"I'm not one-hundred percent sure, but I think John might've been stealing from them. I don't really know what his connection with the Yakuza was, and I didn't like to ask." She gave a small, involuntary shudder as something dark and unreadable flashed across her face. "So, I'm only guessing. You know John was into real estate? I told you that, Sierra, remember?"

"Yes, I remember. You said he owned the biggest business on the island." Her sister's voice was husky, but under control once more.

"Anyway, Yoshio, he's the big honcho in the Yakuza—he's always got at least one or two bodyguards with him wherever he goes. Well, he was one of John's biggest clients. John was always hosting parties for him at our house. Schmoozing him, buttering him up, you know. Him and his friends."

Dalton was still kneeling next to Keira as she huddled in the chair, his hand on her shoulder, to give her comfort. So, that's why he felt, rather than saw, the strange tremor shoot through her body. It was like someone had walked over her grave. He glanced at her face, but it was partly covered by her bangs, which now dangled over her face, as if she were hiding behind it. Something about this conversation was causing her pain. He wanted to stop this interrogation, because that's what this had become. But he needed the information, if he was going to help her. They all did.

So, instead of telling her to stop, that it was all okay, they could talk about it later, he gave her shoulder a gentle squeeze, and said, "What else, Keira?"

She drew in a deep breath. "I think that…perhaps…John might've been laundering money for him."

Dalton heard Reed's quick intake of breath on the other end of the phone, and he wanted to do the same. It was all making a horrible kind of sense. Dalton had never dealt directly with the Yakuza before, but of course, he knew of their reputation. The stories were outrageous and often violent and gory, of how they did business, ruled with an iron fist when things didn't go their way. And even if only half of it were true, then they were a force to be feared. The local police were always on the defensive when it came to catching these criminals. It was nearly impossible to pin anything on them, as they were as slippery as eels. And had plenty of high-paid lawyers in their back pockets.

"I think he'd been doing it for a while. I mean, John…we, always had plenty of money. And he loved to throw it around. He was generous like that. But I noticed in the past few years he became…I don't know, a bit more tight-lipped. But also more cocky, more egotistical. And he really started splashing out with the spending. Buying things we really didn't need. We had four cars in the garage, for Christ's sake. Who needs that many cars? And not just any cars, either. There was a Porsche, an Aston Martin, and I forget what else.

But they weren't cheap, if you know what I mean."

"And you think he was embezzling money from the Yakuza to do all this?" Dalton asked quietly.

"Yes. I mean, it seems pretty obvious, don't you think?"

Dalton hated to admit it, but Keira was probably right.

"Keira, did you report John's death? Did you tell anyone? Phone the police?" Reed's voice was gentle, but Dalton suddenly realized how important this question was and mentally reprimanded himself for not thinking of it himself.

"No," Keira replied hesitantly. Then in a stronger voice, she repeated. "No. I just got out of there as fast as I could. No one else knows John is dead."

"Good. That's good, Keira," Reed soothed. Reed would know it was his sworn duty as a cop to report a death. Especially a homicide. It would be going against all his cop instincts to keep this quiet. But if Keira hadn't told anyone yet, then they had a window of opportunity they could exploit. Because no one would be immediately questioning where John was. Did he have family on the island? As abhorrent as it was to Dalton, to leave a man's body beneath the lava, without a decent burial and without telling his family, this might work to their advantage.

"But the police will be out looking for him, because of Keira being wanted for murder, won't they?" Reed asked the obvious question. "They'll want to question him, see if he knows where you are, or as an alibi, at the very least."

"You're right, they will be looking for him." Dalton mused, almost to himself. "But if what I heard on the radio this morning is anything to go by, the lava flow has cut off all access to the Pahoa area now. The police won't be able to get in. Not by road, anyway. They may not even know if your house is still standing or not. The eruptions will be causing a whole heap of panic and confusion. They'll have their hands full with evacuations, displaced people, looting and all that kind of thing. So, they may not be as focused on Keira, or on finding John, as they might otherwise be."

"That's true," said Reed. "But his absence won't go completely unnoticed, you can be sure of that."

"What about John's family?" Dalton asked. "Is there anyone that'll miss him?" What he was really asking was, how long did they have before someone noticed he was missing. It was a terrible thing to hide from loved ones. The fact that a brother or a son was now dead. But they could deal with the consequences later, if it would buy them more time now.

"Um…" Keira scrunched her eyebrows together in thought. "His mother lives over on O'ahu, in Waimanlo Beach. He only speaks to her every other week or so. But I think she's off on one of her cruises. She does three or four of them a year. His dad died of a heart attack a few years ago. And his sister moved to New Jersey when she got married around ten years ago. They aren't close. They hardly ever talk. She never even rang to find out if the eruptions were affecting us."

It sounded like his family was in short supply, which was a good thing for them.

"What if the mother sees that you're wanted for murder on the news tonight?" Sierra cut in.

"She doesn't tend to watch the news. Says it's full of doom and gloom. I imagine she'd much rather be sipping Mai Tais by the pool on the cruise ship," Keira replied.

"What about the sister? Do you think the news will have reached the mainland yet?" asked Reed.

Keira shrugged and shook her head. "Your guess is as good as mine on that one. Sometimes our local news gets screened on some of the cable news stations. Who knows?"

"Hmm." Dalton frowned. It wasn't ideal, but by the sounds of it, they might have a few days' leeway on their side before people started to get antsy about John's whereabouts.

"What about work colleagues?" Dalton asked.

"He's got a couple of sales reps who work for him, Peter and Tanya. Peter is this brash young bull, who thinks he can do better than John. He only keeps Peter on because the ladies love him. But John still owns the business, and he makes the lion's share of the sales. It's something he's really good at." Keira's lips twisted, as if the words left a bitter taste in her mouth. "I think they're fairly autonomous. They may try and contact him if they have a new listing, but John is often away for a few days at a time. Over on the mainland, or jet-setting around the world. I think Peter would be reveling in the fact he's not around. They might get worried if they see I'm wanted for murder, however."

"Yes, they might. But they don't know anything for certain. So even if they try to contact John, or even if they go to the police, no one will be any the wiser."

"It's certainly not ideal," Reed agreed. "But all this confusion is to our advantage. We may as well make the most of it while we can."

"Oh my God. What if the police think Keira had something to do with John's death?" Sierra squeaked down the line.

Oh, wow, he'd never even considered that scenario. Dalton rubbed a hand over his tired eyes.

"Well, there's no body to be found. It's buried beneath the lava," Keira countered. "So how the hell are they going to pin anything on me?"

"There have been cases where people have been charged with murder, and no body has been found," Reed replied wearily.

Keira looked up at Dalton, naked fear in her eyes. He wished Reed had kept that little gem of information to himself, at least for a while. Poor Keira had gone white as a sheet.

"So, where does all this leave us?" Sierra asked down the phone. "I mean, this is all a little hard to believe. We arrive on the island to come and see my sister, and we find out that not only is she married to a man who's deeply involved with some criminal syndicate, but he's been embezzling their money. And now Keira's a wanted person for some murder she didn't commit, but also, if the Yakuza get their hands on her, she's as good as dead. John is dead, but we hope no one knows that for sure yet, unless the Yakuza spill the beans. And we're not sure how long we've got until someone starts asking the hard questions about where John is, or what happened to him. Then, we have to hope that the police don't start pointing the finger at Keira for John's death, too. Did I get all that pretty much right?"

Keira just gave Dalton an anguished look. Then, she said, "*Was*. I *was* married to an embezzler."

CHAPTER ELEVEN

Keira sat on the floor in the corner rubbing Spike's ears. The dog was curled up next to her, almost as if he realized she needed comfort. His warmth seeped into her thigh, soft fur tickling her bare skin. He was a solid, calming presence, something she could concentrate on. Dalton was still talking to Sierra and Reed, they were both on speaker, but Keira had quietly left the conversation and was listening from her corner, instead. Her mind was too much of a jumble to be able to contribute anything helpful.

It sounded like they'd come up with a rudimentary plan. Reed was going to make some phone calls to his people back in Australia. See if he could find a way to get any inside information on what was going on here. If he could get a connection, through a friend or acquaintance, with an officer here, on the Big Island, then perhaps he could find out what intelligence they had on Keira. What evidence they had that she'd actually committed a murder. Even see if he could track down the real perpetrator. Dalton thought that was a long shot, however.

Keira listened to Reed's voice as he and Dalton talked, wondering what he looked like. He sounded like a cool customer, controlled, asking intelligent questions. She found herself wondering how Sierra had met him. How long they'd been going out? It was amazing her sister had found someone, after so long. She hoped he was treating Sierra well. Did he know about her past tragedy? She wanted to grab the phone from Dalton and have a quiet conversation with this man, Reed, to make sure he understood just how special Sierra was. Keira was suddenly swamped with guilt that she hadn't paid more attention to her younger sister. She wasn't great at keeping in touch with her family at the best of times, but she hadn't spoken to any of them in over six months.

A lump formed in her throat as she thought of her mother and how she hadn't returned any of her phone calls or letters recently. At the time she'd thought it was for the best. Because she'd been ashamed. Hadn't wanted Sierra or her mum to know that her fairytale life here on Hawaii was all a complete sham. But perhaps if she'd reached out to them, they might've been able to help. Instead, Keira had built that wall of silence around herself. Kept her secrets locked safely inside her heart.

"Right, that sounds like a rough plan," Dalton said loudly, and Keira broke off her rumination as the call came to an end. "We'll stay put and wait to hear from you. I'm going to turn this phone off now. I don't think the Yakuza can track it, but just in case, the less we have it on the better. I'll turn it back on at six p.m. tomorrow night. Okay?"

Keira looked up from patting Spike's silky ears. So, they were going to be stuck here for at least the next twenty-four hours.

"Yes. Oh, and, Dalton." Keira could hear Sierra pause, perhaps searching for the right words. "Thank you. You don't know how grateful I am you're helping Keira. She might not be alive without you."

Keira was looking straight at Dalton, so she saw him wince at Sierra's words, color rising up his neck as if he were embarrassed by her gratitude.

"I want to thank you in person when this is all over, but I need to say it now. It takes a particular type of man to help a stranger, and I'm so glad you didn't do what most people would've done, and handed her over to those men with guns."

"Well, now, I'm not sure that's true, but—"

"Yes, it is. So, thank you. Talk to you soon." Keira heard a click as her sister hung up and she was swamped with sudden guilt. She hadn't really thought about it like that before. She'd never once thanked Dalton for all he'd done. In fact, she'd almost taken it for granted he was going to help her. She owed this man her life. And not once had she shown him how grateful she was. All she could do was grumble about the long walk through the jungle, and hadn't even tried to hide her shock and disgust at the state of the cottage he'd brought her to. He was doing everything in his power to help her, and she was doing very little in return. Very little to help herself. How could she have been so selfish? And how could she ever repay him?

Dalton turned her phone off. He glanced in her direction and smiled as he saw Spike curled up next to her. Laying her cell on the table next to his own, he made his way over to her corner and lowered himself gingerly down onto the dirty floor next to her, Spike sandwiched between them.

"This Reed fellow sounds like he knows what he's talking about," he said, almost to himself. "And your sister is going to be an asset as well. Being an investigative journalist, she'll be good at digging out information, getting people to talk to her."

"Yes, she is." Keira didn't correct Dalton. Sierra *had been* an investigative journalist. But that'd been a long time ago. Would her skills still be as sharp? If Keira had kept in touch, then perhaps she'd know more about what Sierra was up to now. Another flash of hot guilt sliced through her gut. If she wasn't careful, she was going to drown in all this self-reproach.

"Dalton." He looked up at her as she said his name. "I want to thank you, as well. I know you were under no obligation to help me escape from Yoshio back then. And your poor truck, oh my God. I can't believe you totaled your pickup."

"Yeah, well, that might not have been my most brilliant moment, driving straight into the rainforest." He gave a wry smile. "But my truck can be repaired. Or replaced. Us humans are a little more vulnerable." He was trying to make light of it, but she needed him to know this was important.

"I know you were under no obligation to save my skin. And I want you to know, you're still under no obligation to continue doing so." Her heart beat out a tattoo of anxiety. She was giving him an out. And a small part of her was afraid he was going to take the excuse and run. And she wouldn't blame him if he did. She'd be devastated. Hated the thought of having to do this without him. "You could just walk away from this right now. Leave me here. I'll be safe enough. Reed and Sierra will help me."

He was staring at her, face blank, eyes shuttered. What was he thinking? She couldn't tell if he was even considering her words.

Finally, he said, "I do need some time to think." His dark eyes wouldn't meet hers.

Oh no, was this it? Was he going to say the words she'd been dreading?

"If I'm going to help you, I've got a few arrangements I need to make. I've got a son. I want to make sure that he and his mother are safe, before I commit to this."

Oh, God. She didn't know which bit of information to process first. The fact he'd swept away her arguments as if she'd never even spoken. Or the fact he'd just announced he had a family.

"Wow. Well, of course you have to contact you family."

Jesus, the idea had never even crossed her mind. That Dalton had a family. She'd known vaguely that by involving him she might be putting him in danger, but she'd desperately needed help and he was the only one around to do it. She'd been selfish and needy. But now he was telling her he had a family. A son. And a wife. Although he hadn't actually said *his wife*. He called her *his son's mother*. But they must still be involved somehow. If not married, then living together. This was spiraling so far out of her control, it felt like she was in the middle of a large vortex that was sucking her inexorably inwards.

"I'm going to make us something to eat, then I'm going to make a few phone calls."

"Right," she said, her voice sounding small, even in her own ears. "Thank you, Dalton. For everything. I can't begin to thank you enough." It was as if her body had gone numb, and she felt robotic, unable to process so much all at the same time. She took a deep breath. And then another one, to try and clear the heavy weight now sitting in the middle of her chest.

"Are you okay?" His large hand landed on top of hers, which was still patting Spike's head. The contact made her flinch. And brought all those churning emotions to the surface.

"I didn't mean to cause so much trouble. I don't want to involve Sierra, or Reed. Or you," she said, holding back the tears prickling behind her eyelids.

"No one thinks you did this on purpose," he said gently.

"I don't want to be such a problem. I just want to disappear. If I could get off this island, then I could go somewhere safe, change my name, go into hiding."

He stared at her, long and hard. Then he surprised her by reaching over and pulling her into his embrace. Spike protested at being squashed between them and wriggled out of the way. "You're not in this alone, Keira. Remember that."

God, his arms felt so wonderful around her. This was nothing like being held by John. Dalton was trying to comfort her. Make her feel safe and secure. He didn't want anything from her, there were no expectations to this embrace, no obligation, no debt. Her heart thundered in her chest. She softened in his arms, accepting his solace. It might be a long time before any other man held her like this again, she may as well welcome what he was offering. He rested his chin on top of her head. It felt as if they fitted together, like a lock and key.

Dalton's words made sense, but a black misery still sat like a hard stone in her stomach. A tiny voice kept telling her she wasn't worth it. She didn't want to put more people at risk, just to save her ass. Well, that was most of it. But there was a small part of her misery caused by the revelation that Dalton had a family. A significant other. And a son. Which meant he wasn't free. Which shouldn't bother her in the slightest. She wasn't about to jump into bed with him. Finding another man was the absolute last thing on her agenda right now. She hadn't even begun to process John's death and what it would mean to her life. She needed time, space, to be by herself before she could do that.

"I'm pretty sure Sierra doesn't see you as a problem," he said softly into her hair. "I can tell just from talking to her, she loves you. You're not in this alone. We'll get you through this. I'll get you through this."

Why did he have to be so damned understanding? Why did he have to make her feel like he actually cared? For a second, she thought about fighting him, pushing him away. It would do her no good in the end to accept his comfort now, if she was just going to have to do this on her own eventually. But she stayed where she was, her body overriding her head, and she remained tucked beneath his chin, absorbing the warmth of his big body so close to hers.

"Thanks," she mumbled eventually.

"I mean it." He pulled back, but only far enough so he could tip her head back and look her in the eye. "We'll find a way out of this. Together."

Her gaze traced his eyebrows, his cheekbones, square and angular, and then went down to his mouth, roamed over the rough stubble covering his top lip and the small triangle of beard forming on his chin. Those lips enticed her in. They curled up ever so slightly at the corners, softening his otherwise serious mouth. The cut on his bottom lip was still red and, while not bleeding, looked sore. She wanted to lean in, and gently kiss those lips. Soothe that cut with her tongue. Felt herself being drawn like a moth to a flame. She watched his pupils dilate as understanding hit him. That she was attracted to him. She wanted him.

It took a mammoth effort of will, but she pulled back and leant her shoulders up against the wall, breaking their connection. Hadn't she just told herself she wasn't getting involved? Not with anyone. And certainly not with a dangerously sexy man all dressed in black with a hero complex.

Using her good leg, she levered herself up. "Show me where the food is, and I'll fix us something. You go and make your phone calls," she said wearily.

"Right." He seemed to shake himself and then he was also standing, Spike dancing around his feet, excited that something might be happening. "There should be plenty of tins over in the left-hand cupboard. I stocked them up last time I was here. It was a few years ago, but they should still be good." Dalton pointed to the small kitchen area. "Don't drink the water out of the tap, though. We'll need to purify that first. I've got another two bottles in my go-bag if you need them."

"Got it," she replied, limping over to the kitchen corner and opening the cupboard door. Yep, there were tins of food, plenty of them. Enough to keep them going for the next few days at least, which was something. At least they wouldn't starve out here. She chose two tins of soup and looked around for a can opener.

Dalton, who'd been watching her silently, pulled an army knife out of his pocket, flipped up the correct tool, and handed it to her without a word. She took it gingerly, making sure their fingers didn't come in contact as he passed it to her.

Then he grabbed his own phone off the table and was out the door, leaving her alone in the dilapidated cottage. How the hell was she going to survive the next few days, cooped up with Dalton in this isolated little shack?

CHAPTER TWELVE

Dalton stalked down the path, away from his father's cottage. Spike followed close on his heels. He would go back up the small incline, there should be good cell reception from the top. He wasn't going far, he would still be able to hear Keira if she called him. And it would give him some much-needed space. Some privacy. Time to breathe and think.

Keira was affecting his brain. Affecting his capacity to concentrate clearly. Which was why he needed to get out of there. The jungle closed around him as he strode up the path. The heat and humidity of the day brought out a hoard of small flying insects, which he waved ineffectively away.

He hurt all over. His leg was throbbing. Even though the cut was minor, it was deep, and he'd need to remember to take some of the antibiotic pills he had in his first aid kit. Wounds could go septic really quickly out here. The bruises on his ribs hadn't been helped by crashing his car through the jungle, either. All his muscles were feeling the effect of fighting with that damned bail jumper yesterday, and were protesting every move he made. Plus, his head still ached, the pills only taking the edge off. Most likely he had a mild concussion. Dalton wasn't usually one to feel sorry for himself, but today, he was definitely feeling his age. A few days in this hut to rest and recuperate might not be a bad thing after all. Perhaps he should give up on the idea of becoming a private investigator and concentrate on his antique business instead.

After a second's contemplation, he shook his head. Who was he kidding, he loved this too much to give it up now. He'd bought the small antique shop as a sideline, a hobby, something to keep him busy in his retirement years. He'd be a bounty hunter for a few more years, yet. As long as Sam wanted him back after the dust had settled from this whole thing, that was.

Thinking about Sam, he wondered exactly what he was going to say to him. He needed to let both Sam and Cane know what was going on. For their own protection as much as anything. They'd want to help. Dalton knew Cane would be chomping at the bit when he found out what was going on. But Dalton still hadn't decided exactly what their next plan of action would be. He was happy to sit tight for the next twenty-four hours, to see what Sierra and Reed came up with. Should he put them in touch with Cane? If he did, they might show up on the Yakuza's radar, because Dalton had no doubt the gang would be watching anyone who was associated with him, just as soon as they discovered his name. Which'd probably happened by now. It would've been easy for them to trace his license plate number back to him.

Dalton decided to keep Sierra and Reed separate for now, let them work behind the scenes individually. He could always call on Sam or Cane's expertise later on.

He'd call Sam soon, but his priority was contacting Flora. To make sure she and Tavi stayed safe.

Her ran a hand through his hair. What in hell was he going to tell Flora? She wouldn't be happy that his stupid need to protect the innocent was impacting hers and Tavi's lives. But she would do what he asked, because, even though she might be angry as hell, she knew better than to argue when it came to Tavi's safety. He'd owe her big time after this. He hoped it wouldn't complicate their relationship. Up until now, they'd remained friends. Good friends. But Flora had always been a little hesitant about his job, said it was dangerous, even when they were going out. Which it wasn't, not really. Because he never put himself in a situation he couldn't get out of. Until today. But when Tavi was born, he'd promised never to involve her or his son. That it wouldn't impact them in any way.

Dalton sucked in a deep breath, counted to three and dialed Flora's number. "Hi, Flip, how's it going?" He tried to lighten his tone but wasn't sure he'd succeeded.

"I'm fine. What's the matter?"

Nope, he hadn't been able to keep the stress out of his voice, she could read him like an open book.

"I'll tell you in a sec. How's Tavi first?"

She gave a deep sigh down the phone. "He'd good. Actually, he's great. He made a new friend down at the park today. A little girl, her name is Amy. Tavi helped her get down the kiddy slide. It was so cute. He was such a little gentleman."

"That's my man," Dalton said, pride filling his chest like an inflating balloon. "Must take after his father. A true ladies' man."

"Ha, I'll be the judge of that," Flora replied, but there was a smile in her voice. This small little thing helped to lift Dalton's mood. But it was time to tell Flora the facts.

"Hey, Flip, I need you to do something for me."

"Uh-oh, what have you got yourself into now?" She'd already guessed there was something wrong, so he may as well tell her the truth. Or as much as she needed to know to stay safe.

"I've got involved in something, and now the Yakuza

might be after me." He winced as he said the words, it sounded ridiculous, even to his own ears.

"The Yakuza? You're joking, right? This is a joke?" Flora laughed down the phone and he didn't blame her. "That's like, Mafia-style shit. I thought they only existed in the movies?" She was still laughing.

How did he convince her? "No, they're definitely real, Flip. I need you to take this seriously. Because if they're after me, it won't take them long to find a connection to you."

She stopped laughing. "Holy shit. You're telling me this is real?" Her voice lowered to a whisper as the truth finally seemed to sink in, and Dalton guessed Tavi must be in the next room watching TV, which was why she'd lowered her voice. "Where are you? Do I need to come and get you? Shit, shit!"

"Calm down. I'm safe, for now. And I'm not going to tell you where I am, for your own security. Okay?"

"Yep, all right. So, what do you want me to do?" She was a smart girl; one of the many things Dalton liked about her was her quick wit and intelligence. She caught on fast, which was good in a situation like this.

"I want you to pack a bag and go and visit Aunty Keaka, over in Honokaa." There was silence on the end of the phone as Flora digested this news. Honokaa was only an hour's drive up along the coast. Away from all the lava flows and eruptions. Flora was lucky to have a large Hawaiian family. And family always came first with Hawaiians. Aunty Keaka would take her in without question. Dalton had met the older lady back when he and Flora were dating. She was a large woman, who wore swathes of floral muumuus, with a smile that matched her enormous size. Aunty Keaka wasn't actually Flora's aunt, the name was used more in Hawaii as a form of respect and honor. Flora's mother had died in a car accident when she was only sixteen and Keaka, as a friend of

Flora's mother, had stepped up and taken Flora in. Looked after her and made sure she finished school.

"For how long?"

"A few days, at least. Pack for a week, just in case."

"Shit, Dalton. What about my job? I can't just up and leave. They might sack me. I need that job."

"Tell them you're sick or something, Flip. This is serious. I'll help you out if they do sack you, you know I will. But you can't risk Tavi's life just to keep your job."

"Sometimes I really hate you, Dalton Kealoha," she barked, her voice rising again now that her temper was taking hold.

"I know, Flip. And you can take all that lovely temper out on me later. But for now, you have to get out of there. Immediately. Do you promise?"

"Yeah, yeah," she grumbled.

"Promise me, Flora." The fact he used her real name, instead of the nickname he'd coined when they were dating, made her stop grumbling.

"I promise."

"And you need to leave soon. In the next hour or so. Okay?"

"Okay. But I really, really hate you. You're going to pay for this."

"Oh, I know," he said in a half-groan. He knew that was an understatement. The other thing he'd always liked about Flora was her feistiness, the fact she didn't let anyone push her around. But when she really exploded, you didn't want to be standing too close. And Dalton knew he'd be on the end of that famous temper of hers when this was all over. "Tell Tavi I love him. I'll see him soon."

"I will, Dalton. He'll miss you."

Dalton gave a small smile. He'd miss his son as well. "I'm going to turn this phone off now, Flip. So you won't be able to contact me. But I'm going to let Cane know what's going on, if you need any help, if anything goes wrong, call him. All right?"

"Yep, got it." Flora only seemed to be half-concentrating on their conversation now, as if she were already planning in her head what she was going to pack. But then, just as he was about to hang up, she called out, "Oh, and Dalton? Stay safe. Tavi needs you. We both need you."

"Thanks, Flip." He ended the call and stood, staring out at the lush, green rainforest. It would've been nice to talk to his son, to hear his childish voice, even for a few seconds, over the phone. Hear him talk about those puppies he loved so much from his favorite show, *Paw Patrol*. Dalton should know all the dogs by name, he'd watched it so many times. But he was usually more interested in his son's antics while he watched the show—he loved to act out whatever the puppies were doing, standing so close to the screen he could reach out and touch it—and Dalton's heart kicked in his chest as he thought about Tavi. He never thought he could ever love another human being so unconditionally. But when Tavi was born, even though he and Flora had decided they couldn't make it work together, he'd pledged to himself he would do everything in his power to protect that little boy. To make sure he felt loved and encouraged, to be Tavi's champion. Dalton cursed under his breath. Holy crap, he was going to miss not seeing him over the next few days. He couldn't remember the last time he'd gone more than a day or two without at least talking to his son. He'd make sure to chat to him next time he called Flora.

There would be time to think about his small family later. Now, he needed to call Sam and Cane to let them know what was up. It'd be another interesting conversation. They'd probably need some convincing as well, this whole thing was just so unbelievable.

Dalton pulled himself up short. Wow, he hadn't realized

until just this moment, but he'd made a commitment to Keira. He was going to help her. Common sense was telling him this wouldn't end well. He hadn't needed any time or space to make the decision. Not really. His subconscious had always known this was going to be the outcome.

The image of Jaimie, at her twenty-first birthday appeared in his mind. She was happy and laughing, so free and young and beautiful. He hadn't been able to save her, but maybe…

Bah. Dalton shook his head. Just because Keira reminded him a little of Jaimie, he wasn't going to find redemption for Jaimie's death by saving Keira. That was just plain crazy.

Dalton turned back to stare at the collection of small buildings, partially hidden by some low-hanging vines. He'd have to go back into the hut at some stage. And now it wasn't just his father's ghost that had him not wanting to return. It was the fact he'd have to spend the night cooped up in there with Keira. Having her so close was going to be one almighty temptation. Hell, he'd already pushed things too far by stripping off in front of her and then almost kissing her. That was out of line, and he'd apologize when he went back in. Admittedly he hadn't known she'd just watched her husband being murdered, but it was no excuse. He'd just have to keep a tight rein on his libido and pretend that his hormones weren't going wild every time she came close. What she needed now was comfort and understanding. Not someone acting like a randy teenager who couldn't control himself. He was an adult and he needed to start acting like one. If only she didn't set off little landmines in his groin every time she looked his way.

Dalton shook his head and thumbed the phone to find Cane's number.

CHAPTER THIRTEEN

Keira stumbled down the steps of the hut, the dewy morning air invading her nostrils, damp and earthy. Another black mark against this cottage on the mountain, there was no indoor plumbing. The outhouse was its own little building beside the main house. But Keira had made her mind up not to grumble any more about all the things that were wrong with this place. She was safe and alive, and that was the main thing.

One thing she had positively refused to do, however, was visit the toilet at night. There was no way she was going out there in the dark. That's when all the creepy crawlies came out. Even though Dalton had laughingly told her he'd cleared the area. Wiped away all the spider webs and swept the floor, checked for any scorpions or centipedes. She'd still waited, her bladder near to bursting, until the first light of dawn had filtered through the window, before she deemed it safe enough to risk it.

Gingerly, with two fingers, she pulled the wooden door open and poked her head inside. It all looked clear. At least they had the luxury of a flushing toilet, courtesy of the rainwater tank attached to the other side of the house, which Dalton had checked to make sure was full. He'd had to unblock one of the pipes, but surprisingly, once he turned the tap on at the tank, everything had worked. Albeit, there was no running hot water, but beggars couldn't be choosers.

She completed her business and was back outside as quickly as possible.

Soft sunbeams pierced through the jungle leaves as the sun rose over the horizon, calling her up the pathway, toward the small rise. Keira loved to watch a sunrise. She was a runner and was often out at first light, on the beach, when no one else was around. It was quiet, and she found running relaxing. It was during her runs that she had truly fallen in love with the Hawaiian landscape. The impossible blue of the ocean against the backdrop of verdant, green-jungle-clad mountains. How could anyone not love the vibrant colors, so alive and kinetic?

Taking a quick glance behind her, she decided Dalton wouldn't miss her for five minutes. So, she walked on quiet feet up the incline, until she could see the valley below through the leaves. The sun was peeking over the top of the next mountain range, painting the dark-green shadows with pink light.

It was so different compared to the Australian landscape. At least, it was different than the coastal vistas around Adelaide, where she grew up. In Australia, the ocean still smashed itself against a rugged coastline, but the beaches were long and golden, filled with soft, yellow sand. And the vegetation was short and impoverished, beaten down by the heat and dry, unforgiving winds. It was still beautiful, at least it was in her eyes. Just in a more harsh and imposing kind of way.

Keira felt a sudden spike of longing to go home. Back to Adelaide, to see her mum. Spend some time with Sierra. And even Logan, her younger brother. She'd been away for so long now, perhaps it was time to go back.

She stood there, drinking in the scene. But after a few moments, her mind wandered back to last night. Dalton had insisted she take the bed, which, if the truth be known, wasn't that much of a compensation. Even after they'd taken the old mattress outside and bashed it to within an inch of its life to get rid of all the dust, and then covered it with an old blanket she'd found in the small wardrobe, it was still lumpy and uncomfortable. At least it was warm enough at night to only need a light covering, and Keira had accepted Dalton's offering of a lightweight cotton blanket he had in that go-bag of his. But Keira couldn't rid herself of the image of bugs and other crawlies hidden inside the mattress, coming out to attack her after the light was out. It hadn't happened. But still… Even though she'd traveled all over the world, she'd never lost her aversion to all things insect. Even though there were no bugs in the mattress, a few found their way into the bedroom, and Keira spent some time slapping away mosquitoes before sleep finally claimed her. A bug net would've been handy, but alas, there were only so many items Dalton could cram into his wondrous bag.

Dalton had shaken out his sleeping bag—another thing he'd magically pulled out of his go-bag—and lay down on the floor, on an old rug at the end of the bed. She'd heard him tossing and turning during the night, and she'd almost taken pity on him and told him to come and sleep on the bed with her. Almost. But then he probably would've refused. He was one stubborn man. She found it hard to read him. Most of the time he was all controlled and professional. But then, like yesterday, that façade had cracked and he'd shown a side she hadn't thought possible. When he'd taken his clothes off and stood in front of her, daring her to do the same, she'd been shocked into speechlessness. After their conversation with Reed and Sierra, he'd apologized for his inappropriate behavior, promising it wouldn't happen again. Keira wasn't sure if she was more relieved or disappointed.

Because it'd showed a part of him that she wanted to get to know. Something deep inside her responded to him. Dalton was like quicksand. No, he was more like lava. She needed to keep a safe distance, so she didn't get burned. Didn't sink into him. His sensuality bubbled underneath the surface like a volcano ready to erupt.

But how was she supposed to keep her distance, when they were cooped up together in this cottage, like two lions in a cage? There was an unspoken tension simmering between them and she didn't know what to do about it.

Thoughts of what she was putting Dalton through invaded her mind. Of how much he was sacrificing to help her. She hadn't been game to ask any more about the *family* he'd mentioned, because his face had been grim and shuttered when he'd come back in yesterday evening after talking to them. Her imagination had been running on overdrive, however. Wondering about the woman he'd called his *son's mother*. And about his son. How old was he? Did he look like Dalton? She thought back to Dalton's house. There hadn't been anything to suggest a child lived there, no toys scattered around the house, either inside or outside. And the place had been a little…austere, seemed to lack that certain touch only a woman could give. But she had only really seen the kitchen and living area, so who was she to make broad assumptions about Dalton's life?

That old, familiar guilt reared its ugly head again, making her wish she hadn't put him, or Sierra and Reed into this situation in the first place. But where else could she go? She had no one else who could possibly hope to help her against the deadly Yakuza.

Her best friend on the island, Francesca, would help her. She would love the fact there was danger and adventure involved. But what help could Francesca give? Besides a place to hide out for a day or two. But that might put Francesca in harm's way as well. She knew she could trust Fran, and there was a part of her that was still telling her to get away from all this. If she could get off the island without being seen, then she could disappear. After that, the options were endless. She could vanish into the deep jungles of Vietnam. Or be swallowed up by the teeming millions in Bangkok. The US mainland was probably out of bounds, as was going home to Adelaide. But what about somewhere else on the Australian continent? Like the isolated city of Perth, or a small country town up in the wetlands of the Kimberly coast? The Yakuza would stop looking for her eventually. Wouldn't they? The idea had its merits, and Fran would be more than willing to help her get out of Hilo, if that's what it took. She could stow away on a boat, or even use a disguise to get onto one of those day cruises to the other islands.

Perhaps she could call Fran and warn her, just in case. If Dalton was calling his family and close associates, then she should, too. After Dalton came back to the hut last night, he'd briefly told her he'd also let his two work colleagues, Sam and Cane, know what was going on. In part, because they might be able to come up with an idea on how to assist with this predicament. They had a connection to the island cops, but it was mainly to give them a heads-up, make sure they kept alert and watchful. Even when, not if—there was no doubt the Yakuza would make the connection sooner or later —Dalton doubted they'd bother Sam or Cane. But it never hurt to be forewarned, and he told Cane, his partner in the bounty hunting business, to keep a close eye on his wife and kids, as well.

If Dalton could do it, then why couldn't she?

She pulled her phone out of her back pocket, where she'd surreptitiously slipped it as she left the cottage this morning. Dalton had warned her not to turn it on unless it was urgent.

But this was urgent. She pushed the on button and then glanced guiltily behind her to make sure Dalton wasn't charging down the path toward her. He'd looked to be asleep when she left the room, but looks could be deceiving. He might've been playing possum and could right at this very moment be readying himself to come looking for her.

Her phone's screen lit up and she quickly scrolled through until she found Francesca's number. It rang and rang. Damn, was she ever going to answer?

Finally, a sleepy voice came on the line. "Keira. What the hell? Do you know what time it is?"

Oops. She'd forgotten, it wasn't even six a.m. yet. Fran was never out of bed before nine, if she could help it. She could imagine Fran sitting up in bed, long blonde hair in disarray around her shoulders, her sweet, pixie face screwed up against the early morning light. "Sorry, Franny," she apologized in a whisper. "I lost track of time, I've been a little preoccupied lately. But I need—"

"Oh fuck, Keira." Fran's voice lost all its sleepiness as she seemed to suddenly snap awake. "I've been trying to call you. Fuck, Keira, the police are looking for you. I saw it on the news last night. Are you okay?" Her words tumbled over each other as she tried to get them out in a hurry, and Keira had to hold the cell away from her ear, so she wasn't deafened.

"I'm all right at the moment. I'm somewhere safe, where the cops can't find me." Well, she hoped that was the truth. "And before you ask, no I didn't kill anyone." She was still whispering, keeping her eyes glued to the door of the cottage, just in case Dalton came charging out.

"I never thought you did," Fran said, a touch indignantly. "So, what's going on? Is there anything I can do to help?" Just as Keira had predicted, Francesca's voice had brightened at the prospect of doing something illegal or reckless.

"Thank you for the offer, Fran, you're a star. And who knows, I might even take you up on that offer. But I'm safe, for now. I can't tell you where I am, or much of what's going on, though." A sudden thought occurred to Keira. "Is there anyone else there with you?" Fran didn't have a boyfriend as such at the moment, but it wasn't for want of trying. She often had at least one or two love-starved men trailing after her, or in her bed.

"No, I'm alone."

"That's good. Because the main reason I'm calling is to tell you to take care." How did she put this so it didn't sound completely far-fetched, as if she were talking about the plot of some really bad movie? "Franny, you need to be careful. Don't go out unless you have to. Don't let any strangers into your house. Actually, maybe you should move out for a few days, go and visit—"

"What are you talking about, Keira?" Fran's tone was incredulous, and Keira knew she wasn't doing a good job of convincing her.

"I'm being hunted by the Yakuza." There, it didn't sound quite so bad when she said it quickly. "They want me because of something John did." Oh, Jesus, Fran didn't know about John. She would freak out when she found out he was dead. But Keira plowed on anyway. Now was not the time to be going into details about her dead husband's exploits. "They framed me for the murder of that girl, whoever she was. And now I'm hiding from them and from the police."

"Fuck." Fran's voice was only a whisper, but at least she sounded like she believed Keira now.

"I'm worried the Yakuza might find out you and I are friends. That they might try and hurt you to get to me." A cold sliver of apprehension slid down Keira's spine. Up until this very second, she'd known in an abstract kind of way that all these things were possible. But it wasn't until the words actually left her mouth it became a reality. Fran could actually be in mortal danger. And it was because of her. Her hand began to tremble.

"Oh, wow!" Keira wished Fran didn't sound quite so enamored by that idea. Fran always had her head in the clouds. A true artist, she always thought the best of people, but also was easily taken in by the whole sensational thing. She thrived on melodrama.

Keira sighed. "I've got to go, Franny. You take care. I'll try and stay in touch. And, Fran, you have to take this seriously. Maybe you should leave your house for a few days." Keira cast another nervous glance toward the cottage. She'd been out here too long now, she really needed to get back.

"I'm not going anywhere," Fran said stubbornly. "But I will look after myself. You know you can always count on me, Keira. I'll do anything I can to help."

"Thank you. Talk to you soon." Keira hung up but wished she could reach out and hug her friend. Tell Fran how much she meant to her. It was nice to know she still had someone she could turn to. Someone who was on her side. Of course, she had Sierra and Reed, she could trust them implicitly. But it was also gratifying to know she had a plan B if she ever needed to use it.

Quickly, she powered the phone off and slipped it back into her pocket. Then made her way on silent feet back toward the hut in the jungle.

* * *

Dalton glanced through the door, to where Keira was kneeling down, dragging leaves and dust out from under the bed with a broom. Then quickly wished he hadn't. Because she was down on her hands and knees, butt in the air to get farther under the bed, giving him a perfect view of her nicely shaped ass. She was still wearing the cut-off shorts from yesterday. But unlike yesterday, when she'd had on a more sensible T-shirt, today she was wearing spaghetti-strap top that barely covered her midriff, and showed off her lightly tanned shoulders. She said it was the only other top she had in the small backpack he'd allowed her to retrieve on their mad flight from his house. Most of her spare clothes were in the suitcase, which was way too big and unwieldy to bring with them.

Dalton found his gaze often stealing to the length of her bared collarbone, tracing it down to the sliver pendant, and then lower, to the swell of her breasts. He gave himself a mental shake and forced himself to look away.

When she'd first come out of the bedroom this morning, he'd been shocked to see a tattoo, high up on her left shoulder. It was the Wonder Woman symbol, and as she walked past him with a swish of attitude, he decided it was appropriate.

"I was young and thought I was invincible," she said as she passed him, knowing without him saying a word, he was looking at her tat. Judging her. "But I still like to think everyone has a small bit of Wonder Woman buried deep inside them."

He gave a surprised laugh. But then, the more he thought about it, the more he agreed with her. It went together with the tattoo of the butterfly on her ankle, to paint more of personality on that blank canvas of hers.

It was now midafternoon and the heat was becoming almost unbearable. It often got stifling hot up here in the mountains; with no sea breeze to cool it down, the air became oppressive and even more humid in amongst the rainforest. Early this morning, he'd done a full reconnoiter around the perimeter of the shacks. Checked out all options for escape routes, in case they were needed, and made sure they really were alone. Which they were. None of the paths into this place looked like they'd been used in years. They were overgrown and in some places, the path was almost impossible to see, if you didn't know where you were going. He was convinced they were safe. For now. Each time he'd made sure to wear his gun, just in case. He'd been out three times since then, and done the check all over again.

Around half an hour ago, Keira had announced that she couldn't stand it, all this waiting around doing nothing. So, she'd found an old broom and a few rags and started cleaning up. Dalton didn't see the point. This place was a nightmare. It deserved to be bulldozed. Actually, when he got back home, that was the first thing he was going to organize. Someone to come and tear this place down. Get rid of it once and for all. It held too many memories of his father.

He heard her start to rattle the doors to the old wardrobe in the corner of the bedroom and he got up and began pacing the floor. Items of old clothing and bed linen began to appear on the floor behind Keira as she emptied the cupboard. Spike danced around his feet, hoping they might be going outside.

"No such luck," Dalton said quietly, as he ruffled the dog's ears. They'd agreed to wait until tonight to get back in contact with Sierra and Reed. But this waiting was killing him. There were only so many times he could run a perimeter check. His leg was still sore, but Keira had checked it earlier today and it wasn't abnormally red or inflamed, which was a good thing. One thing was for sure, he wasn't looking forward to sleeping on the floor again tonight. He'd gotten soft in his old age. When he'd been in the Navy, a night spent on the floor wouldn't have bothered him in the slightest. But today his back was stiff, and his neck and shoulders could do with a good massage to get rid of all the knots.

"Hey, Dalton," Keira called from the bedroom.

He looked up, but she still had her head buried deep in the wardrobe, so he couldn't see her face. "What?"

"Come and look at this." He sighed. He didn't want to look

at anything she might've found in his father's old wardrobe. He didn't want to be reminded of his father, full stop. But his feet turned towards the bedroom anyway. He stood in the doorway and watched her cute butt waggle as she struggled with something obviously heavy in the closet.

"Wait, I'll give you a hand." He pulled the wardrobe door open as far as it would go and pushed his way in beside her, trying to peer over her shoulder to see what she'd found. And he got the surprise of his life. The wardrobe had a false back. A little alcove had opened up in the wall, between two shelves at the back of the wardrobe, and Keira was struggling to pull out what looked like a heavy, metal box wedged inside. "What the…? How did you find that?"

She finally straightened up so she could look him in the eye. "I don't really know. I was banging around in there with the broom, trying to knock the dust off the shelves and something suddenly came loose. I wiggled this piece of board and voilà, this little secret space appeared." She gave him a wide grin, full of mischief.

She obviously thought this was a bit of fun, an adventure. But she was in for disappointment. Because, knowing his father, there would be nothing of interest in there. His dad was the farthest thing from sentimental a person could get. Knowing his father, it was probably drug paraphernalia, to feed his drug habit. Or perhaps a stash of guns or ammunition.

"Are you going to bring it out?" Her grin began to fade as he continued to stare at her, unmoving.

He pursed his lips, went to tell her it was better left where she found it, but then changed his mind. He'd only met Keira yesterday and didn't know her well, but he would bet his life that she'd never let him hear the end of it, if he didn't pull the damn thing out of the wall.

"Move out of the way, then," he said, and she stepped

sideways to give him access to the wardrobe. The metal box had a handle on each side, and he bent in, grasped the handles and hauled on the box. Holy crap, it was heavier than he expected. He braced his back, straightened his legs and tried again. This time the box moved, and he lifted it slowly out of its little hidey hole, struggling to maneuver it out between the doors, and finally dropped it on the floor next to the bed.

"What do you think is in it?" Keira was already on her knees beside the box, wiping the dust off with one of her rags. "Can we open it? Does it belong to your dad?"

Dalton gave a shrug and said, "Sure, you can open it, if you want. I have no idea who it belongs to, but it's probably a good guess that my father was hiding something in there."

The box had a latch, but wasn't locked and it wasn't in too bad condition, considering it'd probably been here for nearly twenty-five years. Keira gingerly pried the lid up. It stuck at first, there was a little rust around the edges, but after a second attempt, the lid lifted, leaving a shower of dust to rain down on the contents inside. Dalton couldn't help himself. He dropped to his knees beside Keira to get a better look. There was a layer of soft fabric covering whatever was inside, and Keira pulled it back with gentle fingers.

"Books. It's full of books," Keira said softly. She touched the top one with her fingers, as if she were loath to pull it out.

Books? What the hell would his father want with a pile of books? He began taking them out, one by one, laying them on the floor next to him.

There had to be ten or twelve books, all old, maybe even first edition, probably worth some money. Some of the titles he recognized. *Of Mice and Men. The Old Man and the Sea. 1984* by George Orwell. And he'd taken some care to make sure they were preserved, each one wrapped lovingly in a piece of black fabric. Why would his father do this?

Dalton stood, a sudden, inexplicable anger coursing through him. He didn't even want to touch them. If his father had owned them, they must be tainted in some way. He went over to stand in the doorway, away from the reminders of his dad.

"These books are amazing. Was your father a scholar?" Keira exclaimed, not catching on to his angry mood. "Look at this," she held up an old, bound copy of *Moby Dick*. "Oh, look at this." She picked up another book from the bottom of the box. It had a dark-red leather cover. "It looks like a journal."

Dalton froze. His father wouldn't write a journal, would he?

Keira wasn't aware of how still he'd become. He felt like a tightly wound statue, with a bomb hidden inside, just waiting to explode. She opened the journal and a letter fluttered to the ground. She picked it up between thumb and forefinger and exclaimed, "Dalton, this is addressed to you. I think this is a letter from your father."

"Burn them. Burn it all," he snarled and turned away, practically running out of the door.

CHAPTER FOURTEEN

Keira watched Dalton storm out of the room. He slammed the front door open and walked out into the enveloping jungle. She stared after him, dumfounded. This was the first time she'd seen Dalton truly angry. But why? He was normally so self-controlled, so proficient and even-tempered. What had got him so riled up about finding a box of old books?

The letter that'd fallen from the journal was still in her hand and her eyes began reading the words almost without her permission.

Dear Dalton,

I hope one day you find this letter, but I'm not sure you ever will. I want you to have these books. They were my prized possessions. When I was reading these timeless pages, I became lost in another world. And I was able to imagine a very different life, where I hadn't made the stupid choices I did.

I'm so sorry. I screwed up in so many ways. Dalton, I want to apologize to you, for everything I've done...

There was more, a lot more, but Keira stopped reading, suddenly feeling like she was intruding on something intimate and private. Dalton needed to read this letter. It wasn't her place to dig into his past. But one thing was for sure. She couldn't let Dalton burn these books. At least not until he'd read the letter.

She opened the journal and tucked the single sheet back in the front. Her fingers flipped quickly through the pages. They were all full of small, messy handwriting, with dates going back nearly thirty years. Dalton's father seemed to have documented his life in here. She winced, trying to put herself in Dalton's shoes. Would she want to know the intimate details of a loved one if they had lived a life of crime? Had betrayed her like Dalton's father seemed to have? Maybe Dalton didn't want to read the journal right this minute, but one day he might change his mind.

She glanced through the doorway to see Dalton seated on the top step of the sagging front lanai. He was leant over, elbows on his knees, head in his hands. His hair fell over his face, hiding it from view. He suddenly looked less like a big, tough man who could handle a group of Yakuza all shooting at him, and more like a little, lost boy. Keira's heart ached for him. Spike was lying in the shade of the step, eyes locked onto his master, looking just as miserable as Dalton.

Fran had often accused her of being too softhearted. Of wanting to help everyone, even if it was to her own detriment. But it was instinctual to Keira. If someone was in pain, she wanted to help them ease it, in whatever way she could.

She got to her feet, placing the leather journal carefully back on top of the other books, and went outside. The wooden step was green with moss, but she sat down next to Dalton anyway. Close, but not touching him. She could feel the heat of his body. Neither of them said anything for a long time.

She could feel the pain emanating from him and had to stop the urge that would have her running her fingers through his hair, smoothing those messy locks back into place; touching his shoulder, or his back, to offer comfort.

Finally, she said, "I'm sorry, Dalton. I didn't mean to cause any trouble."

He lifted his head and stared out into the surrounding greenery. "It's not your fault, you weren't to know. Crap, I wasn't to know. It just goes to show, I should've torched this place a long time ago."

So, he was still talking about burning things. Not good. His finger tapped agitatedly on his knee and on instinct she took his hand in hers. He stiffened slightly but didn't withdraw it.

"But you didn't. You hung onto it for a reason. So, why do you keep this hut if it bothers you so much?" It was a dangerous question, and he might well fly into a rage again and tell her to mind her own business. But she had a feeling he wouldn't. She had an innate ability to tell when someone just needed to talk, to get something off their chest.

"I don't know," he replied at last, voice low, as if his mind was somewhere far away. Almost as an afterthought, he turned his hand palm up and threaded his fingers through hers. She was humbled by this small gesture. "My father was a deadbeat. He was sent to jail when I was twelve. And he died in jail when I was eighteen. I had nothing to do with him when he was serving his time, and I want nothing to do with him now."

"But he left you this place. Surely that counts for something," she said softly, not wanting to break their fragile bond.

"Not in my mind, it doesn't. And he never made it obvious he'd left me this cottage. I didn't even know it existed till I was searching through some of Grandfather's old documents. You know, trying to decide whether to keep them or not."

Keira nodded, not daring to interrupt him now the story was coming out.

"It was about six months after I moved back to Hawaii, and I was starting to clear out all my grandfather's things.

Renovations on the house were beginning in a few weeks. And I found this deed of ownership made out in my name, tucked in amongst all the invoices for stock and tractor parts, as if it wasn't worth anything. It showed the transfer of ownership from George to me. I was shocked. I wondered why my grandfather had never mentioned it. But then I guess he was as ashamed and disgusted by George's activities as I was."

There could be numerous reasons why his grandfather hadn't alerted Dalton to the fact he'd inherited this piece of land. Maybe Dalton was still too young or angry to appreciate it back then. Maybe the grandfather was biding his time, waiting to tell Dalton when he was more sympathetic or understanding.

"Sounds like Karma was on your side on that day. Sounds like you were meant to find it," she replied.

"Hmm," he rumbled darkly. "Anyway, I asked Aunty Lei if she knew anything about it, and in her unhurried way, she finally said she remembered George had a place somewhere. She wasn't exactly sure where, because her memory wasn't good anymore. But after a few days, she came up with an old map with all my grandfather's land holdings on it. And there were some coordinates listed for another, unnamed piece of land up here on the mountain. When Aunty Lei saw those, she said she remembered now, and told me how to get here." His hand tensed in hers and she glanced at him from below lowered eyelashes. She could feel the slight rasp of the calluses on his palm against hers. It sent a tingle of awareness up her arm. But he wasn't looking at her, his thoughts were still back with Aunty Lei.

"Weren't you just a little bit excited about that? Surely you must've been curious about what kind of place it was? Where your father lived that last chunk of his life?"

He looked at her for the first time since he'd stormed out

the door. His bicep brushed up against her arm, and the tingle turned into a slow burning fire through all of her nerve endings. "To tell you the truth, I made no attempt to contact George after he abandoned us in LA. And he never tried to contact us, either. Not before, or even after he was sentenced to twenty years in jail."

Keira grimaced, trying to concentrate on his words, and not the sensations caused by his touch. That must've been hard for a young boy, to feel like his father had abandoned him. But she kept her mouth closed, because the look in his eye said he didn't want her sympathy. He just wanted her understanding.

"I never cared whether he was alive or dead. That might sound harsh, but it's reality. And I never gave much thought as to where he might be living while he was back here in Hawaii. So, I guess, to answer your question, yes, I was taken aback to find out he'd had a hideout. And even more shocked to find out he left it to me."

"I can imagine," she said. She couldn't let go of his hand, even though she probably should, it was as if her hand were glued to his.

"I had to see it for myself, so I hiked up here. It took me a while to find it, and I knew what I was looking for, so at least we know it's well hidden from the rest of the world. I only came the once. That was enough for me. I brought a whole lot of food with me, because I wasn't sure how long it would take me to find it, or how long I'd stay. But as soon as I got here, I knew I couldn't stay more than one night. So, I left all the food behind, which is why you found the cupboards stocked."

Keira nodded, trying to see things through Dalton's eyes. It was no wonder he hadn't found the metal box back then. It sounded like he'd scampered as soon as he could. One idea kept rolling around in her head, however. "It must've been very isolating, to be up here, all on his own. I wonder if he was lonely. Maybe that's why he had all those old books. Maybe they were the only friends he truly had. Perhaps—"

"Please don't start feeling sorry for him, Keira. George was not a nice man." Dalton lowered his eyebrows at her, and she knew she was about to cross an unwritten boundary. But even though he was frowning at her, he didn't release her hand. Was that a good thing? Did he even realize he was holding it? Squeezing it?

"Maybe not," she replied. Although, what she wanted to say was that maybe Dalton had painted such a picture in his own head of what he thought his father was like, that there was no room for the truth. Not even for some sort of compromise between the truth and Dalton's reality. Unwritten boundary, or not, she suddenly decided Dalton needed a shove in the right direction. "But you might find some answers in that journal."

"Answers to what?"

"I don't know. Answers to questions you never even realized you wanted to ask."

"I'm not reading that journal, Keira, and that's final. Got it?" His dark eyes suddenly bored into her, and she wanted to squirm like an insect pinned to a board. It was definitely not the time to ask him if he minded her reading it then.

He stood up, breaking their connection, and began pacing back and forth across the small, cleared area in front of the lanai. Spike jumped up, eager for some action.

It took her a few seconds to get over the shock of losing the warmth of his hand. She opened her mouth to argue, then shut it again. Who was she to tell him what to do? She'd known him less than two days. His father was most likely the ruthless drug smuggler who lived like a savage that Dalton made him out to be. He was sentenced to twenty years in jail, after all. So, he must've deserved it. But something about that pile of books inside told her there was more to the story. Much more.

CHAPTER FIFTEEN

Dalton tapped his finger on the tabletop, ignoring the plate of food in front of him. He wasn't really hungry, even though he knew he should eat, keep the body refueled and ready for action. But his mind was too preoccupied with other things to have much of an appetite. He'd lit two of the storm lanterns, and now they were eating in the soft, yellow light cast by the one he'd hung above the table. At least all the windows in this hut remained essentially intact, otherwise they'd be completely swarmed by flying insects. As it was, there were still plenty that'd found their way inside.

They'd had a phone call from Sierra and Reed earlier, and he was still going over the ramifications of everything they'd said. He'd put Keira's phone on speaker, so they could both hear what was being said. Reed had done most of the talking. After making a few phone calls late last night—because of the time difference back in Australia—Reed had found someone with enough leverage to get him an introduction to the police captain on the Big Island, Joe Chin. They'd had a meeting with him this afternoon, but as Reed already guessed, Joe wasn't about to give them much information on the case against Keira. Reed didn't have any authority in Hawaii, but he was still working with his Australian connection to see if they could arrange a collaboration. But these things often took time to set up. However, Reed still thought their meeting with the captain was a good start, at least now he'd planted the seeds of doubt in his mind by telling him Keira wasn't actually responsible for the supposed murder.

Keira had been quiet and subdued ever since. At first, he'd thought she was the same as him, inundated with too much information. But now he looked at her properly for the first time in over an hour, and he could see there was something else going on behind those chocolate eyes. The phone call had affected her, but in a different way to him.

"You okay?" he asked through a mouthful of re-heated freeze-dried beef stew.

"What?" She lifted her eyes from the dinner she was also picking at with little enthusiasm. "Oh, yes. I was just thinking about what Sierra said."

Reed had done most of the talking, but toward the end, Sierra had come on the phone.

"Hi, sis," she'd said brightly. "How are you doing?" Keira had given an automatic reply, and Sierra had gone on to say, "I found out some things, too, while Reed was doing his thing. I contacted Stacy, a journalist who's been filing reports with her newspaper on the murdered girl. Once I confirmed who I was, she was most forthcoming. She gave me lots of interesting facts and details about the murder, and when I pushed her, she admitted that things didn't seem to quite add up. I've got a face-to-face meeting arranged with her tomorrow morning, and I'm hoping I might be able to recruit her to help us track down the real killer."

"You need to keep your heads down," Keira had warned. "Don't be attracting any attention. If the Yakuza find out you're connected to me…" She hadn't finished her sentence.

"I know all that," Sierra had huffed, but Dalton had seen the real fear on Keira's face. She seemed to be more scared for her sister's wellbeing than her own. "I just want you to know that we'll get you out of this predicament. I promise. Okay? I…we, are going to move mountains if we have to. You're going to be all right."

Dalton knew Sierra was only trying to reassure her sister, to buoy her sprit so she didn't fall into despair. But it almost seemed to have had the opposite effect on Keira.

"Everything they told us was positive," he replied. "They've made some good headway, we just have to sit tight for a few more days and let them work their magic."

"Yeah, I guess," she said, dropping her fork in her half-eaten food.

"So, what's the problem?" he asked, also laying his fork down.

Her luscious lips pursed into a bow as she stared out the window, not meeting his eyes. "I don't know. I just feel…bad, guilty, ashamed, I'm not really sure what it is. Sierra hasn't had it easy over the last ten years. She lost her baby girl in a car crash, and then she and her husband divorced soon afterwards. And now it sounds like she and Reed are an item. I'm so glad for her. She deserves to be happy. She doesn't need this. She doesn't deserve to be dragged into this shit with the Yakuza. I could be putting her and Reed in real danger."

Chocolate-brown eyes finally turned to meet his and he was startled to see how sad they were. As if she truly felt like she was a burden. Like she was unworthy of everyone's concern. She was such a beautiful; vibrant woman, what'd happened to her to make her doubt herself this way?

"And now it feels like this big freight train that's going full-steam ahead. You, and Sierra and Reed, are all so determined you know what's best for me; how to help me. But what if I don't want help? What if I just want to get off this roller coaster? It might be better if I was on my own. I could disappear easier that way, then the Yakuza would never find me."

How the hell did he start to refute everything she'd just said? It stunned him to think that she might reject his help. Reject her sister's help. That she felt her life wasn't worth the trouble they were going to.

When he couldn't come up with an answer straight away, she stood up and walked over to the window to stare outside at the darkness. But not before he saw a single tear run down her cheek.

Last time she'd cried, he'd resisted the urge to take her into his arms and comfort her, because he'd thought she was a killer on the run. This time…he could do better. In three strides, he was standing behind her. He could see her eyes widen as he approached in the reflection of the glass.

"Don't," he said. "Don't do this to yourself." He took her hand, turned her around to face him, and enfolded her in his embrace. A zing of something, the same one as when she'd held his hand earlier today, zipped through his fingers, igniting a slow-burning fire low in his belly. At first, she resisted him, remained inflexible, like a piece of wood in his arms.

"You need to believe you are worth saving," he said into her hair at the side of her face. A small part of him took note of how tall she was, how he hardly had to dip his head to whisper in her ear. How she fit nicely against his body.

A low sob was muffled by his shirt, as she leant her forehead against his shoulder. "I'm not so sure… You don't know me. You don't know what I've done. What I'm capable of doing…"

Whatever she was trying to say, it wasn't making a whole lot of sense. What was clear, however, was how his body was lighting up like a Christmas tree along all the spots where he touched hers. With only the strappy top on, her beautiful tanned shoulders were bare, and all that skin called to him. He wanted to run his fingers over the nape of her neck, across the mound of her shoulder and down the hollow of her collarbone. He forced his mind back to their conversation. Whatever she thought she'd done, it couldn't be as bad as she was imagining. How could he convince her to stop feeling so sorry for herself? To want to fight for her freedom? To give her back her confidence? That her family loved her and deserved to be allowed to help her.

"Come look at this." He turned toward the bedroom and she gasped as he jerked her, almost roughly, after him. Spike followed them into the room, but Dalton gave him a command to lie down in the corner, which he did with a grunt of displeasure. It was gloomy in the bedroom, with no storm lantern set up in here yet. But there was enough light for them to make out the pile of books on the floor as he pointed a finger.

"I grew up without my father around. Thinking my father didn't give a shit about me. I learned to be strong on my own. Learned to be a man on my own. I had no other brothers or sisters to turn to when I was lonely. And this is the legacy he left me. A pile of old books. All I've got is my hate for him and a pile of stinking books." He speared her with his gaze. "What you have with Sierra is priceless. You have a family who cares about you deeply, and that's not something to be scoffed at. They would be devastated if something happened to you. Imagine what it'd do to Sierra, or your mother, if you just disappeared without a trace. They'd never stop looking for you. Do you want to leave them with that legacy?" The words were on the tip of his tongue to say, *I care about what happens to you, too,* but he bit his tongue. Because that revelation scared the hell out of him. He needed time to digest where that thought had come from.

Instead, he went to wrap his arms around her again, but

she held him at bay with a hand on his chest. "None of them would care, if they knew what I'd done. What he made me do."

The hairs on the back of Dalton's neck stood up. What had she just said? He kept pulling her in closer. She was shaking in his arms now and the tears were flowing freely. He wanted to ask her what she meant, but something made him hold back the words. She was like a lost, little girl in his arms, wanting absolution for her sins.

Whatever the case, she was in no state to say anything. Her chest was heaving as she began to sob, like an inconsolable child. So, he led her over to the edge of the bed and sat down, pulling her into his lap. He settled her against his chest and held her tight, both arms wrapped around her back. "I didn't want to," she gurgled between sobs. "I never wanted to do it."

He held her tighter, letting her ride the wave of her sorrow and pain. Over the top of her head, Dalton could see Spike's eyes glinting in the dark, as he watched them. But he was smart enough to stay in his corner, didn't try and garner Dalton's attention. It was as if he knew Keira needed Dalton right now.

It took a long time for her sobbing to abate. But finally, her sniffles lessened and at last she looked up and drew in a deep breath. "Jesus, look at your shirt," she said.

She'd soaked his T-shirt with her tears, but he wasn't worried. "Come here," he said, shuffling backwards until his back was up against the wall, his legs spread out long on the bed. She crawled in next to him, put her head on his shoulder and curled up into his chest. It was an innocent action, one he wouldn't have dreamed of doing a few hours ago. But all kinds of barriers had been broken down between them. You didn't hold a sobbing woman in your arms and not feel something toward her. Not that he hadn't had feelings toward her before. But now, his head understood there was nothing sexual in this embrace, that she was seeking comfort, nothing more. If only his body would listen.

He could feel every inch of her long legs, as they lay alongside his on the bed. The spot where her breasts were pushed against the side of his chest was on fire with molten heat. The feel of her breath across his neck as she nestled in closer was driving him to distraction.

"Thanks." Her voice was hoarse from crying. "I'm sorry you had to witness that. I haven't cried like that in…I don't know how long."

"You don't have to thank me. You obviously needed to let go of some baggage."

"Obviously." She tried to laugh, but failed, her throat still thick with tears. They lay in silence for a moment and he let her compose herself. He studied the shape of her figure, her profile, in the weak, yellow light. Traced the line of her slightly upturned nose. The only sound was the buzz of a lazy mosquito, and her occasional sniffle. Spike gave a resigned sigh from his spot on the floor, and Dalton smiled at his dog's forbearance. Keira's fingers began to absentmindedly pluck at her necklace.

"What is this pendant you wear around your neck? And the rings on your fingers?" It was a question he'd been meaning to ask for a while now.

"This?" She held it up, so the light from the other room made it glint dully. "I made this. I'm a jeweler." Her long fingers traced the curved lines of the mandala. "I love the plumeria flower. In Australia we call them frangipani. It looks so fragile, but it's not. It embodies the blue skies, and the crashing waves, and the beaches of Hawaii, don't you think?"

"Yes, it's beautiful. A jeweler huh? Do you sell your creations?"

"Yes, mainly online, though. I sell some of it through a little artisan shop in Hilo. Leeana sells works from quite a few local artists on the island."

"I think I know it," he said. "Is it that little one on the corner of Mamo Street, called Lucky in Love, or something like that?"

"Yes, that's it." She sat up a little higher, so she could look him in the face. "How do you know? I wouldn't have thought that kind of thing would interest a big, tough bounty hunter." Her smile was weak, but at least she was trying for humor.

"I own the antique shop three doors down."

"What?" The soft light flickered in her eyes as she stared at him. "Well, that's a little…unexpected."

"Not really. My mother is into antiques. Her house is full of them. I learned to appreciate the beauty of old things when I was still young."

"Wow, I'm discovering a whole new side to you. I guess I'm surprised. But maybe I shouldn't be." Her fingers dropped the mandala and landed on his chest, tracing the line of his sternum through the black fabric of his T-shirt. "You are certainly a man of many talents." There was still a huskiness in her tone, but now Dalton heard a nuance that hadn't been there a few minutes before. A sensual undertone which set his heart pounding beneath her hand.

In the space of a split second, their embrace went from consolatory and warm to hot and erotic. All those nerve endings he'd been doing his best to dampen down suddenly flared to life. Those skillful fingers sketched around the muscle of each pec and then ventured down, flowing over his abs, one by one.

He sucked in a breath. Then brought his hand up and captured hers. "What are you doing?"

"Something I've wanted to do almost from the first moment I met you." Her eyes were dark and luminous in the dim light. "Don't you feel it, too, Dalton?"

Oh God, yes, he did, but someone needed to be the voice of good sense here. "There are so many reasons why we should stop this right now." The main one being that he wasn't the type of man who'd normally take advantage of an emotionally vulnerable woman. Which was clearly what Keira was right now.

"I know. And yet, I don't want to stop."

Neither did he.

Her face was so close to his, the soft curve of her cheek almost resting against his roughened one. Without conscious thought, he brought his palm up to cup her chin. Tilted it upwards just a little. So, he could claim her mouth. Would she let him? His whole body was alive, thrumming. Something about this woman was doing things to his brain that he'd never encountered before. As if a voice deep inside her was calling to him. Telling him not to lose her. She was important.

"But I do have one question," she said, and Dalton liked the breathy tone of her voice so much he could hardly grasp the meaning of her words. "You mentioned you had a family…" She hesitated, and immediately he knew what her question was going to be.

"Flora is the mother of my son, Tavi, but we're not together, if that's what you mean. I'm not committed to any relationship. I'm a free man," he reassured her.

She gave a small smile of relief. "That's good." Her tongue darted out to wet her lips and her eyes, as big as the moon, watched him, waiting. He wanted to moan deep in his chest. That one tiny gesture had his mind turning to mush. All he could think about was following that tongue back inside her mouth. To find out what she tasted like.

His self-control broke, like a dam bursting its banks, and he let his lips descend the final few inches onto hers. She gave a tiny murmur of pleasure, which drove him on. Their first tentative kiss deepened, and she closed her eyes and groaned.

He needed to feel her body, all of it. Without breaking their kiss, he levered himself onto his elbow and slowly edged himself up and over her, until she lay beneath him. He savored the impression of her body beneath him. All her curves seemed to fit directly into his. She must've been able to feel his erection pushing into her abdomen; he was so hard all he wanted to do was unleash himself from behind the zipper of his jeans.

"Take it off," she said, her words muffled by his kisses. The urgency of her fingers plucking at the bottom of his T-shirt told him what she wanted. He sat up, straddling her thighs, and shrugged out of his tee in one fluid movement.

"Oh, yes." Keira's hands roamed freely over all his newly-liberated skin. Over his abs, up to his chest, around his nipple and then back down, to the edge of his waistband. "Just as good as the first time," she purred, and he remembered with a spike of guilt how he'd undressed in front of her yesterday. Trying to get a response out of her. But he was getting a response out of her now, and it was nearly blowing his mind.

Before he even had a chance to ask, she was trying to sit up, tugging at her own shirt. He obligingly helped her pull it over her head. When she lay back down on the bed, he was hit by the sight of a tanned and well-defined stomach, and her full breasts, almost breaking free of the lacy, black bra.

There was a glint of silver, and he saw she had a belly-button piercing. He ran a finger around the cool metal ring. It set off her flat stomach, and he decided he liked it.

"Nice," he said.

"Why, thank you, kind sir," she shot back. "Now stop ogling my piercings and come here." With that, she dragged his head back down toward her, hungry lips open and ready for his kisses.

He explored her mouth, her neck, down between her

breasts. Tasted the skin on her shoulder, licked the Wonder Woman tattoo. She arched up into his mouth as he went lower, down over her abdomen, then lower still. Those shorts needed to come off. The button was slippery beneath his fingers and it took him a few tries to get it undone. Then he was tugging the denim fabric down her legs. He may as well get rid of his own jeans while he was at the end of the bed, so he dropped them in a puddle at his feet. Belatedly, he remembered the condom in his wallet and quickly retrieved it, putting it on the corner of the bed, within easy reach.

For a second, he allowed himself to glory in Keira's body, laid out on the bed. Long legs led up to slim hips and a muscular belly. She must work out to have a body that toned and fit. She still had on her bra and panties, but he would make short work of those when he was ready. Her head was turned to the side, so he couldn't see her eyes, but he could imagine the yearning in them. There for him.

He crawled back up the length of her body, planting kisses on the way. Stopping at the top edge of her panties as he slipped a finger underneath the elastic. Keira tensed slightly and he raised his gaze to look at her. But her head was still back on the bed. Taking his time, he worked his way up over her belly ring, licking and tasting her skin as he went. Keira lay still, her hands by her sides, and it finally dawned on him she wasn't responding as she had only moments before.

Balancing on his hands, he dragged himself the rest of the way up the bed, until he hovered over her, looking down into her face.

"Hi," he said, raising an eyebrow.

Instead of the hunger he'd expected to see in her gaze, there was an almost empty expression. As if the real Keira had left the room, leaving a cardboard cutout in her place. What'd happened? Something had changed in the time it took him to take off his pants and come back to her. But for the life of him, he couldn't figure out what. Her gaze flickered to him, then went back to rest on the ceiling above his head. The fire that'd been flaming so hot in his belly suddenly grew cold.

"Keira?"

"Hmm," she gave him a vacant smile.

"What's the matter?" Was it her husband? Was she thinking of her dead husband? He couldn't blame her, was somewhat shocked she'd made it this far. All the reasons they shouldn't be doing this in the first place came flooding back.

Laying down alongside her, he took her chin in his hand and tipped her face toward him. "Talk to me, Keira."

"Nothing's going on, I'm fine. Why did you stop? I was enjoying that."

But Dalton didn't believe her, not for one second. Her voice had taken on a robotic tone, as if she were speaking from force of habit.

"Maybe you were enjoying it, until about two minutes ago. Then something changed. What was it?"

Her eyes finally focused on his face. The blank look was replaced by one of fear and then self-loathing.

"Oh God, Dalton, I'm so sorry." She rolled away from him, curled into a ball on the bed, with her back to him.

"It's okay. I understand. You're still thinking about your husband."

"No, that's not it. Well, yes, it is, but not in the way you mean."

"What's the matter?" he asked again.

"You won't want me if I tell you. If you find out what I've done, you'll be repulsed by me." Here she was, going on again about something she'd done, something she was ashamed of. With gentle hands, he rolled her back towards him on the bed, and they lay facing each other, his forehead resting against hers.

There were no tears this time, her eyes were dry. But there was a faraway, haunted look to her face. Her normally full lips were stretched into a line, pulled down at the corners. And her cheeks seemed hollowed out and pale.

"Tell me, Keira," he prompted.

She wouldn't meet his gaze. Bit her lip and then closed her eyes. "John used to give me to his guests. If I didn't do what he wanted, he would…make me pay afterwards."

"What?" His mind took a few seconds to catch up. Give her to his guests…? Then it hit him like a ten-ton truck.

Holy crap, her husband had used her as a prostitute. To keep his clients happy. Bile rose at the back of his throat, and a sudden urge to punch something overwhelmed him.

"That fucking bastard," he roared. No longer able to lie still he got up and began pacing the floor, heedless of his nakedness.

CHAPTER SIXTEEN

"Dalton, please, don't," she implored. He was pacing the floor like a caged animal, and poor Spike was cowering in the corner, afraid of his master's fury.

Dalton was angry at her. She knew he would be. Why, oh why had she blurted out those words? She'd managed to keep that secret for so long now. Managed to keep her true heart silent. But for that split second, with Dalton, lying in his arms, she'd felt safe, sheltered.

But now he hated her. And he had every right. She was damaged goods. Not worth anything to anyone. What husband would give his wife to be used as a sex toy, just to help him close a deal? And what wife would let him?

She curled into the fetal position. The only thing left to do now was wait out Dalton's rage, and then pack her few meager things and leave. Because there was no way he would want anything to do with her. She was on her own again. Lying there in her underwear, she no longer felt sexy and empowered; now, she now felt exposed and barren. Bereft and desolate.

She heard Dalton stop his pacing, but didn't lift her head to see what he was up to. The bed dipped as he lowered himself on to it and she flinched away from him. And then, wonder of wonders, his arm came around her shoulder, pulled her toward him. What was going on? Why wasn't he yelling at her to leave? That she was a lying little whore and she needed to get out?

"Sorry," he whispered into her hair. "I'm so sorry." He was apologizing to her. But why? "Don't be afraid, I'm not going to hurt you. I was just so mad. I can't believe your fuc—" He drew in a sharp breath. "Never mind. What I think of your husband doesn't really matter," he finished brusquely.

Dalton's arm was warm, like a soft blanket around her shoulders. But his words surprised her. It sounded like he was angry at John. Not at her. She lifted her head and chanced a glance at his face. His dark gaze bored into hers, with an intensity she'd never encountered before.

"I can't believe you've been through all that. And you think you're not worthy because of it." A tension was thrumming through his body, she could feel the almost imperceptible tremble, as if he were holding in so much more he wanted to say.

Her head was still trying to make sense of it all. She'd been vulnerable, he'd broken through her defenses, and that's the only reason she could think to justify why she'd opened her mouth to tell him about her life with John. And then, as soon as the words left her lips, she'd regretted them. Because of course, Dalton was a man. And like every other man she knew, he would blame her for her own predicament. Tell her she deserved it. When he'd leapt out of bed in a rage, she'd assumed the worst. Because that's the way it'd been for as long as she could remember. As long as she'd been with John.

But Dalton wasn't like any other man she knew. Here he was, holding her, giving her refuge, and telling her it wasn't her fault. It was hard for her to process. She didn't know where to start, but she owed him something.

"I've never told anyone before," she whispered.

His arm tightened around her. In the dim light she could see his jaw working, but then he let out a breath and said, "You can tell me. I won't judge. And it might help to…you know…deal with it a little better."

Could she? Should she? Would it make it better or worse to tell all? Let it all out, like draining poison from a wound.

Dalton shifted slightly, and she remembered he was still naked. The rasp of his legs as they covered hers, the flex of his abs as he pulled her in tighter against his body, it all felt so good, so right. Perhaps she could trust him to hear her words.

Tilting her chin toward the ceiling, she let his warmth invade her core. Then slowly the words formed. At first, her thoughts were a ball of heat and pressure, pushing from inside her chest. A burden so immense it felt like she might burst if she didn't release it. But in the second she decided to tell him, gave herself permission to let the secret out, the words tumbled up out of her throat and onto her tongue, almost before she knew what was happening.

"After the first time, John promised it'd never happen again. It was so important for him to close this deal he had going. It was a twenty-million-dollar property on the line. And the guy was so close to signing. But he said he'd only do the deal if John would give him this one little thing. And that thing was me. I knew he'd been watching me all night. Kind of predatory, you know. I think I was in shocked disbelief when John told me—and also more than a little drunk at the time—and maybe that's why I agreed. But I felt so dirty afterwards. And I made John swear he'd never do anything like that again." Keira's stomach clenched painfully as the memories of that night swirled. At the time she'd been so distraught, felt so betrayed and soiled. As if the whole thing had somehow been her fault. But then John had been so loving afterwards, so solicitous and devoted, acted as if nothing had happened. And stupidly, she'd forgiven him.

"But it did happen again?" Dalton prompted quietly.

She closed her eyes, unable to look at the empathy shining from his gaze. Now she'd started, she needed to tell the whole story.

"Yes, a few months later. This time with Yoshio, the Yakuza gang leader. When John told me Yoshio was coming for dinner, and what he expected of me, I flat-out refused. We argued, and he got so mad. I'd never seen him so mad. He didn't hit me. Instead he went into my jewelry studio and destroyed my tumbler. It's a machine I use to polish my gemstones. He threatened to break it all, all my tools, my workbench—reduce it all to rubble, he said. So, I gave in. I drank myself into oblivion that night, and let Yoshio have his way."

"That doesn't sound like the end of it, though?" Dalton asked.

"No, it wasn't," she admitted. "Yoshio came more and more often to our house. At first, it was every two or three months, but it soon became monthly. I think John began to hate him for his obsession with me. But what could he do? He was the one who'd offered me in the first place." Keira let her gaze find the ceiling, trying not to let the memories overwhelm her. "I never told John exactly what went on behind those bedroom doors, and he never asked. But Yoshio was becoming more…twisted in his tastes. Maybe that's why John started stealing his money, as a way of getting back at him. I'm not exactly sure what would've happened if Yoshio hadn't found out John was taking his money." She gave a small shudder. "In some ways, I owe my freedom to John and his greed and ambition."

Dalton was stroking his hand lightly down her back, sending small shivery tingles up her spine. "I can't believe there are actually men alive in the world who are capable of such…atrocities. Do you mind if I ask, why you stayed with him for so long?"

"It's hard to explain. Even I'm not sure exactly why I complied to his wishes. It was as if John knew how to press all my buttons. He told me I was an undeserving wife, that if I truly loved him, then I'd do this one little thing for him. It wasn't asking so much was it? And it wasn't like I was cheating on him, because he condoned it."

"It's called emotional blackmail," Dalton said darkly.

"And now I realize that John was very good at it. But back then…I don't know…I wanted to please him. There were other things, as well. He was financing my jewelry making, helping me to turn it into a reality, building up my business. You see, when John wasn't using me to buy him favors, everything else about our life was normal."

"Mmhmm."

It didn't sound like Dalton really believed her. But it was the truth. If she mentally blocked out the fact John was using her like his own personal prostitute to get further in business, then John was mostly a loving husband. He helped her with her business. He cooked dinner for her most nights, especially if she was working late in her studio. He bought her gifts, flowers, clothes, gold and diamonds, an expensive car. Rubbed her feet if she complained her shoes were hurting. Brought her a cup of herbal tea in bed every morning. And when they had friends around for a meal, he was the consummate host. Treating her with affectionate ease. And there were so many other little ways to justify it. At least he wasn't using real prostitutes, like he'd threatened to do.

"I was making plans. I was going to leave him."

"That's good. It means you were starting to stand up for yourself. Now that he's dead, at least you can begin to find your self-esteem again."

"I'll certainly try. I want to be that woman I was before I met John. The one who had the courage to travel the world on her own, to experience everything life had to offer. I really do."

Dalton's hand had dropped lower down her back, and now he was tracing small circles in the dip just below her waist. Small shock waves of sensation spread out from his fingertips, and she suddenly couldn't concentrate on what else she wanted to say.

For the second time that day, she let her eyes roam over him, pushing herself up on her elbow to get a better view. He was definitely the whole package, when it came to manhood. Just looking at him caused a warmth to pool low down in her stomach. It was funny, half an hour ago she'd felt so... ravaged, scorched by her admission, questioning her whole sense of self-worth. Expecting Dalton to treat her with the distain she deserved. But now...

Now, everything had done a sudden about-face. The opposite of what she'd expected had happened. Dalton respected her courage, had empathy for her plight. Had offered her support instead of condemnation. It was liberating and invigorating. Her body was re-awakening, his touch igniting that yearning deep inside.

What would it be like to have sex with a man to whom she was actually physically attracted? On her own terms, rather than under someone's command. And she did want him. Not only because he was a physically perfect specimen, but because his heart called to her. He cared. About her wellbeing.

She lowered her head, until her lips hovered mere millimeters above his, letting a slow smile curl her lips upward. Dalton's fingers stopped their lazy circles, as his eyes widened with surprise.

"Kiss me," she demanded.

"Are you sure?" He licked his lips and she could see how much he wanted to. How much he was holding back. "I mean…"

"Yes, I'm sure." She dropped her head the last little bit and met his mouth with hers. At first, he was tentative, in case she changed her mind. In case she was confused. But she wanted to taste him. His body set her on fire and for once, in a very, very long time, she was lusting after a man. And it felt good.

With a twist of her hips and a push on his shoulder, she was suddenly sitting astride him, had propelled him onto his back. She sat there staring down at him, enjoying the view. His big hands came up and grabbed her hips, but other than that, he remained perfectly still, watching her with dark, brooding eyes.

She ran a fingernail down the length of his chest, watching for his reaction. He never moved a muscle, but she could feel all that restrained energy, buzzing just below the surface.

She liked that she could have this effect on him. How her touch could affect a man like him. So big and strong, yet he stilled beneath her hands. A slight catch to his breath was all that gave him away.

Reaching behind her back, she undid her bra and watched his face as she slowly lowered it. A muscle in his jaw flickered.

Taking one of his hands from her hips, she placed it on her breast, letting his long fingers cup her fullness. A zing of pure desire shot straight to her core as his erection pulsed beneath her.

"You're an extremely beautiful woman, Keira." Dalton's voice was husky as his gaze roamed over her, hovering for a second over her breasts, before coming up to meet her eyes. Showing her he liked what he saw. Once he was sure he had her attention, he added, "Both inside and out."

And at that particular moment, she did feel beautiful.

* * *

Dalton groaned and opened his eyes the merest slit. Daylight poured into the bedroom. It must be almost mid-morning. They'd slept the morning away. Then Dalton smiled as he remembered their night together. They hadn't fallen asleep until the early hours before dawn, so it was no wonder they were tired.

Keira stirred in his arms, gave a sleepy murmur and snuggled in closer to his chest. They were both completely naked, but he'd draped the blanket over them as the night began to cool. He ran a lazy hand over her hip bone, which was jutting into his stomach, and then down her thigh. In some ways, he lamented only having the one emergency condom in his wallet. But then another smug smile lifted the corners of his mouth. Without another condom, they'd had to get rather inventive with their lovemaking. He stretched gently, trying not to disturb Keira, and was surprised at how stiff some of his muscles were. He could blame the previous few days, a fight with a bail jumper and a car crash for some of his injuries. His leg was sore today, too, telling him he might've overdone it just a little. But perhaps he was also just a tad out of practice in the sexual department.

He looked down at Keira's sleeping face. Would it be stupid to hope they could have more than one night together? It had been a night full of revelations. He still couldn't believe what Keira had told him about her husband; the way he'd treated her. It was no wonder she was confused and wary. It'd take time and some counseling for her to come to terms with what he'd done. She struck him as such a giving person. An idealist, who relied on her intuition to connect with people. Last night, she'd revealed she was an artist, a jeweler, and when she'd said that, certain things about her became clearer for him. Most of the artists he knew tended to live in their imagination, more so than in the real world. They had a way of retreating from reality, getting lost in their work. Was that what'd happened to Keira? Had she somehow pretended what her husband was doing wasn't really happening? And that bastard had captured her soft, trusting soul, and taken advantage of it. Used his cruel intentions to control her. Dalton squeezed his hand into a fist at the thought.

Suddenly, Spike, who'd been lying at the bottom of the bed, sighing every now and then in a vain hope his master would finally get up and let him outside, gave a low growl. Dalton stiffened, and listened intently, wondering what his dog had heard.

The dog got to his feet, his deep growl becoming more menacing.

A muffled, male voice sounded outside the front door. "Dalton, are you in there?"

Spike started up a loud, sustained, barking and Keira jerked awake in Dalton's arms. "Is it them? Have they come to get us?" Keira asked, pushing her mussed hair back from her face, fear replacing sleep in an instant.

"Get dressed, quickly," he said, leaping out of bed and pulling on his jeans.

She was scrambling out of bed behind him. "Oh, God, what are we going to do?" she moaned.

"I'm not sure, but I think I might know who it is." He took her by the shoulders and forced her to look at him. "Stay in here, out of sight. If I yell, you climb out the window and run like hell, okay?" It was a terrible plan, but it was all he had. Hopefully that voice belonged to the person he thought it did, and there would be no need for running and hiding. Spike was still barking, so whoever was outside would be left in no doubt someone was inside. But the fur along the red dog's back, which had been standing up, was now lying flat, and his bark lost its menace. As if he knew the person on the other side of the front door.

Dalton pulled his T-shirt over his head and grabbed his gun from the little side table next to the bed, tucking it into the waistband of his jeans.

Keira was still struggling to get her top over her head, not bothering with her bra, and Dalton caught one last glimpse of those luscious breasts before he left the room, closing the door softly behind him.

Instead of opening the door straight away, Dalton crept around to one of the front windows that afforded a view of the lanai. Slowly he peeked around the edge of the window, hand on his gun. He let out a rush of relieved air, just as more loud banging started up on the door.

"Let me in, Dalton, I can hear your bloody dog." It was Cane, and he was alone. Although how he'd found this place was one of the first questions he was going to have to answer, because even as one of his few friends on the island, Dalton still hadn't told him of the existence of his father's hut.

Dalton unlocked the door and ushered the other man in, taking a quick look outside before shutting the door firmly.

"Goddamn, you're a hard man to track down." Cane gave Dalton a slap on the back as he took a look around the room. "Shit, what is this place? How come you never told me about it?"

Cane was pretty much a carbon copy of his father. He wasn't a tall man, but he still managed to be imposing; all muscle, with a thick neck and fierce expression. Indomitable. The only difference between him and his father was Cane had no distinctive scars on his face. Sam had been attacked by a knife-wielding felon early on in his career as a bail bondsman, and had been left with three scars on his face. Sam always like to joke that he still got his man, even though his face looked like a bloodbath. And they gave him a fierceness that Cane never seemed to be able to emulate.

"Too many questions," Dalton growled. "Sit down." He gestured to the small table and chairs in the corner. Cane did as he was told and Dalton stood over him, arms crossed, gun still nestled comfortingly in the back of his jeans.

Dalton wasn't sure, but he thought Cane's gaze may have lingered on the bedroom door just a little too long. When he'd called Cane, to warn him to watch out for the Yakuza, he hadn't told them everything. He'd kept his involvement with Keira a secret. Instead he'd said that he'd gotten mixed up with something bad, something the Yakuza might not like, and to watch their backs. That he'd get in touch with them if he needed help. And he'd made sure they wouldn't try and contact him, that he was hiding somewhere safe for now. But neither Sam nor Cane knew about George's hideout.

Cane was his friend, but he had a lot of talking to do as to what he was doing here, before Dalton relaxed. He resisted the urge to glance at the closed bedroom door, just hoped Keira would do as she was told and stay put. Until he made damn sure this wasn't some kind of setup.

Spike had his head on Cane's knee, begging for a pat. But when he saw Dalton's belligerent stance, he backed away under the table, tail between his legs. Dalton could see the confusion in the dog's eyes, almost as if he were saying, *but this man is a friend, isn't he?* Dalton had to make one-hundred percent sure.

"What you doing up here, Dalton?" Cane asked, with a large dollop of detachment that had Dalton's internal radar going off. Cane was always a little too cocky for his own good. Most days Dalton ignored it, because sometimes you needed that arrogance to get what you wanted, especially in their line of work. But when he intentionally downplayed it, like now, Dalton became worried.

"I'll ask the questions," he snapped, and for the first time, Cane really looked at him, surprise in his features.

"Look, man, I didn't mean—"

"Shut up for a second, will you?" Dalton kept his voice soft, but there was no mistaking the menace in his tone. He was ready to take his friend down, if he didn't answer his questions properly. You could never be too careful, not when the Yakuza were involved.

Cane reared back, hands up in the air, as if in surrender.

"How did you find me?"

"Can I get a glass of water? It was a long walk up here."

"Not until you answer me." Dalton took a step toward him, arms still crossed, brows lowered in a frown.

"Fine," Cane said, putting his hands on the table. Which was good; Dalton wanted them where he could see them.

"There's been a whole heap of crazy stuff going on in town."

Dalton just nodded and let Cane keep talking.

"Me and dad were worried about you. When the police called and told us your car was halfway down a mountain side, that it'd been run off the road and you were nowhere to be found, we were shitting ourselves."

"I phoned you," Dalton said, more calmly than he felt. "To let you know I was okay. To warn you."

"Yeah, you did, but that was nearly forty-eight hours ago. We haven't heard a peep out of you since then. I was worried, Dalton. Me and dad decided I needed to come and find you. Especially when you said the Yakuza might be after you. Goddamn, what did you do to get mixed up with them?"

"I'll tell you later. First of all, you need to explain how you found me."

"Why are you treating me like I'm the enemy?" Cane pursed his lips and raised one stocky hand, palm outwards.

"Because I can't trust anyone at the moment."

"Surely, you can trust me. We're partners. I've worked side by side with you for the past four years." Cane's mouth took on a slightly sulky tilt.

"Mmhmm." Dalton considered his friend. Why was he being so distrustful? Cane was right, he was only here to help. "Just tell me how you found this place, first."

"All right. It wasn't that hard, and there's no woo-woo conspiracy going on here, if that's what you were thinking. I went and talked to Aunty Lei. I knew if anyone had a clue where you'd gone, it would be her."

Dalton blew out a breath. She was the only other person who knew about this place; knew that if Dalton needed somewhere to hide, then this might be the spot he'd come to.

"How is she? Is she okay?" Dalton had thought about warning his aunt, but it would've done no good, she would've raised her chin and told him in that unhurried way of hers that no one on the Big Island would ever dare hurt Aunty Lei. And she was probably right.

"Yeah, she's all good, man. But she was crazy mad when she found out you were missing. I thought she was going to kill me. She has good aim for an old bird." Cane mimed ducking under the table to avoid a precisely thrown saucepan.

Yep, that sounded like Aunty. Dalton tipped his head back. He really wished Cane hadn't let on to her about all this, now she would be worried. And he hated to worry her for no reason.

"So, now do you believe me?"

Dalton took a step back and uncrossed his arms. Cane wasn't here for any other reason than he wanted to help. Why had Dalton even second guessed him? It was stupid.

"How long were you planning on hiding out up here? You can't stay here forever, you know," Cane continued.

Dalton shrugged. He hadn't really considered how long he was going to stay up here. At the moment, they were relying on intel from Sierra and Reed before they made any decisions. Things with Keira's sister weren't moving as fast as Dalton might've hoped, but he was still willing to give them another few days yet to come up with a plan. And on one point, Cane was wrong. George had hidden up here for years without being found. So, it was feasible for him and Keira to stay here for as long as they wanted, as long as they re-stocked their food supplies.

"Can I have that glass of water now?" Cane asked.

"Sure." Dalton felt a twinge of guilt twist in his chest. He walked over to the pot of filtered water they kept on the bench and poured some into a battered tin mug, which he and Keira had been taking turns to drink from. Dalton avoided looking directly at the bedroom door as he passed it, praying silently Keira would remain hidden. He still wasn't sure whether he was going to reveal her presence to Cane, or if he'd try and get rid of him, with him none the wiser. It might take some fast-talking, but it was a definite option. The fewer people who knew where Keira was, the better.

"There's more," Cane said, as Dalton put the mug down on the table in front of him. "I have to tell you, there are rumors flying all over town. It's not hard for people to put two and two together. There's something else you need to know. The Yakuza have put a bounty on your head. A big one." Cane narrowed his eyes at Dalton, his blue eyes going hard. "And on the head of the girl. The one the police are after. The one that, if I'm not sorely mistaken, you're shacked up with." Cane raised an eyebrow in the direction of the bedroom door.

Holy crap, Cane knew she was here. Dalton hadn't been able to hide anything. He'd known all along.

CHAPTER SEVENTEEN

Keira followed Dalton down the path. Sometimes he was hard to spot in the deep shadows, dressed all in black. Spike was even harder to see as he trotted, wraith-like, at Dalton's feet. Cane was in front, leading them down, Keira could see splashes of color from his bright floral shirt in amongst the leaves.

Keira was still coming to terms with Cane's arrival, and the news he'd brought with him. She'd listened with her ear to the door as Dalton let him in to the hut and then interrogated him, her heart beating a staccato tattoo, adrenaline making her jittery. Dalton had circled Cane like a wary tiger, waiting for one wrong move from his prey to pounce. Which surprised her, because from what she understood, Cane was a friend, a work partner. But he was treating him like he was a threat, and it hit her like a brick wall that she'd have to be very careful with who she trusted now, too. Especially now that there was a bounty on her head.

That bit had shocked her the most. When she'd heard Cane utter the words that the price for her life was one-hundred-thousand dollars. It made everything more real. It meant not just the Yakuza were pursuing her now. But many other, unsavory people would go out of their way to hunt her down, to get their hands on that substantial sum of money. She shouldn't be surprised, after all, she'd heard plenty about the Yakuza tactics, but it'd all seemed like a fantasy, things people made up to go in movies. It didn't happen in real life, not to normal, law-abiding people like herself.

In the end, after Dalton had asked her out to meet Cane, Dalton told her he trusted the man. He was a good friend and they should probably listen to what he had to say. Then Dalton had filled him in on everything else, including the fact Keira thought the leader of the Yakuza, a man Keira had named as Yoshio, wanted her to access John's bank accounts to get all his embezzled money back. Cane had suggested if Keira just gave up the bank details, then Yoshio might leave her alone. Which might well have worked, except she had no knowledge of them.

Up in front, Cane came to a halt, waiting for them to catch up. Cane reminded her of an eager puppy, full of energy, pumped up, as if on an adrenaline high. Keira would have to remember to ask Dalton if he was like this all the time.

"We should probably take a bit more care from here on," Cane said in a low voice as soon as both of them were close enough.

Keira eyed him without saying a word, then took a swig from her water bottle, readjusting her backpack. The only person she was going to take orders from was Dalton.

She gave Spike a drink of water out of her hand, listening to Cane as he continued, "My car is parked at the end of a dirt road, about a kilometer down from here." Cane had told them he'd taken no chances, made sure he wasn't followed and was driving a borrowed car. "Aunty Lei told me where to find the start of the trail up to your hut," he added in a hurry, when Dalton shot him a sharp look. "There's no way I would've found it otherwise."

"Lead on, then," Dalton said in a deadpan voice. Dalton

had been acting as if he were on edge ever since Cane had arrived, and Keira was finding it hard to read him. After their night spent together, she'd felt like they'd forged such a strong connection. But this new Dalton, well, she was struggling to figure him out. And it hurt just a little, even though it shouldn't. They hadn't made any promises to each other last night, far from it. But she'd told him her secrets, and to an extent so had he, revealing his inner feelings about his father.

Cane gave them both a speculative look, before hoisting his small backpack higher on his shoulders and continuing down the path. As soon as Cane had his back to them, Dalton surprised her by taking her hand and giving it a quick squeeze. It was over in a second, almost like it never happened, but it was enough to lift Keira's spirits. Enough to know he was thinking about her. He cared.

Her thoughts skittered guiltily to the red journal she'd stuffed into the bottom of her backpack. Dalton would not be happy if he knew she'd brought it with her. But Keira hadn't wanted to leave it; who knew when the next time Dalton, or anyone else, would go up to that hut again? There was important stuff in there that Dalton should read. If not now, then sometime in the future. Perhaps it might help him deal with this hate for his father that was eating him up inside, even though he would never admit it.

Keira gave a small shrug and upped her pace, ignoring the slight twinge in her twisted knee. They had a plan in place. They were going to Francesca's house. Keira had already called to warn her. Cane had given a very persuasive argument and eventually convinced them to go back into Hilo. Said they were way too isolated and vulnerable up here on their own. Which Keira had thought was the whole point of the thing, but she'd kept her mouth shut. Cane argued that if they were in town, he and Sam could help protect them, and they were closer to the police. Dalton was also worried about his Aunty Lei, because as he pointed out, if Cane could use her for information, so could Yoshio. Cane was going to settle them at Fran's place first and then go and look after Aunty Lei.

When Keira first heard of Cane's plan, she'd baulked. He'd asked her if she had any friends on the island who weren't connected to John in any way. Immediately, Fran sprung to mind. "But won't Yoshio be watching her? Won't we be putting her in danger?" she'd argued.

"No, I don't think so. They'll be looking at your husband's connections. I'm assuming you had a lot of friends you socialized with as a couple?" Keira nodded. She thought about Eva and Gianna and their husbands. Would Yoshio be brazen enough to pay them a visit, or just discreetly watch them, waiting for Keira to turn up on their doorstep?

"Who else knows about this Francesca?" Cane asked.

"Well, John knew about her, of course. She and I were roommates for a while, but that was ten years ago. I guess after I met John I saw a lot less of her." It was true, she really only saw Fran when John wasn't around. If she was in town, she might meet her for lunch, or go and visit her at her studio-cum-gallery. It wasn't that John didn't like Fran, but now Keira thought about it, he'd never fostered her friendship either, as if deep down somewhere, he didn't believe Fran was good enough for her. "You're right, not many people would be able to connect me with her." And most of those people had known them ten years ago, when Keira first moved to Hawaii. When she worked at the real-estate office. Keira had lost touch with all of them since then.

"Besides, it will only be for a day or so, then we'll move you somewhere more suitable. Perhaps even be able to get you off the island," Cane said.

Keira looked at Dalton, to gauge his reaction. Now they

were even talking about getting her off the island. Which meant they thought they couldn't get around the Yakuza, not even with Sierra and Reed's help.

Dalton nodded slowly. "It makes sense," he replied. "And Cane's right. I should get closer to town, more involved in this. There are people who might be able to help us. But I'll need to talk to them face-to-face. Even though it's a little riskier being in town, I think we should move."

For some reason, Keira didn't feel like she agreed with him. But who was she to argue? She knew nothing about espionage, the rules of engaging with villains, or how to evade the long arm of the Yakuza. She had to trust them. The one ray of sunshine in this whole thing was she would see Fran again.

"Once we're sure the place is clear, we should probably get Sierra and Reed to come and meet us as well," Dalton said.

"Really?" Keira's heart skipped a beat. To be able to see her sister. Now that would be something special.

* * *

Dalton sat in the passenger seat of Cane's borrowed truck. He was trying damn hard not to show how tense he was. Cane was driving fast, but that wasn't what was bothering him. Even though Cane had made a lot of sense and Dalton understood that moving back to the city would be best, it still felt like he was being railroaded by his partner. Perhaps it was because he wasn't in complete control of the situation anymore. He had been called a control freak on more than one occasion. Dalton's head told him to trust Cane. After all, he'd spent nearly five years with the guy in the Navy, and then another four years working in bail bonds, so he knew Cane was as solid as they came. Dalton squashed that tiny shadow of a doubt wriggling in the depths of his soul. This whole thing was one big fuck-up. Nothing was ever going to feel completely right until it was over. One way or the other.

"Take a left here," Keira directed from the back seat. Spike sat next to her, his head hung out of the partially open window, enjoying the new smells immensely. At least one of them was happy about the new situation.

They were a couple of streets back from the main drag, only a short walk to the beach and the main shopping hub.

"Slow down," Keira said as she peered out the window. "It's up here, just opposite the school... That's the one, number two hundred." She pointed eagerly at the ramshackle little cottage hunkered down in a meadow of tall weeds. Dalton held in a grunt. This place wasn't much better than his father's hut. But looks could be deceiving.

Cane pulled into the drive. "You guys get out, I'm going to park the car down the next side street," Cane said. "Just in case."

"Good idea," Dalton replied. "Wait a second," he cautioned Keira, who was already opening her door. "Let me check it out first."

She huffed in frustration and narrowed her beautiful brown eyes at him but stayed in the back seat. Slowly, Dalton got out of the car and walked to the end of the drive, surveyed the street both ways with a practiced glance. Nothing moved, except an old guy using a walking cane a few doors down. It was mid-afternoon in Hilo, but this street was still quiet. *Good.* The less witnesses to their arrival, the better.

"Right-o," he said, and the back door sprang open and Keira dived out, Spike following at her heels, and was up the two small steps to the main door before he could say anything more. A petite, blonde woman opened the door and took Keira into her arms before she'd even stepped into the house. Dalton watched the two women embrace, Keira towering over her friend, her long legs glowing in the afternoon sunshine, her short, auburn hair mixing with the light-blonde locks of her friend.

"Thank you so much," Keira said, "You are literally a life saver."

"No probs, Kez. Come in."

Dalton followed them into the slightly cooler, dim interior. Inside the house was a riot of color, as if the woman who lived here couldn't decide which was her favorite, and instead used every hue of the rainbow. One of the walls was red, the one next to it a bright purple. The furniture was old and worn, but everything in sight was draped with patterned scarves and rugs, so it looked like a carnival had thrown up all over the house.

Keira turned around and caught his eye. She was worried, but he wasn't sure about what exactly.

"This is the man who's helping me. The one I told you about. Dalton, meet Fran," she said, stepping back so they could shake hands. The petite lady had the brightest blue eyes he'd ever seen, and she raked her sapphire gaze up and down his body as their palms came together.

"Ooooh, he's yummy. Nothing like John, mind. Can I have him?" Fran leaned in and whispered the last bit into Keira's ear, but it was still loud enough for him to hear. Keira looked at him and blushed. He gave her a rakish smile.

"And who's this?" Fran asked, not waiting for an answer as she bent down to pat the dog's head.

"That's Spike. I hope it's okay if he stays, too?" At Fran's wide grin of acceptance, Keira grabbed her by the arm. "Come on, Fran, we need to talk." She steered her towards what looked to be a bedroom at the back of the house, and Dalton guessed she was going to tell Fran about John.

Dalton decided to leave the two women to their difficult conversation and went into the kitchen to see if he could find the makings of a coffee. He would kill for a real coffee right now.

About a half-hour later, he and Cane—who'd found a good place to park the truck, not too far if they needed a quick getaway, but far enough to evade suspicion—were sitting at the small Formica table in the kitchen when Keira and Fran emerged. Both women were red-eyed, and he knew it must've cost Keira dearly to come clean to her longtime friend about what John had been doing to her.

Keira took a seat at the table next to Dalton, absently playing with the ring on her finger, leaving the introductions of Cane to Fran for Dalton to do.

"I've called Sierra. They're coming over. They'll be here in ten minutes or so." Dalton watched Keira's face. He wanted to make her smile. He liked it when she smiled. And he knew that bit of news would pick her up.

"Really?" she breathed. "Oh God, you don't know how much I want to see her."

"I've given them an address a street over. They can park their car, and I'll go over and collect them," Dalton said.

She raised her eyebrows at him, but at least the desperate sadness had abated.

"We can't be too cautious, Keira," he said, unconsciously reaching for her hand to stop her twisting her ring as if she were going to pull it right off.

"I know, I guess I'm just not used to all this clandestine stuff." And then she did smile. Just for him, and for a second he was drowning in her eyes, lost in the memories of what they'd done together last night.

"Ahem." Cane cleared his throat and Dalton's awareness snapped back to the here and now. That's when he realized he was still holding Keira's hand, and both Fran and Cane were staring at them, Cane with surprise, Fran with amused curiosity.

Dalton opened his mouth, unsure of exactly what to say, when his phone rang. It was a burner phone he'd asked Cane to stop in and buy on their way into town. He had another two stashed in his bag, along with his personal phone. Keira also had a new burner phone. Who knew if the Yakuza had the technology to track phones? The police could do it, but only if they had a warrant. But Dalton wasn't taking any chances.

"Yes," he answered in clipped tones. After a few seconds he hung up and started towards the door. "I'll be back in a minute." He only felt a slight twinge of guilt that he was leaving Keira to explain their moment of intimacy to the other two. Hopefully she could bluff her way out of it.

Two minutes later, after checking not once, or twice, but three times that the coast was clear, Dalton strode around the corner of the block and saw a couple standing next to a nondescript white sedan. Reed and Sierra. He could see the likeness of the two sisters immediately. They both had dark-auburn hair, but Keira's had hints of lighter brown and red through hers, giving her a softer look. Sierra was more angular, and where Keira had luscious curves, Sierra could only be called athletic. But as he got closer, Dalton made out her face and saw that she was also a sultry beauty. He kept his eyes peeled for anything untoward, making sure they were alone and hadn't been followed.

"You must be Dalton." Reed took his hand in a welcoming grasp. Keira had already told her he was from New Zealand, but the man could almost pass as having Hawaiian heritage; he had coffee-colored skin and a slight slant to his serious, dark eyes. Reed also had that straight-backed stance, reminiscent of cops and military men. Sierra shook his hand and then stood back and crossed her arms, surveying him. It was good to know they were a little wary of him, just as he was of them. Trust needed to be earned in these kinds of situations.

"Good to finally meet you both," Dalton replied. He knew

how impatient Keira would be, so he dispensed with more small talk. "Follow me."

They followed without comment, and soon, he was opening the door and ushering Sierra past him.

Keira was waiting at the end of the corridor. There were silent tears spilling down her face. The sisters embraced for many long moments, and Dalton had to turn away from the love and regret so clearly evident on Keira's face, as a lump formed in his chest. If he achieved nothing else good today, the fact he could help Keira reconnect with her sibling was enough. He cleared his throat and led Reed into the kitchen, to give the two sisters time on their own.

CHAPTER EIGHTEEN

"Are you limping?" Keira asked. She turned just before she sat at the table in the kitchen and caught Sierra's quick glance at Reed. He pulled out a chair for her and then stood behind it, almost as if he were on guard.

"Yes, I broke my ankle a few months ago. You probably haven't heard." She glanced down at her offending leg and then back up at Keira, something unfathomable in her eyes.

Keira shook her head. Heard what? The way Reed laid his hand protectively on Sierra's shoulder, the way they looked at each other, as if they shared a secret, it was all a bit curious.

"We've got a lot to tell you," Sierra said. "It's one of the reasons I've been trying so hard to contact you. But you never answered my texts or my emails. Or my phone calls." This time, Sierra speared her with one of her best journalist stares, and Keira wriggled uncomfortably in her chair. It was true, she had been actively avoiding her sister. Her whole family. Because she was too ashamed to let them in to her life, which had become a living hell. Dalton gave her a sympathetic glance. He was seated opposite her at the kitchen table, and she wished he was closer, so she could touch him, gain some comfort from his closeness. But she was on her own.

The little kitchen was getting overcrowded. Cane was

leaning up against the Formica counter in the corner. She, Sierra, Reed and Dalton were all squeezed around the table, with Spike huddled underneath at Dalton's feet, and Fran was doing the hostess thing, bustling around making coffee and opening a packet of cookies.

"I know, I'm really sorry, sis. It's just that…" She searched for the right words. Searched for any words to get herself out from beneath her little sister's piercing gaze. Sierra shifted slightly and laid her hand over the top of Reed's, which was still on her shoulder.

Keira let out a squeal of delight that had Dalton jumping up from his chair in fright. "Oh, my God. Is that a ring on your finger?" Keira was standing now, leaning over the table to get a better look. "It is. That's an engagement ring. Are you two engaged?"

Sierra snatched her hand away, but it was too late, and so she also stood up, giving Keira a quick, sheepish glance. "Yes," she admitted. "One of the many things we have to tell you. It only happened last week…" Sierra faltered, and Keira was stunned that her normally composed sister was actually at a loss for words. She must really be in love with this guy to be rendered speechless. Sierra leaned back a little to rest her shoulder against Reed's chest, and his hand snaked around her waist. A lump formed in Keira's throat. It was such a small gesture, but one that Keira understood. Sierra was seeking his touch, his comfort, taking some of his strength. And Reed was letting her know he had her back. This simple move told Keira more about their relationship than any words could've done.

"I'm so pleased for you," Keira said and elbowed Dalton out of the way—he had to stand up and go and lean against the counter with Cane—so she could come around and hug her sister. "This is the best news ever." She pulled back so she could look her sister in the eye. "I mean it. You deserve to be happy." Then she leaned in and pulled Reed into a three-way hug. "I guess that means you're going to be my brother-in-law, huh?"

"I guess so," he replied, with a grin that showed off a charming dimple in his chin.

Keira hadn't had much time to study Reed. Apart from their quick introduction today and the few random things Sierra had told her over the phone, she knew hardly anything about him. He was originally from New Zealand, and she could see his Maori heritage in the slope of his cheekbones and the color of his skin. He was also a cop on Kangaroo Island, had been in the force for a long time. He was tall, with dark hair he dragged back with his hand whenever it fell over his face, and deep-brown, piercing eyes. And he couldn't keep his gaze off her sister. Which was a really good thing, as far as Keira was concerned.

"Well, I'll look forward to some interesting conversations, then," she warned. He gave her a quick, wary glance and she smiled. "Don't worry, you've already passed my rigorous testing regimen. You're okay in my books," she joked, backing away from their embrace and taking her seat once more.

"Wow, this is all fascinating," Fran broke in. "I've never had this much excitement and good news in my house all at once." She beamed, taking everyone in with her charismatic smile. "And I hate to interrupt, but the coffee's made, so come and grab a cup, everyone."

Keira was dying for a good cup of coffee, she hadn't had one in over three days now, and could quite possibly be going into caffeine withdrawal. There was lots of shuffling, and people bumping into each other, as they all were handed a cup and grabbed a cookie or two.

While everyone was getting resettled, Dalton spoke above the noise. "I know you all have a lot of catching up to do." He nodded at Sierra and Keira. "But I think we should talk strategy, first. Sierra and Reed shouldn't stay long. We can't afford to draw attention to ourselves. And while it's amazing Fran is letting us use her place as a safe house, the less the neighbors have to talk about, the better."

Dalton's words brought Keira tumbling back down to earth. She played with her ring under the table, out of sight. Even though what Dalton said was true, she wanted a few more hours, just to pretend everything was normal. To talk to her sister, find out what was going on in her life, re-establish that fragile bond they'd always had between them.

"Things have come to a head today. Cane finding our hideout tipped our hand. I'm not sure if I'm grateful to Cane for bringing us back to civilization, or not." Dalton lowered his eyebrows in Cane's direction. "But this is a good chance for us to collate all our knowledge, find out what everyone knows, and see if there are any cracks we might be able to capitalize on to get the Yakuza off Keira's back. Who wants to go first?"

After a second or so of silence, Sierra said, "I've got some interesting information." She glanced over at Dalton and he nodded for her to continue. "I had a meeting with Stacy Wong, she works for the *Hawaii Tribune-Herald*." Both Cane and Dalton groaned in unison, and Sierra held her hand up. "I know, their paper doesn't have the best reputation. Actually, they usually concentrate on local Hilo matters, and not much else. And they're not known for their spectacularly accurate reporting, either. But this lady used to work for the *Chicago Tribune*, and she has some good journalistic chops behind her. Stacy moved here to be closer to her ailing mother, but she loves to keep her journalistic skills up to par, if she can."

"Yep, I met with her as well, this morning. She struck me as a very intelligent lady. Sharp, and to the point," Reed said into the small silence that followed Sierra's declaration. "She wouldn't be giving us information if she thought it was incorrect or irrelevant. She also values her reputation, and she's not going to be running off to the police to tattle on us. Plus, she seems to have a special dislike for the Yakuza. She's been quietly amassing a whole stack of information on them, and their dealings on the Big Island. One day she hopes to expose them. I'm not sure why she hates them so much, but from the little she's said about it, I gleaned that her mother might've been tricked into selling her house by someone connected to the Yakuza. She thinks they might be dabbling in real estate as a way to launder money, perhaps. But whatever her motivation, I do trust her."

"That's good to know," Dalton said quietly. "Cane, I'd still like you to check her out, do a background check, that kind of thing, when you get back to the office."

Keira froze for a second. This journalist might not know it, but she had inadvertently stumbled on the truth about the Yakuza laundering money. She might get more than she bargained for, if she tried to break this story wide open.

"Will do." Cane inclined his head, and readjusted his hip against the counter.

"Don't get me wrong, though," Sierra interrupted. "She's also in this to get the scoop on the story, whichever way it happens to end. She's not just doing this out of the kindness of her heart," she warned. "But I do agree with Dalton. We can trust her."

"Anyway," Fran chimed in impatiently. "What did she have to say? Did she have any information that might help clear Keira's name?" Keira was thinking the same thing herself and gave Fran a hopeful smile by way of thanks.

"Yes. And no." Sierra stood up, as if she were too agitated to remain seated any longer. "The name of the murdered woman still hasn't been released by the police, as they haven't been able to notify her family yet. They also haven't made it public as to how she died. But Stacy managed to find out that the girl was called Penelope Opūnui. She worked for Cinderella Escorts." Sierra let the words hang in the air for everyone to digest. "Stacy contacted the agency this morning, they're really just a high-class brothel, and, after a few…shall we say…inducements, the Madam in charge revealed that John was one of the dead girl's clients. I'm sorry, Kez." Sierra stopped her pacing and put both her hands on Keira's shoulders. "I know you probably didn't want to hear that."

Keira swallowed heavily and looked down at her clenched fists in her lap. No, she didn't want to hear that her husband had been seeing a prostitute. It was a shock to have those words said out loud. But it also wasn't much of a surprise. Because, while she'd never considered John might be unfaithful, it didn't surprise her to hear he was getting his sexual urges served elsewhere. Dalton, who was now sitting next to her at the table, gently unclenched her fingers and took one of her hands in his, resting it on his knee beneath the table. She was grateful for his support; it soothed her agonized mind a little.

Sierra continued, but left her hands comfortingly on Keira's shoulders. "This is both good and bad news. Good news because we have a definite connection to John now. But bad, because we have a definite connection to John. Which is why the police are looking at you, Keira. As the scorned wife."

"And it made the Yakuza's job that much easier," Reed added sourly, "for them to frame you for the murder."

Yes, she supposed it did. Yoshio must've known what John was up to behind her back.

"I procured one more bit of info from Captain Chin, which, unfortunately, puts another nail in Keira's coffin," Reed continued.

"What's that?" Dalton asked, suppressing a heavy sigh, but not letting go of her hand.

"Even though it's not public knowledge, he let it slip the cause of death was poison."

"Oh, crap." Dalton pursed his lips and looked at Keira sideways.

"Why crap?" she asked.

"Because poison is the number one murder weapon chosen by women. That's why the police are so keen to talk to you," Dalton said.

Keira snorted. "As if I had it in me to murder anyone."

"Yes, but the police don't know that. Keira, you need to take this seriously," Sierra reproached.

"I am," Keira replied. Of course, she was taking it seriously, it was her life on the line, after all. She said nothing more for the next ten or fifteen minutes, as Reed and Dalton argued back and forth, discussing the finer points of what the journalist told them, weighing it against the information Reed gleaned from Joe Chin, with Sierra and Fran sometimes adding their thoughts.

Keira was getting that feeling again, that it might just be better to quietly disappear. As she sat, only half-listening to the debate going on around her, she noticed Cane remained quiet throughout the whole debrief. She studied him for a few seconds out of the corner of her eye. Cane was relatively good-looking, in a rough diamond kind of way. He was stocky and well-muscled, with a square face. But there was a look in his eye that Keira found disturbing. It was the way he was watching Dalton, when Dalton wasn't aware of it. Almost slyly, furtively, as if he resented Dalton. He was certainly twitchy about something. But in the end, Keira put it down to the fact he was worried. Anxiety sometimes manifested in odd ways. Again, she decided, if Dalton trusted him, then so did she.

Her hand remained inside Dalton's, even while he gesticulated with the other to make a point. It was large and warm, and she could feel a line of callouses along the ridge of his palm. Her mind returned to their night together—was it only last night, it seemed like forever ago—and how gentle he'd been with her. After her revelation of what John had made her do, he kept asking her if this was what she truly wanted. He was more worried about her state of mind than about his own needs. And that had touched something deep inside her. As well as being an even bigger turn-on than that delicious body of his.

Then she heard someone say something that caught her attention.

"I like that idea," Keira said, breaking into their conversation. "Whoever said that? The one about smuggling me out on a boat."

* * *

Dalton stared out the front window, lost in his thoughts. The streetlamps outside were beginning to flicker on as dusk descended. Cane was sitting in a single chair on the other side of the living room, tapping away on his phone, probably sending texts to his wife, or checking Twitter. He was Twitter-mad, but it was one of those many social platforms Dalton would never understand. He could hear Fran humming a happy tune as she bustled around in the kitchen, making them all dinner. Sierra and Reed had left an hour earlier. And Keira had asked if she could use Fran's shower.

He would need to go next, to wash off all the sweat and grime of their tramp through the jungle this morning. Even though there was tank water available at the hut, there was no running shower. So, both he and Keira had taken turns to use a bucket and some soap out in the back of the cabin. It wasn't nearly the same as having a nice, hot shower.

Images of Keira in the shower, all soapy and slippery,

invaded his mind. A vision of what she would look like, head tipped back, letting the water run down her sleek, brown hair, over her tanned shoulders, and then cascade over her breasts and—

"That feels better," Keira announced, shaking him out of his train of thought. Which was a good thing, because any longer and he might have had to cover his lap with a pillow. "There's nothing like a hot shower to make you feel human again," she continued. Dalton glanced at Cane to see if he'd noticed Dalton's distraction. But Cane wasn't looking at him, he was staring at the woman standing in the doorway. Dalton followed the direction of his gaze.

"What?" she asked dryly. "It was the only clean piece of clothing I had left in my backpack. All the rest of my clothes are still locked up in your machinery shed." She cast an accusing look at Dalton. But he was too busy drinking her in to notice.

Her freshly washed hair was shiny and sleek, sitting in a brown halo around her face, which looked natural and glowing. And she had on the most amazing red dress he'd ever seen. Spaghetti-straps with a low, scooped neckline, the hem kicked out a little and reached to just below her knee, allowing her nicely toned calves to show beneath. It was floaty and flirty, very summery, and hugged every single contour of her body. And he wanted to undress her here and now. Tear that red dress off and reveal the curves hinted at below.

"Wow," he breathed. "That's a...nice dress."

Keira did a self-conscious little twirl, and then caught Cane staring at her as well and blushed. "Fran loaned me a pair of her sandals to go with it," she added coyly.

"Yeah, nice dress," echoed Cane. But there was a smirk to his lips that Dalton didn't care for.

Dalton frowned and was about to open his mouth to say

something, when Cane's phone rang.

Cane looked at his cell and pursed his lips. Then his face paled visibly. "I'm just gonna take this outside." He was on his feet and headed for the back door before Dalton could ask who it was. The back of Dalton's neck prickled; he wasn't sure why. It was probably Alani, his wife calling to find out what time he would be home. There wasn't much else any of them could do tonight, so he would get Cane to check in on Aunty Lei and then head home. There was no point in disrupting Cane's life, too. He had two young kids, and Dalton knew Cane liked to be home to put them to bed as often as he could.

Dalton wandered over to the side window and stared out at the overgrown grass in the backyard. He could just make out Cane, pacing to and fro in a small patch of bare earth in the corner of the yard. Every now and then he waved an agitated hand in the air, and once he glanced quickly back toward the house.

Keira came over to stand next to him. "Everything okay?"

"Yeah, sure," Dalton replied, and then was distracted by the red dress again. "This was really all you had to wear?"

"Yes, why?" But the slow grin spreading over her face told him that she knew exactly what kind of effect it was having on him. Had she worn it on purpose?

"You know why," he growled and encircled her waist with one hand, tugging her slowly closer. He let his eyes rove over her face, taking in her high, arched eyebrows, delicate cheekbones and full lips. Lips he wanted to kiss. Lowering his head, he hovered over her mouth, waiting. He felt the soft exhale of her breath over the side of his neck. He closed the final few inches and tasted her. She leant into him, her hips resting against his belly, and his cock stirred at the softness of her.

All of a sudden, the back door banged open. Dalton's head

sprang up as Keira flinched in his arms. Cane strode into the living area, eyes wild, mouth twisted with what could only be called panic.

"I'm sorry, Dalton. You have to take this." Cane held his phone out to him.

Fran appeared in the doorway, come to see what all the commotion was about.

Dalton took the phone, but held it away from his ear. "What in hell is going on?" he asked, voice calm and controlled. It took a lot to rattle Cane, but the man was more than rattled now. "Has something happened to Sierra? Or Reed?"

He heard Keira gasp, but didn't look around at her.

"No, they're safe. You'll find out if you answer the phone."

Why was Cane being so cryptic? And why was he so tense? The man looked like he was a stick of dynamite, ready to explode with one touch. He stood in the doorway, legs akimbo, hands clenched at his sides. And Dalton suddenly recognized the stance. Cane was expecting a fight.

He held the cell to his ear. "Dalton here. Who's this?"

A voice he didn't recognize came down the phone. There was a definite accent, Japanese, if he wasn't mistaken. "Good evening, Dalton. It's so nice of our mutual friend to have brought you to my attention."

"What are you talking about? Who is this?" But Dalton had a sick feeling he already knew the answer.

"My name is Yoshio. You may have heard of me." Dalton suddenly found it hard to breathe. Keira came up and placed a hand on his arm, a silent plea in her eyes. He couldn't look at her. Instead, he directed a death stare at Cane. His friend flinched, but didn't look away. The fucking traitor. Dalton was going to kill him.

"Cane was moving too slow for our liking, so we've upped the ante. Added some insurance, if you like," the voice on the other end of the phone continued. "I've got someone here I'd like you to talk to."

"What the hell are you—"

"Hi, Daddy."

Tavi.

It was his son.

Dalton stilled. His whole world distilled down to this one point in time. There was nothing else, no one else. "The man said you wanted to talk to me," Tavi continued. There was a tremble in his little voice and Dalton suddenly wanted to smash something. "Daddy?" Tavi said again, and Dalton realized he still hadn't said a word. Keira's grip tightened and there was fear in her eyes. But he couldn't worry about her right now.

"Hi, buddy. Are you okay?"

"Yes, this man said he was taking us to see the lava. But I want to go home now." Dalton could tell his son was close to tears. And Tavi had said us, which meant Yoshio most probably had Flora as well.

Before he could answer, however, Yoshio's voice replaced that of his son's.

"So, you see, I have all the aces up my sleeve. Things can go one of two ways. The easy way, or the hard way. It's your choice, Dalton." The smooth voice of the Yakuza mobster sounded like he might've been ordering a pizza, not talking about life-and-death scenarios. "Here's what I want you to do." Yoshio talked, and Dalton listened.

CHAPTER NINETEEN

As Dalton hung up the phone, he moved so fast, Keira almost didn't see him. He shoved Cane up against the wall, one hand on his throat, his other on his right arm, twisting it up and away. Away from a gun, Keira suddenly realized.

"You fucking bastard. How could you?" Dalton yelled into Cane's face.

"I didn't know, I swear. I didn't know they were going to take Tavi." Cane was struggling to talk, because Dalton's grip on his throat was so fierce.

What were they talking about? "Dalton, you're scaring me. What's going on?" Keira sidled around to where Fran was standing in the kitchen doorway, mouth open. The two women clung to each other. She kept well away from the men. Dalton was so mad, like an enraged bull. His rage was normally the ice-cool fury that bubbled dispassionately beneath the surface. This was an entirely new Dalton. She was guessing, but she thought he might only be holding back from killing Cane by the barest of margins. Spike hovered by her legs, as unsure as she was about what was going on.

Beads of sweat stood out on Cane's face, but he wasn't letting Dalton intimidate him, he stared him straight in the eye, almost daring him to take a swing.

"Dalton," Keira was yelling now. "Please, tell me what's going on."

Dalton's gaze never left Cane's face, but slowly a change came over him. He loosened his hold on Cane's neck but didn't let him go completely.

"You fucking bastard," he snarled, getting right up into Cane's face. Then he let go of Cane's other hand and reached around and plucked his gun out from behind his back. Keira hadn't even suspected it was there, wouldn't have even guessed. Then he slammed Cane once more up against the wall, before letting him go with a snort. "Sit down in that chair, and don't move a fucking muscle," he demanded. Cane hung his head and wouldn't meet anyone's eye, like a beaten dog.

"Dalton, please tell me what's going on," Keira implored,

He swore and ran a hand through his hair, tugging at it so hard, Keira winced for him. "They have my son, Tavi. And Flora." Dalton's gaze met hers. The anguish in his face nearly broke her heart.

"What?" She must've misheard him. Sinking into the closest chair she pushed her hair away from her eyes.

"They want to trade both of them, for you."

"Oh." Her word was merely a breath. Everything suddenly became crystal clear. Cane had betrayed them. She wasn't sure how. Or why. Perhaps to get the large bounty that was on both of their heads? It didn't really matter anymore.

Yoshio had Dalton's son. And the mother of his child. Two people's lives now rested in her hands. Surely Yoshio was only bluffing? He wouldn't kill an innocent young boy and a woman for no reason. Would he?

Frantically she sought for answers. They needed to think, to come up with a plan to rescue his little boy. She glanced up at Dalton, trying to gauge if he had any new ideas. And that's when she saw the fear in his face. And pain. Their gazes locked, and she stared into the depths of his gorgeous, brown eyes for many long seconds. And she knew. Knew what Dalton was going to do. Knew what she had to do. It was the only option.

It was up to her to take the lead. To take the decision out of Dalton's hands. It was the least she could do. His mind would be a complete mess. Dalton had morals, he was principled and incorruptible. And his protective instincts for her would be warring with his unconditional love for his son. His head would be at war with his heart. But she knew which one would win in the end. And so, she made the decision for him. So he didn't have to say the words. Because it would destroy a part of him to do that. To tell her in the end, he had no choice.

But deep down, right in her very soul, where no one would ever see it, the betrayal hurt, like a knife blade to the heart. Even though she knew it was never an option for Dalton to choose her, a tiny part of her still wanted him to. Because she'd been so close to believing she could trust a man again. That Dalton was that man. But now, she knew it'd always be her, on her own. She had to save herself, because no other man would.

She stood up. Pulled her face into something she hoped looked like determination. "All right. Let's go. Where is this swap supposed to take place? And when?"

Dalton only stared at her, didn't say anything. He still had Cane's gun dangling from his right hand. He looked so big and strong and so out of place in Fran's small living room, all dressed in black. Like a dark demon in amongst all the bright, rainbow decorations.

Fran began talking at the top of her voice, almost hysterical. "What are you thinking? You can't do this. They'll kill you."

Keira went over and took Fran by both shoulders. "What

choice do I have? You would do the exact same thing."

"No. No, I wouldn't. There must be another option. Can't we come up with a plan?" Fran looked beseechingly at Dalton, who'd moved to stand directly behind Keira.

"Yes, you would. Fran. It's a little boy. Dalton's little boy. I can't risk his life. And neither could you."

Fran seemed to shrink in front of her, tears running down her cheeks. She shook her head in denial, but Keira could see the understanding growing in her friend's eyes. Then Fran enveloped her in a hug, crushed her to her chest so hard, Keira almost couldn't breathe.

Keira knew she would never know the exquisite love and connection between a parent and a child Dalton was feeling right now. But she could guess. Perhaps fortuitously, she and John had never had children. At first Keira had thought about it, a lot. But John was never keen, using the age gap as his excuse. He said he'd never had an interest in kids, which was one reason he was still single when they met. After his subtle abuse started, she'd given up the idea, knowing she never wanted to bring a child in to that kind of perverted lifestyle.

Dalton still hadn't said a word. Hadn't drawn a breath to protest that she didn't need to do this, that they would find another way. Something inside Keira felt like it'd died.

"This was all your doing." Fran let go of Keira and advanced on the hapless man still sitting in the chair. "I'm not normally a violent woman, but with someone as disgusting as you, I might just change my mind."

Cane cowered back into the chair, as far away from the irate woman as he could get. If the situation hadn't been so dire, Keira might've laughed at the lunacy of the whole thing. Her diminutive friend looked like she was about to punch a man, nearly twice her size, in the mouth. And Keira wanted to urge her on.

"Much as I'd like to see you hurt him, Cane has to drive us, it was one of the demands." Dalton finally spoke, his deep voice stopping Fran in her tracks.

"Are you serious?" Fran whirled around, directing her anger towards Dalton now. "Are you seriously going to let Keira do this?"

Dalton clamped his mouth shut. Keira could tell he didn't want to say the words, to admit the truth. But his lack of denial was the same thing. He wasn't going to stop her.

Keira was about to say she was just going to get her backpack, to go and change out of her dress into something more appropriate. But then realized there was nothing in the bag she would need, nothing more appropriate for her to wear. She wouldn't need a purse, or money, or a driver's license, or lipstick or a comb. Not where she was going. Yoshio wouldn't care what she was wearing when he killed her. She watched numbly as Dalton turned and emptied the bullets out of Cane's gun, then scooped the ammunition into his pocket and left the gun on the table.

"You need to let me explain—" Cane began to say, but Dalton whipped around so fast, he shut his mouth with a click.

"You don't get to explain anything. You don't get to speak. There is no excuse in the world that will justify your betrayal. You're just a fucking *hapa*." The hatred burning in Dalton's eyes was extraordinary. "You'll be lucky if I don't kill you afterwards. You put my son in danger. You are the scum of the earth. And now, you've put Keira in danger."

Keira said nothing as Cane stood, and Dalton ushered him toward the front door. "Don't try any funny business," he growled at Cane. Cane shook his head, but had the good sense to remain silent. And what else could Cane do? It seemed Yoshio might've outfoxed even Cane. If Cane hoped to get any of the promised bounty money, he would need to come with them. Would have to play along with this little game for a while longer.

"Tell me where the meeting point is," Dalton demanded of Cane.

"Yoshio told me not to tell you. He also said not to involve the police, otherwise—"

"I don't fucking care what Yoshio said, you will tell me," Dalton roared in such a loud voice it made Keira jump.

"He said to drive out on Kahakai Road," Cane replied sullenly. "That we would know when we got there. It would be obvious."

Dalton merely grunted in reply.

Fran came over and hugged Keira, but she couldn't return the hug, felt oddly detached and remote from everything that was happening around her. Fran was crying, but Keira only wiped at the tears, not feeling any of the emotion so evident on her friend's face. What was wrong with her? Was this how a condemned person felt, on their way to the gallows?

"I'll look after Spike for you," Fran said in a whisper, and Dalton merely nodded. They couldn't take the dog where they were going.

Then Keira was out the front door and down the steps before she even knew what'd happened, Cane a few steps behind her. Dalton's voice pulled her up short. "Wait a second, I forgot something." He ducked back through the door. But neither Keira nor Cane needed to be told not to follow. It was if she were on autopilot, programmed to move mechanically when commanded, but not to feel anything. Not to think anything.

"I'm sorry," Cane muttered to her back. She didn't turn around. He was nothing to her. A bug to be stepped on. No, even less than that. He was the man who would hand her over to Yoshio. Who had taken away her choices. Had taken away Dalton. Had cut off her only chance at love. Because in her detached frame of mind, it all became clear. She could've easily fallen in love with Dalton. It was already starting to happen. But that was not to be.

* * *

Dalton sat in the passenger seat watching Cane's every move. It was taking all his will power not to make him stop the car and force him to get out. So he could beat the absolute crap out of him. Hit him until blood sprayed from his nose, pummel him until his face was unrecognizable; beat him senseless. But even then, he wasn't sure that would satisfy his rage. He couldn't begin to process how furious he was at his supposed friend's betrayal.

"Why are we meeting him here?" Dalton barked.

"I don't know," Cane replied dispassionately. "Yoshio said something about it being appropriate. Something about the fact Keira could join her husband."

Icicles ran down Dalton's spine. Was it because Yoshio knew John's body now lay underneath the lava? Was he intending to do the same thing to Keira? Let the lava dispose of her body, of the evidence? Keira didn't respond to Cane's words, and Dalton couldn't see her face, hidden by the night's dark shadows, in the backseat of the borrowed car, as they drove deeper into the surrounding Hilo hinterland.

Dalton went back to staring out the windshield. His window was down, letting the humid night air flow over him. It was warm, a beautiful night in Hawaii. Alight with a carpet of stars in the sky, the sound of soft trilling crickets in the *pilli* grass as they swept along the road. He should be out walking on the beach, his arm draped around Keira's shoulders. They could be doing the normal things that lovers do on a night like tonight. Not driving to her certain doom.

But Dalton could see no easy solution. In his head the words, *don't hurt Tavi, don't hurt Tavi,* rolled around and around on a loop, so loud they just about drowned out any other thoughts. All his Navy training, his ability to think logically and coolly, especially under pressure, had gone out the window when he'd heard his son on the other end of the phone. Tavi was his light. And his dark. He would do anything for his son. He would give his life for his son. But the question was, would he be prepared for someone else to give their life for him as well?

This was crazy. Yoshio wanted Keira for one thing, and one thing only. Access to John's bank accounts. What would he do to her when he found out she didn't know the passwords? The answer was obvious, even to Dalton. He'd kill her. But would he leave her alive, even if she did give him what he wanted? Probably not, she'd be too much of a liability. Knew too much about him and his gang. Either way, this wasn't going to end well for Keira. Not unless she could convince Yoshio she was somehow valuable to him.

And now they were headed back towards Pahoa, back towards the still-active lava flows, to meet Yoshio and his men, so he could get his son. This road was one of the rear roads into Nanawale Estate, a relatively new development, only a few years old, and full of large, opulent houses of the rich and famous. But Dalton knew from the news reports that most, if not all, of this estate had been destroyed by the encroaching lava flow. Everyone would've been evacuated. They'd already passed through one blockade, where local police had tried to close the road with wooden sawhorses, but they'd been easy to push aside and keep driving. He couldn't figure out why Yoshio would go all the way out here. It was pitch black, with no streetlights, no light at all from any of the few scattered houses along the road, either, which had all been abandoned.

Suddenly he saw an orange glow light up the night. Bright sparks flew into the sky like fireworks. Was that lava spewing into the air? Were they that close to one of the new eruption sites?

"Jesus, did you see that?" Cane said in astonishment and slowed the car.

"Shut up," Dalton replied. "And keep driving."

Keira remained silent and pensive in the back seat.

The car swung around a corner, and the road continued in a straight line. Off in the distance, white light spilled across the road. As they got closer, Dalton made out two sets of headlights from two cars parked across the road, facing them.

"Slow down," he ordered. This must be it. This must be Yoshio. And his son. He was suddenly terribly unsure how to proceed. What should he do? He'd never done a hostage exchange before. *Whoa.* The thought pulled him up short. A hostage exchange. But that was exactly what it was.

He glanced into the backseat. Keira's face was lit by the advancing headlights. Her features were pinched and drawn, her face a pale oval in the flickering light. What was he doing? He couldn't do this. He couldn't hand her over to Yoshio like she was some kind of chess piece. A pawn in the Yakuza game. Especially not now that he'd gotten to know her. He would never forgive himself if he did this.

As if she was reading his mind, she said, "Don't worry, Dalton, none of this is your fault. Let me do all the talking, okay?" But she wouldn't meet his eyes. She leaned forward so her head was between the two front seats, and peered through the windshield. "I can see four of them. They all look like Yoshio's men. Do you think they've got your son and his mother?"

He didn't want to look away from her, wanted to say all the words that were on the tip of his tongue. But her distraction worked, and he couldn't help it, he turned to look through the front window. Yes, there was four of them, all wearing those blasted tailored, black suits, as if they were harmless businessmen here to do a deal, rather than deadly killers. They hadn't discussed what was going to happen once they got to the rendezvous spot. Every time Dalton tried to get the words out, they stuck in his throat. And neither Keira nor Cane spoke for the whole trip, both lost in their own thoughts. But now that they were here, Dalton admonished himself for not being more prepared.

Cane had slowed the car and was pulling over onto the verge, ten meters or so in front of the other cars. Dalton could make out the figures a little clearer now, backlit by the bright headlights, arrayed across the road in front of the cars. None of them had their guns drawn, thank God. But their stances were aggressive and antagonistic. There was no sign of either Flora or Tavi. Should he be worried? Or were they stashed safely in one of the cars?

While he was still weighing up the men, weighing up his next move, Keira got out of the car and began walking towards the men. "Keira, wait." Holy crap, she was a stubborn woman. Dalton scrambled to open the door and follow her. "Stay here," he yelled to Cane as he shut the door, hoping like hell the man would do what he was told for once in his life.

But he was too late. Keira was already halfway to the men.

"Where are they?" Keira demanded. "I'm not giving myself up until I see the boy."

Dalton walked swiftly up behind her, feeling the comforting weight of the Glock in his waistband. Not that he would be able to do much. Four against one wasn't good odds.

A man—Dalton supposed it was Yoshio, because it was hard to make out any of their features—got out of one of the cars and stepped forward. "How nice to see you again, Keira. You look lovely tonight. That red dress becomes you. But then again, you always looked lovely." There was an edge to Yoshio's words Dalton didn't like. A smug familiarity. And after Keira told him what John had forced her to do with

Yoshio, Dalton wanted to go and wipe that smugness right off his face, forever.

"Cut the bullshit, Yoshio." Keira's voice was steely and controlled. She stopped in the middle of the road and he nearly bumped into her. How was she managing to stay so calm? "Show me the boy, or Dalton will shoot you in the head." Holy crap, those were fighting words. He really hoped it didn't come to that. One of the other men, the one closest to Yoshio, put his hand under his jacket, reaching for his gun. Even though he didn't draw the weapon, he made it very obvious he would do so at any provocation.

Yoshio must've smiled, but it was hard to make out in the bright lights, all Dalton could see was his face distorting. "Much as I'd like to see him try, we might save it for another time." Yoshio motioned with a flick of his hand toward one of his men. The gangster slowly backed up toward the car on the left and opened the rear door. The man reached in and pulled someone out by the arm.

"Let go of me, you oaf." It was Flora, and Dalton nearly fell to his knees as sweet relief flooded through him. Flora smacked the man's hand away, glaring at him, then reached back inside the car. When she re-emerged, she had Tavi balanced on her hip. Tavi's eyes were huge and round, but he kept his mouth closed, didn't cry or complain. He was such a good boy. Clutching him close, she held her chin high and walked toward Yoshio, but only after giving the Yakuza gangster a glare that would cut a normal man to ribbons. Dalton's chest went from being tight and heavy to feeling warm and bursting with love. Love for his son.

"Stop there, if you please." Yoshio's words were a command, not a request.

Flora stopped walking and stood flanking Yoshio in the middle of the road. She stared directly ahead, meeting Dalton's gaze. Now he was closer, he could see Yoshio's suit was, in fact, gray pinstripes, not black like his underlings. Just the same as three days ago, when Dalton had first encountered him in the middle of the road. Before he launched his truck off a mountain. The similarities weren't lost on Dalton.

"As you can see, Keira, they are both well. Unharmed and eager to go home. I am assuming we can do this like civilized people. No need for any fuss or fanfare." Yoshio's voice was polite, as if he were having a conversation at a dinner party. But there was a dangerous edge to it Dalton didn't miss, and he understood the warning. *Don't screw this up, or someone will die.*

"Right, let's do this," Keira said, so softly Dalton almost missed it.

"Keira…" He grasped her hand, not wanting her to go. She pressed her palm into his. Dalton could feel the imprint of each of her fingers on the back of his hand, the blood pounding in her veins beating against his own skin. She was terrified, he could see it in her eyes, but she kept her head up, shoulders straight. The red dress flowed around her, glowing, lighting her up like a halo in the bright headlights.

"I know," she said. Then gently tugged her hand from his and walked towards Yoshio.

At the same time Flora began to make her way to Dalton. His eyes flicked from Keira's back, to his son's face, and back again. Then Flora was in his arms and Tavi was clinging to his neck. The smell of his little boy, of talcum powder and chocolate, hit him like a punch to the gut. He was safe. Tavi was safe.

By the time he remembered to look up, Keira was stepping into the back of the Cadillac.

"Mr. Mano, if you want your money, you'd do well to come with us." Yoshio gestured toward one of the large sedans. Cane got slowly out of the borrowed truck, and walked towards the gangster, hands in the air. He gave Dalton a fleeting glance on the way past. There was abject fear in his eyes, but Dalton didn't care. The man deserved whatever was coming to him. If the Yakuza killed him, then Dalton wouldn't mourn him. And if he did survive and managed to get the bounty money, then he'd better watch his back, get the hell off this island, because Dalton wouldn't rest until the bastard was either dead, or in jail.

"Don't try and follow us, will you?" Yoshio called back over his shoulder, almost as an afterthought. "After all, I know where you live. I know where your family live." The softly delivered threat turned Dalton's blood to ice in his veins.

He, Flora and Tavi stood at the side of the road, forming their own little tableau as they watched everyone climb into the two cars. Then they backed up and turned around, drove off down the road, towards the fiery lava.

The three of them stood in the dark, watching the double set of taillights disappear down the long road, carrying Cane and Keira away. It was too late. There was nothing he could do for Keira now. Dalton hugged Tavi even closer to his chest. Flora clung to his arm like he was a lifesaver.

"I was so fucking scared," she said on a shaky breath.

"I know. I'm truly sorry. You'll never know how sorry I am."

"What the fu—" Flora glanced down at Tavi, who still clung to Dalton's neck. "Tell me what's going on," she ground out between clenched teeth. Oh yeah, Flora was beyond mad. In an unconscious move, Dalton went to cover his groin area, because he'd seen her like this only once before, and his balls still ached at the thought of it.

"I'm sorry," he apologized again. "I thought you'd be safe at Aunty Keaka's place."

"Yeah well, we weren't. Cane must've told them where to

find us. You have a lot of talking to do, mister."

"I know," he soothed, leading them toward the truck, hoping Cane had the sense to leave the keys in the ignition.

Now that Tavi and Flora were safe, his mind began working properly again.

He needed a plan to rescue Keira. But how he was going to do that when they didn't even know where Yoshio had taken her was beyond him. There was one little ray of hope. It wasn't much, but Dalton was hoping Fran had gotten a message through for him.

The keys were indeed still in the car, and so he placed Tavi in the backseat with his mother. They were his first priority. He needed to get them somewhere secure first, to know they couldn't be used against him again. Dalton started the car, but couldn't bring himself to turn around. His gaze stayed locked on the strip of road disappearing into the pitch black. Following Keira's last journey.

CHAPTER TWENTY

Keira sat in the dark car, not moving and not speaking. She couldn't believe how calm she felt. As if walking up to Yoshio and getting in the Cadillac had been the easiest thing in the world to do. As if leaving Dalton behind had meant nothing to her. When in fact, it'd meant everything.

One of Yoshio's thugs sat next to her in the backseat, but she studiously ignored him. Much as he ignored her. Keira had been surprised when Yoshio told Cane to come with them. She'd watched him walk meekly over and get in the other car. Of course, they were keeping them separated. Didn't want to take a chance that Cane might change his mind and try something dodgy, like help her escape. But there was no chance of that. As far as she was concerned, Cane was a greedy, egocentric, backstabber, who was now beneath her consideration.

She wanted to ask where they were going, but knew it'd be a waste of her breath. Instead she thought back to the many times Yoshio had *visited* her and John, to see if she could come up with any details. She'd been trying to do this while Cane drove her out here, so she could tell Dalton where they might be taking her, but her mind refused to work properly. All she could think clearly was that she was handing herself over to the Yakuza. And Dalton was letting her.

Now the swap was over, however, her mind had cleared. They were driving down a little-used road, a back way into the Nanawale Estate, if her sense of direction wasn't too far out. From radio reports she and Dalton had listened to today, this estate was also being swallowed by the new lava flows, which were continuing, but had slowed somewhat from the first few big eruptions. This was backed up by the glow that lit up the night sky in front of them. Fresh, molten, lava flows making their slow exodus towards the ocean.

Something tugged at the back of her mind and she thought she remembered Yoshio and John discussing a property purchase in this estate a while ago, when it was first being built. This wasn't Yoshio's main residence, that was a palatial mansion over in Puako, on the other side of the Big Island. But perhaps he used this as a bolt hole, or safe house, or whatever he called it when he needed to get out of sight quickly. He probably had lots of these places scattered all over Hawaii.

Sooner than she thought, the car slowed and then turned into a driveway almost hidden from the road. The glow from the lava was closer than ever now. The dark shape of a house loomed out of the night, but it was hard to see properly. There were no lights on inside, the headlights from the cars the only form of illumination.

The thug sitting beside her exited the car and was around to her door before she had time to think. Yoshio got out more slowly from the passenger seat. Neither men spoke, but the bodyguard took her arm and roughly guided her over a manicured lawn toward what she assumed was the front door. She tried to shake him off, but his grip was like iron, and the more she struggled the tighter his fingers became, until she almost gasped in pain.

"Amida, Jiro, you're on guard," the guy holding her arm

said over his shoulder. Two of the wraith-like thugs from the other car peeled away and headed into the garden. Probably to stop anyone attempting to break into the house—or come and rescue her—and also to warn them if the lava got too close. As it was, Keira had a strange feeling of déjà vu. It reminded her of the evening John had been killed; she'd been filled with the same unresolved dread that they wouldn't escape from the lava then, too. But even back then, there had been worse things to worry about than the lava.

She could sense, rather than see, Cane and Yoshio behind her. But everyone remained eerily silent. They opened the door and all filed in, but much to her surprise, no one turned on a light. Instead they made their way in complete darkness down a long corridor. This was crazy. What was Yoshio up to?

The thug pulled sharply on her upper arm, and this time she did gasp in pain. It was almost impossible to see in the dark, but she thought they'd stopped outside a doorway. The thug fumbled around in the dark, and eventually she did indeed hear a door click open. This time, he also flicked on a light switch, which was a good thing, as directly in front of her, a steep set of stairs descended down into the depths of the earth. She took an involuntary step backward. A tumble down there in the dark would've definitely resulted in death, or at the very least serious injury.

"Hurry up," Yoshio said from behind her, and the thug manhandled her down the first few steps.

Luckily, there was a handrail and she used it to steady herself. Everyone crowded in behind her and she had no choice but to keep going down.

"Shut the door, quickly," Yoshio growled. Keira couldn't understand his sudden urgency, but had to keep all her focus on the steep steps so she didn't plunge headlong down them, taking her guard with her. It was only once she reached the bottom step, she began to understand what Yoshio had been up to. They were in a basement room. But this was no ordinary basement, this looked to be twice as deep as any other she'd ever been in, and three times as large. And it was decked out in the most luxurious of decor, it reminded her of a penthouse suite in a five-star hotel. It was done in the Japanese style, minimalistic but beautiful, in natural, muted colors. There were thick, rattan mats on the floor, a couple of low couches, a matching coffee table, and some expensive antiques lining the walls. The only difference was the lack of windows. Three doors clustered together at the other end of the large room. Keira wondered where they went. Bedrooms perhaps. Or a bathroom.

Keira had heard of things like this. In the movies, they were called panic rooms. A room sealed off from the rest of the house, with steel doors, completely soundproof, where no one could get in. Or out. If that were the intention. Keira began to sweat, even though the room was cool.

The thug let go of her arm so quickly Keira stumbled slightly.

Yoshio came up behind her. "I had this house specially designed. That's why I bought it off the plan, so I could make the needed…adjustments to the building. That way, I don't call any undue attention to the house." And Keira suddenly understood. If no lights could be seen in the house, then no one was likely to come and investigate. And no sound would escape from this deep underground. It would look like this was any other house on the street, abandoned and empty.

Goose bumps raised up all over Keira's skin and she suddenly felt a little ill. It was all becoming very, very real.

"Take a seat, my little *tenshi*." Yoshio gestured towards one of the expensive-looking, cream leather couches. She shivered at the use of the nickname he sometimes used for her. He'd told her it meant angel in Japanese. "You look pale, can I get you something to drink?"

She shook her head.

"Right, well, let's get down to business, then," Yoshio said.

Keira started and looked up at him. But Yoshio was nodding in Cane's direction. She'd almost forgotten Cane was there. He stood up a little straighter. Yoshio's thugs arranged themselves around the room. One stood unobtrusively in a corner, and the other perched himself on the edge of a divan chair at the other end of the room. Like two black-suited statues.

"Over here," Yoshio pointed to a tasteful table in the corner, with two chairs set around it and a laptop in the middle. Cane took the seat farthest away. "I'm assuming you have an account somewhere I can transfer the money to?" Yoshio asked casually.

"Yes, sir, I do," Cane replied.

"Good. Dai, you will do this." Yoshio motioned to the laptop as if it were something beneath his contempt. Of course, he wouldn't get his hands dirty, couldn't be seen to be doing something as menial as transferring two-hundred-thousand dollars into a traitor's account. Keira looked away as the thug who'd manhandled her down the steps came over to the table and opened the laptop.

"Transfer one-hundred-thousand dollars," Yoshio said coolly.

"What?" Cane exclaimed, half-standing again. "I brought you both of them. Just because you let Dalton go free, that's not my problem." He narrowed his eyes at the Japanese man.

"I think it's more than fair." Yoshio glared back at the stocky man. "After all, it was my *insurance* that really reeled them both in."

"Now hang on a second, I had a good plan in place. I was going to bring them both to you tomorrow, just because you —"

"That's enough," Yoshio roared, making Keira jump. Cane also flinched but took his seat again. He knew better than to argue.

Tuning out the muttered conversation of the other men, she focused on her own problems. When Yoshio was finished with Cane, it would be her turn next. What was she going to do? Cane wasn't going to help her, the asshole. And Dalton…? Even if Dalton intended to come after her, he wouldn't be able to find her now. There was going to be no miracle rescue. She was on her own. Should she admit she didn't have the slightest idea how to get into John's accounts? Or should she try and bluff her way through, pretend to log in and when it wouldn't connect tell him it must be a bank error? But even if she did that, how long would Yoshio keep her alive before he got tired of her game? She knew from past experiences he wasn't a patient man. That cool, calm exterior was only for show.

She needed to convince Yoshio to keep her alive. And there was only one thing she knew she had to give. Only one thing might keep her alive. But it would mean not only giving up her body this time. It would mean giving up her soul. Because if she offered herself to him as a bribe, he wouldn't accept that half-there person she'd been whenever he took her before. This would be for real. He would see through her bullshit. There was no John to hide behind anymore. Not that he'd protected her exactly. Not once had he interfered in Yoshio's little games. But there'd always been the expectation she would go back to him afterwards. That she belonged to John, and he was loaning her to Yoshio.

But this time, if she offered him her body as payment, she knew he wouldn't hold back.

Was it worth it? The price of her life, for the price of her dignity? Her very soul?

*　*　*

We've found them.

It was the text he'd been waiting for; hoping for, and Dalton nearly jumped for joy at those three little words. He stopped pacing long enough to type back.

Where?

He was parked in a spot off the road, the car tucked behind a large bush off Kahakai Road. And it was so dark he could hardly see his nose in front of his face. But that was a good thing, because it meant if any of Yoshio's gangsters cruised by, then they wouldn't see him, either.

Tavi and Flora were safe, for now. Hidden away in a small hotel on the outskirts of town, Dalton had booked them in under a false name, and promised he would be back for them soon. Flora had wanted to go straight to the police, but after Keira's declaration that the Yakuza might have at least one Hilo police officer in their pockets, he decided not to trust the police. Not yet, not until he had more information. The detour had taken him twenty minutes, and then he'd circled back, near to the spot where Yoshio had taken Keira. He figured Yoshio had taken her somewhere into the Nanawale Estate and he wanted to be as close as possible when the he got the news.

While he waited for the answer to come through on his phone, Dalton thought back to the few seconds when he'd run back into Fran's house tonight, leaving Cane and Keira standing out the front on the path. It'd been a spur-of-the-moment decision, but it'd been the only thing he could think of at the time, and it looked like it'd paid off.

"Fran, you have to do something for me." Dalton had grabbed a pen and a scrap of paper from the hallway table. "Here is Sierra's number. You need to phone her and ask her to contact her journalist friend, Stacy." Dalton had quickly explained to Fran what he wanted from Sierra. The conversation had only taken a few seconds, and he hoped

Cane hadn't got too suspicious. He hadn't dared to ring Reed or Sierra himself, or contact them in any way, not in front of Cane. The last thing he needed was Cane giving anything else away to the Yakuza. Dalton had no idea how much info Cane had passed on. But he was hoping Cane hadn't had time to let Yoshio know about Sierra and Reed's presence, since Cane only learnt about them while they were all at Fran's place.

An address came through on his phone, and he was already in the car with the keys in the ignition. It'd taken Sierra longer than he anticipated to get back to him and he'd been about to jump in his car and drive around the back streets of the Estate to look for Keira on his own. Which was a stupid idea, because it would've been like looking for a needle in a haystack, as well as tipping Yoshio off.

Then another text pinged on his phone.

We're at the house already. There are guards. Leave your car at the last bend and come the rest of the way on foot. We'll meet you at the bottom of the drive.

Dalton's heart leapt in his chest. What the...? That wasn't part of the plan. Reed and Sierra were supposed to stay at their hotel and relay him information from there. When he'd asked Fran to phone them tonight, he'd been acting on a hunch. Something Reed had said about the journalist, Stacy, had stuck in his head. She'd been amassing a pile of information on the Yakuza. Information to do with real estate. It was a long shot, but he wondered if she could find an address or a sale, something linked to Yoshio in the Estate.

And it looked like his hunch had paid off.

But that was as far as Sierra was supposed to take it. What the hell did they think they were up to? They could be putting Keira in jeopardy. Reed might be a cop back in Australia, but he had no dealings with people as violent and immoral as the Yakuza before. Not that Dalton had ever dealt with the Yakuza, either. But he'd had a lot more experience with terrorists and other high-tech drug gangs in his time in the Navy.

Dalton put his foot on the accelerator and the car took off like an arrow down the dark road.

Ten minutes later, he heard a soft, low call and a figure loomed out of the tall grass. Dalton drew his gun. It was instinctive. But then he noticed the rounded curves of a woman in the darkness and he let out a quiet gust of relief.

"It's me," Sierra whispered.

All of the reprimands he'd been thinking of on the way up the road sat on the tip of his tongue. But none of them would make Sierra turn around and leave now, because Dalton understood that if she was anything like her sister, stubbornness was an ingrained trait. She tugged on his shirt, pulling him back into her little hidey hole in the tall grass, out of sight.

Once they were hidden, he whispered back, "Fill me in."

"This driveway is long, and the house is set right back, practically hidden in the jungle. Reed is stationed up in a tree near the north corner of the house. They've left two guards on patrol, and he can see both of them most of the time from his high position. There are no lights on in the house and no movement we can make out. No noise either. We're not sure, but we think he might either have a basement, or some kind of sound-proof, light-proof room." Sierra reported all this slowly and quietly and Dalton was impressed by her logical coolness. Perhaps they wouldn't be such a liability as he first thought.

"We need to take care of those guards, before they can raise the alarm," Dalton said.

"Yes, Reed and I came to the same conclusion."

"I have a spare gun I'm going to give to Reed."

Dalton heard her sigh of relief. "That's good. I know we need to take these guys down quietly, and we shouldn't use a gun anyway, but I'll feel better if Reed is armed."

It was Cane's gun. He'd retrieved it from the table at the same time he'd dashed back in to talk to Fran. Dalton didn't think now was the time to tell her that he really hoped Reed didn't actually need to use the gun. Even though Reed was a cop, he wasn't recognized as such in Hawaii. If he discharged the gun, or even worse, killed someone, he might be in deep trouble. Dalton was sure Reed would understand the rules, even without him having to say it. But, like Sierra said, it was better that he was able to defend himself. Better off in jail, or barred from ever working as a cop again, than dead.

"Just warn him, if the police do turn up to ditch the gun. He shouldn't be caught with it, okay?"

Sierra nodded her understanding. Then she said, "Reed tried to call Joe Chin. He couldn't get through. But even if he had, I'm not sure if the Captain would've taken him seriously."

"I don't think the police would be of any help in this situation," Dalton replied thoughtfully. "If anything, they might make it worse. And if they spooked Yoshio..." He didn't need to finish that sentence. They both knew if the mob boss felt threatened, he might try to kill anyone who was a witness to his crimes. Which would be Keira. And perhaps Cane, but Dalton didn't give a shit about Cane right now.

Reed was using his phone to text them the position of the guards, as he followed their progress around the house. They had a set route, which kept them at opposite sides of the house most of the time.

"Can you climb trees?" Dalton asked, an idea forming quickly.

"Funny you should ask that," Sierra replied, a humorous tone to her voice. "Remind me to tell you just how well I do climb trees, and what I caught one day when I jumped out of one."

"Deal," he replied. "But right now, I want you to go and swap places with Reed. Then you can guide us, we can take down a guard each." Well, he hoped they could take them down. He hadn't seen Reed in action, so he was wishing on a wing and a prayer that he was as good as he seemed.

A few minutes later, Dalton found himself waiting silently behind a hibiscus bush for his allotted guard to appear around the corner of the house. From his crouched position behind the bush, he could no longer see the low-rise around a kilometer away. But the image of the lava rolling over it in white-hot waves was still ingrained on his retinas. They didn't have very long. Yoshio surely couldn't have planned to be here for much longer. Even if his basement or bunker or whatever it was survived the intense heat of the lava rolling over the rest of the house, they would be entombed in there forever. A slight breeze rustled the leaves in the trees all around him. That breeze was his friend, it'd help to mask any small sounds he might make.

A sound alerted Dalton to the presence of the guard and he tensed, checking for the weight of the Glock in the back of his jeans. He really hoped he didn't have to use it.

The guard came around the corner and stood on a small lanai, not three feet from where Dalton was hiding. He stared out, straight over the top of Dalton's head, probably assessing how close that lava was getting. He was small and chunky, but Dalton didn't underestimate him, even for a second. The smaller guys were often faster and more agile when it came to a fight. A semi-automatic rifle dangled from a strap over the man's shoulder. He obviously thought there was no threat, no need to keep it in his hands. Then wonder of wonders, the guy took out a cigarette and a lighter, and turned his back, shielding the cigarette with his body from the wind so he could light it.

Dalton was up and onto the lanai, grabbed the man around

the neck, before he could even cry out. Dalton used a choke hold to cut off the air to the man's lungs, rendering him quickly unconscious. The guard struggled to get a grip on his weapon, but it was all too little, too late. He was out cold in a matter of seconds and then Dalton tied his hands together quickly. His job done, he texted Sierra to let her know. Now it was over, he had time to wonder how Reed was faring with his guard.

Finally, a text came through and Dalton gathered the guy up and threw him over his shoulder in a fireman's hold and headed back towards the lookout tree.

Reed was already there with his guard, who was much taller than the short guy here, and Dalton was impressed that Reed had been able to handle him with seeming ease. Although his guard looked a little worse for wear; he was limp and unconscious, with a runnel of blood smeared down his face, and Dalton surmised Reed had to hit him to subdue him. Hard.

"Wait here for me," Dalton commanded. "Wrap these guys up good and tight. I'm going inside for a look." It was a risky move, but they had no other choice. They couldn't wait for Yoshio to come out, it might all be too late by then.

Dalton finished his reconnoiter of the house. It took him a while in the dark, but it was clear. Not a soul to be found. Completely empty. Sierra was right when she'd guessed there must be a hidden room somewhere. And Dalton had found the likely culprit, a large metal door leading off the corridor. Dalton felt his way around every inch of the door. It was solid and immovable. There was no way they were going to bash their way through that. Certainly not without warning Yoshio what was going on. He made his way back to the edge of the garden, where Reed and Sierra were holding the two gangsters and filled them in. His night vision was good now, after so long without any light at all, and he could make out the other two fairly well against the backdrop of the trees.

Reed handed him a two-way radio. "They've both got one of these," he said, not taking his eyes off his captives. And every time Sierra went too close to one of them, he glared at her until she moved away. Reed clearly wasn't happy about Sierra being here. But he also clearly had no option. Sierra wouldn't have it any other way.

Dalton looked down at the two-way radio and then back up at the two Yakuza guards. The one Reed had hit over the head was still out cold, but the smaller one had recovered from Dalton's choke-hold, now glared at him over his gag. Scenarios began to play out in his head. He could try and persuade the little guy to talk Yoshio out of his bunker. But could he take the risk the man might say something in Japanese, or warn his boss somehow that this was a trap? Neither he, Reed or Sierra spoke Japanese, let alone sounded like they could pass as one of the two guards. Which didn't leave them too many options. And even if they managed to get through the door to the basement, they were likely to be met by a barrage of bullets. Yoshio would make sure his panic room was impenetrable.

Dalton's stomach was in knots, he knew they'd taken longer than he'd hoped to secure the house. They had no way of knowing what was going on down in that basement room, and he was terrified of what they might find if they ever got in. Keira could already be dead. Or she could be fighting for her life at this very second. If she'd told the truth, told Yoshio she didn't know the passwords, he might not believe her. Would he stoop to torturing a woman to get what he wanted? Dalton had a horrible feeling that he might.

A slight orange glow lit up the sky behind the house and a waft of sulphur made his eyes water, reminding Dalton the lava was still on its slow march toward them. How long did they have before it got here, an hour, maybe less? Yoshio would be hoping to have his business over and done and then leave before then. Was he planning on leaving Keira's body here, to be covered when the lava eventually destroyed the house? The same way it'd done to her husband? The idea was abhorrent, and Dalton tried not to think about it. But suddenly with the images of lava flowing through his head, a notion began to form. Yoshio would have no idea how close the lava actually was. He was relying on his guards to warn him.

Quickly, he sketched his plan out to Reed and Sierra. He wanted to keep Sierra as far away from the action as possible, knowing Reed would be distracted if he thought she was putting herself in danger. He also needed Sierra to be able to escape if this all went south. He knew that would be what Keira would want. Actually, she would probably kill them all if she found out what he had planned; what they'd already done. Dalton was continuously surprised by Keira and her sister.

They both eventually agreed to his plan, with Reed adding a few minor touches to make sure they had the upper hand, and Sierra arguing she could be of more help. But in the end Dalton got his way. Dalton and Reed grabbed a Yakuza guard each under the shoulders and dragged them backwards into the thick jungle and dumped them, out of sight. Tall Guy still hadn't stirred, and Dalton quickly checked him for a pulse. He didn't really want the man dying on him. There was a heartbeat, and so he left him lying next to his gagged mate.

They all moved to their allotted positions, communicating via text message when they were in place. Dalton made sure his phone was safe in the front pocket of his pants, and the voice recording app was turned on. He wasn't sure if this part of his plan would pan out the way he wanted, but the recording app might help them to corroborate their stories to the police later on, if nothing else. Then he put the two-way up to his mouth, took a deep breath and began speaking.

CHAPTER TWENTY-ONE

"Lava…it's co…time…lea…"

"What was that?" Yoshio demanded, leaning away from Keira so he could glare at his henchman.

Keira sucked in a great gulp of air, thanking God for this one small distraction.

"I don't know," Dai, the guard who'd manhandled her earlier, said. He shook the two-way radio and glared at it, as if that would make it somehow work better.

"Well, find out," Yoshio said, his voice deceptively quiet. He hated any situation where he wasn't in complete control. That calm masked a boiling rage inside, and woe betide anyone who messed up. Yoshio lifted his hand from where it'd been resting on Keira's knee, to point at the unfortunate thug. It was also the hand that held the knife. Keira felt a surge of relief the knife was no longer touching her skin.

Dai shot him a quick, unreadable glance, then said, "Repeat. Amida, say again. You're breaking up."

There was a lot of static coming from the radio, but nothing intelligible. Just as Dai looked like he was going to throw the radio away in disgust, they all heard the word, *lava* clearly down the line, before more static took over.

Dai stared at Yoshio, but said nothing. They'd all heard the warning, but this was his boss's call.

"Sounds like we should get out of here." Cane had been sitting at the table, not saying anything. Actually, he'd been extremely quiet for the past half hour. Keira hated him even more for his silence. He was a coward, and he was going to let Yoshio get away with whatever he wanted when it came to Keira. Why should he care? He had his money, the transfer had been done. He'd said nothing when Yoshio started to hound her for the bank details. Yoshio hardly ever yelled, it was beneath him, but he had an icy coldness to his voice that was perhaps even worse. Cane also said nothing when the mobster began to idly play with a knife as he stalked back and forth across the basement floor, the implied threat obvious to Keira. And Cane hadn't even said a thing when Yoshio sat down next to Keira on the cream couch, pulled up her red dress and began running the knife up and down her bare thigh. She had frozen, like a rabbit caught in a snare, the cold brush of the steel taking away all coherent thought.

But now, here was a form of salvation, in a static-filled warning from one of Yoshio's thugs. She daren't say a thing, not with Yoshio sitting so close, that knife now waving dangerously in the air. Yet, she willed Cane to speak up, to get them out of here.

"Are you sure that was Amida?" Yoshio questioned sharply. "Why doesn't he come down here and tell us? That was the plan."

"I don't know, boss." Dai shook his head warily.

"Come on, what are you waiting for?" Cane stood up. "I'm not going to stay down here and be buried alive by lava." Cane was already halfway to the stairs before Yoshio got slowly to his feet.

"Stop."

Cane glanced back in time to see Dai pointing his gun straight at him, and halted with one foot on the first step.

Yoshio sighed gently. "Just when I was getting to the fun part." Keira's gut twisted in fear. He was a monster. Part of her had known all along, but had never really accepted just how depraved he was. He was going to cut her with a knife, and he was going to enjoy it. She felt a sudden urge to vomit. "Oh well, we'll have to carry out our little…talk somewhere else." He made it completely clear this was merely a reprieve, but she'd take anything she could get right now.

Yoshio didn't need to say anything more, just motioned with his chin, and the two thugs were already halfway up the stairs. Yoshio pointed for Cane to proceed him as well, then he hauled Keira up off the couch and steered her towards the stairs, her elbow held in a vise grip in one hand, the knife pressed into her ribs with the other.

"Wait here," he growled, and yanked her to a standstill at the mid-point on the stairs. "You too," he told Cane.

Cane shot him a look that spoke of his disdain and looked as if he were about to disobey. It would be more than obvious to Cane that Yoshio was holding her at knifepoint, but that didn't seem to bother the man at all. Threatening Keira's life was of no substance to Cane. Yoshio couldn't use her to control him, because he had no interest in whether she lived or died. She had to resist the urge to spit in his face. If she ever got out of this, she was going to throttle him with her bare hands.

They waited in the dim silence, Keira straining to hear what was going on up top. Finally, a shout came from the corridor just outside the heavy, metal door. "All clear, boss. You can come up."

They climbed the rest of the stairs and emerged into the dark main house. They still hadn't turned the lights on. Cane stopped in the hallway and Yoshio pushed him forward, closing the basement door behind him. She could just make out a thug guarding either end of the long hallway, guns at the ready.

"Out the front, boss," Dai said. Yoshio shoved Cane again, and then he and Keira moved towards the tall guard.

"Where are Amida and Jiro?"

"I haven't seen either of them yet, boss, I—"

There was a scuffling noise and then gunshots sounded, loud and horrifying from behind her. Keira sucked in a sharp breath. What was going on? She couldn't see what was happening.

"Ambush," Dai yelled.

Was it Dalton? Or the police? Keira wanted to cry out for help, but Yoshio pushed her forward so hard she stumbled, almost going down on her knees. But Yoshio's rough hand on her arm yanked her back just in time.

"Move," he shouted. She shook her head, refusing to budge. She wasn't about to run full tilt into a gun battle. But he grabbed her by the hair and began to pull her along the hallway. She screamed at the searing pain in her scalp, but had no choice but to go along with Yoshio. It was so dark she couldn't see her hand in front of her face, or a wall for that matter. She careened into one wall and bounced off as her shoulder hit. Next, she was seeing stars as her forehead slammed into the edge of the doorway at the end of the hallway. The world spun hazily, and she thought she might black out. She struggled desperately against Yoshio's grip, but his fingers were entwined in her hair, and it felt like her whole scalp was going to be yanked off.

"Stupid fucking bitch. Move," Yoshio was yelling now, all pretense of his cool façade gone.

"This way," Keira heard Dai's voice come out of the dark. Where was Cane, she wondered vaguely? And Yoshio's other thug? They were at the front door now, she could see outside, the stars giving enough light to show shapes of trees and shrubs, the pathway. Then she realized, it wasn't just the stars providing the light. There was a strange, reddish glow around the house, like an orange fog was descending to cover everything with its tendrils. Shots rang out from somewhere in the house behind them.

Yoshio let go of her hair, but grabbed her by the arm again before she could even right herself. The knife was back in her ribs, sharp and cold.

"You go to the car, boss, I'll cover you," Dai whispered from somewhere out on the front lanai.

"I should just kill you now," Yoshio hissed into her ear. "You did this. You and your fucking husband, you did all this." He pulled her toward the steps and down onto the gravel driveway.

A voice came out of the darkness. "Stop, or I'll shoot."

Relief nearly melted her bones. *Dalton*. That was Dalton's voice.

Things happened in a blur then. Dai raced in front of his boss, firing as he came, and Yoshio dragged her backward, away from the gunfire and towards the rear of the house, into the darkened jungle of the backyard.

She fought him. Dalton was here to save her, she wasn't going with him. Then the knife bit deep across her forearm and she screamed in pain and stumbled.

"Keep up, or the next one will be in your carotid artery," Yoshio snarled. He kept moving at a surprising speed, dragging her past a resort-style pool and gazebo, and onto a beautifully manicured lawn. Her arm throbbed, and she could feel the wet warmth of the blood running down her wrist. Her lungs began to burn now, as she gasped for air.

The orange glow got brighter, and choking smoke made her cough. Then a tree a hundred meters to the left of them burst into flames.

"Yoshio, stop. The lava. We can't go this way," she pleaded. It was hard to see from inside the wall of garden shrubs exactly which direction the lava was flowing. Was it coming straight for the house, or was it going to miss it and flow off down the slight incline?

Yoshio did slow his stride and glance over his left shoulder, as if he hadn't noticed the deadly, molten lava up till now.

"We have to go back, or we'll be trapped."

"I'm not going back," he said, so matter-of-factly, he almost sounded like he was talking about going for ice cream at the beach. Another large tree, closer this time, erupted into flames. Where was Dalton? What'd happened back there by the cars? She couldn't hear any more gunfire. Had Dai shot Dalton? And what had happened to Cane?

"Actually, that would be quite ironic, don't you think?" Yoshio continued. "If I were to throw you into the lava. A befitting way to die, so you could go and join that fucking deceitful husband of yours."

"No." Keira tried to yank her arm free, but it was as if his fist was an iron claw. Then, he began to drag her across the lawn, towards the flames and heat. He was completely mad, Keira decided. Only a madman would run towards free-flowing lava. He obviously had no care for his own safety anymore.

"Stop right there."

Yoshio hauled Keira around in front of him, like a shield, the cool, metal blade so tight against her neck she hardly dared to breathe.

Dalton was holding one arm into his side, like it was hurting him. Oh God, he'd been shot, she suddenly realized. And that's when she noticed he was also unarmed. Why didn't he have a gun? But there was no time to ponder that.

"If you throw her in the flames then I will kill you with my bare hands."

"Yes, but she'll already be dead. And I'm sure that's not the outcome you were hoping for."

"Even if you escape, the Yakuza will never have you back. You're a disgrace. You've dishonored yourself and your gang."

Keira wondered where Dalton was going with this conversation.

"The police were closing in on you anyway. They have information that links you to the death of the escort."

"Ha, they know nothing. I didn't kill her."

"Well, yes, technically that's true. You'd never stoop to getting your hands dirty like that. But we can link you to the man you ordered to kill her."

The heat of the encroaching lava was seeping through the back of her dress, the red fabric warm against the back of her legs. She could feel it, even though Yoshio's body was screening most of the heat; it was as if there was a giant bonfire behind them. It was hard to breathe, noxious gases from the lava filling the air around them.

"That can't be true. I know Dai, he is meticulous with his… skills. And if it is true, and he were indeed foolish enough to leave any evidence behind, then he isn't fit to serve me, anyway. In which case, I'll have to terminate his employment."

Why were they having this conversation right now? Keira didn't see how this was going to get Yoshio to set her free. Was Dalton buying time? If so, what was he waiting for? "Does it really matter anymore who gave the order for the prostitute to be murdered?" she asked loudly.

"Exactly, my little *tenshi*. Even though my plan to get the police to do my dirty work, when I planted the seed of suspicion about the identity of the murderer, didn't have the outcome I wished for, you are still here in my arms now. At my mercy. Perhaps we can die together, my sweet. Two star-crossed lovers."

He really had gone mad. If he wanted to commit hara-kiri,

then he could do it on his own, because she wasn't about to stand around and wait for it all to happen. Every other time Yoshio had dominated her, she'd let him get away with it. Some part of her always thinking she deserved to be treated that way. If her husband valued her so lowly, then perhaps she was worth nothing at all.

But now, John was dead. And through Dalton's eyes, she'd begun to see she wasn't as worthless as she thought. Memories of herself ten years ago, back when she'd been strong and independent, floated up to her mind. She could be that person again, if only she let herself.

A flicker of a memory of a long-ago, martial-arts class startled her with its clarity. It was a women's self-defense course she and Fran had signed up for, back when they were roommates. Keira had forgotten about that class, never thought in her wildest dreams she'd ever need to use it.

Until today.

Her arm where he'd sliced her with the knife felt like it was on fire, but she'd need to ignore that if her plan was going to work.

Raising both hands, as if in a gesture of surrender, she started talking really fast, saying a whole lot of nonsense in a bid to distract Yoshio.

"Maybe you're right, Yoshio. Maybe we are two star-crossed lovers. Meant to be together all along. My husband did you wrong, but he's paid for his sins now. So, if you were to forgive me, then we could be together. I mean really be together." She tried to turn around slightly, as if to look Yoshio in the eyes as she continued to babble.

"Stop wriggling, woman. And stop talking bullsh—"

His concentration was broken for a split second, but that was all she needed. Her right hand snaked up and grabbed the hand that held the knife and hauled it down and away from her neck with all her might.

Yoshio grunted in surprise and brought his other arm around her throat to try and subdue her. But she was ready for this, and she bared her teeth and bit down hard on the bare flesh between his hand and the cuff of his tailored suit. At the same time, she slammed her foot into the bony part of his shin. Stilettos were the best shoe to create the maximum amount of damage in this maneuver. She was only wearing sandals, but they had enough of an impact so that he howled with the combined pain in both his shin and wrist.

Then he did what she was hoping and praying he would. His grip loosened. It was all she needed to swing her body sideways away from the knife, still keeping a stranglehold on the hand that wielded it. In the exercise they'd practiced in class, she was supposed to then be able to pull the assailant's hand up and around, behind his back. But Yoshio was strong. Stronger than she expected. And while she'd had the luck to surprise him before, he'd quickly regained his composure. They stalled in a kind of checkmate, her with both hands on his wrist, staring up into his face. His dark brown eyes glowed with a hatred she'd never encountered before. Slowly, ever so slowly, he forced his arm up towards her chest, and she knew she wouldn't be strong enough to stop him from stabbing her in the heart.

Out of nowhere, something knocked her out of the way, and, with a grunt, her hold on Yoshio was broken as she landed on her side on the grass. When she scrambled to her feet, all she could see was a writhing mass of limbs and shadows, as Dalton and Yoshio struggled for ownership over the deadly knife. She could only stand and gape, not even sure who was who in the dark of the night, hoping against hope Dalton hadn't misjudged Yoshio and his determination to win at all costs.

Grunts of exertion filled the night as the two men fought. Suddenly there was a howl of pain, but from whom, Keira couldn't tell.

"Dalton," she screamed.

A figure stood up, the other man remaining prostrate on the ground. Then a flood of relief rushed through her. She would recognize those broad shoulders, that stance anywhere. It was Dalton. He was okay.

Dalton raised a foot and placed it on the feebly struggling man's chest.

"Stay down, or I'll do it again," he panted. She caught the glint of metal in his left hand. Somehow, he'd managed to wrest the knife from Yoshio. She wanted to go to him, wanted to feel his wonderful, strong arms around her, holding her, telling her it was safe. But she didn't dare yet, in case Yoshio broke free. And besides, Dalton was favoring his arm again, and Keira was suddenly worried.

"Dalton, what happened to your arm?"

"That guard winged me and I dropped my gun. It's not bad, it just grazed my arm, I'll be okay."

Keira let out a sigh of relief. But they still needed to get him to a hospital. Come to think of it, she probably needed to get to a hospital, as well. In the heat of battle, she'd been able to block out the pain from the knife slash in her arm, but now the burning sensation was coming back with a vengeance.

A voice came from around the edge of the house. "Dalton, Keira, where are you? What's going on?" It was Sierra, and there was more than a little edge of hysteria to her voice. What in hell was Sierra doing here?

"It's okay," Dalton replied. "We've got the bastard, and Keira's here, too."

"Oh, thank God." Her sister appeared out of the dark, jogging up the path that led around from the side of the house and onto the lawn. She ran straight to Keira, taking her in a fierce hug that nearly bowled her over. She didn't say anything; there was no need for words. And Keira accepted the hug gratefully. There would be time for words later. Lots of words, like what the hell did she think she was doing, putting herself in all kinds of serious danger to come out here and help rescue her? But that would be much later on.

"Did you get it?" Sierra stared intently at Dalton.

"Yes. At least I hope so." Dalton patted a phone-shaped bulge in his pocket.

But before Keira could ask what she meant, Sierra spoke up again. "Good, because we need to move. That lava will be here any minute," Sierra said, breaking away from Keira. "We've got the keys to one of the cars, and Reed's around front waiting." There was a tightness to Sierra's voice that made Keira wonder what'd gone on around the front of the house while she and Dalton had been preoccupied with Yoshio. It was all starting to make sense now. It must've been Reed who'd fired the shots from the back of the house, engaged the other thug, while Dai led her and Yoshio out the front.

"Is Reed all right?" she asked.

"I think so," Sierra said. "He's a little groggy, but he can stand, so that's good. That fucker friend of yours, Cane, knocked him out and made a break for it. The coward. He waited until Reed went to check on the other guard—he's dead by the way—and while he was leaning over him to check his pulse, Cane jumped him, hit him over the head with a rock, and disappeared into the night like the dog that he is." Keira had never heard so much venom drip from Sierra's tone before. But she agreed with her; Cane was a cowardly, traitorous human being.

"Have you got something to tie this sack of shit up with?" Dalton asked.

"Yep," Sierra replied, and much to Keira's surprise, she whipped two long cable ties out of her back pocket. It looked like her sister came prepared tonight. She'd better remember not to mess with her little sis from now on. "Help me get him up," she commanded when she'd finished, and Keira knelt down. They both hauled on an arm each, until they had the mobster boss strung up between them. He howled again in pain, but then gritted his teeth and glared at the both of them.

They all stumbled around the side of the house, back toward the cars.

"I'll drive," Sierra said, with an air of authority that said she wasn't going to take no for an answer. And it was probably a good idea, as none of the rest of them were in any state to drive. Reed was leaning against one of the cars, holding his head. Dalton was cradling his arm. And she had begun to shake like an autumn leaf. Shock, she knew. Coming down from the huge adrenaline rush of being held at knifepoint. Of overcoming Yoshio.

"What shall we do with him?" Sierra asked.

"Put him in the trunk," Dalton replied. "He'll be safe in there, and we'll be safe, too."

"What about the other guards?"

Dalton stopped to consider this. "I was going to call Joe Chin and tell him to come and get them." He glanced over the rooftop of the house, to the shallow hills behind, alight with the fire in the sky from the oncoming lava. "But I think we'll have to let them go."

"You're kidding," Keira blurted out before she could stop herself.

"I'm not sure about you," he said softly, "but I couldn't live with my conscience if we left them tied up here and the lava got them. We have to let them go. They can take the other car."

Keira was about to argue. Those thugs had been implicit in Yoshio's plan, had carried out his orders, had manhandled her and would've killed her without blinking an eye if Yoshio had told them to do it. They didn't deserve their freedom. But then again, Dalton was right. They didn't deserve death, either.

"If the police are any good at their jobs, hopefully they can round those men up soon enough," Reed said, joining in their conversation.

Reluctantly, she had to agree.

She helped to bundle Yoshio into the trunk of one of the large black sedans. He wasn't happy about it, but even though he struggled, his attempts were weak and pathetic. They probably needed to get him to a hospital, as well. Keira wasn't sure exactly where Dalton had knifed him, it was hard to see anything, what with his gray suit in the dark of the night. The cops could deal with him, she decided. And if he happened to die on the way back into town, she wouldn't be shedding any tears.

Dalton and Sierra went over to free the other two guards, Dalton pointing the gun at them while Sierra cut their bonds. Then they watched as the two men, both with surprised expressions on their faces, hightailed it out of there, fishtailing the car down the long driveway. They decided to leave the two dead guards where they were. If the police were lucky, the lava might not make it all the way down this side of the hill, and the bodies would still be here in the morning.

They all climbed wearily into the car, Sierra in the driver's seat and Reed beside her in the passenger seat. Leaving Dalton and Keira to settle themselves into the luxurious interior of the rear. But Keira took none of it in. All she cared about was Dalton. The fact he was sitting beside her, warm and solid and strong. She drew in a deep breath. Then another. She was alive. And so was Dalton. At the moment, that was all that mattered.

CHAPTER TWENTY-TWO

Dalton watched Keira, who sat on the edge of his hospital bed, staring out the darkened window into the night. Her red dress was torn and muddy, but she didn't seem to have noticed. He took the opportunity to study her profile. She looked a little lost, waif-like even, her dark-auburn hair mussed and untidy, her face pale and eyes sunken. The white bandage on her forearm stood out starkly against her buttery, tanned skin. But even with all that, she really was a beautiful woman, and his heart began to thud in his chest at the sight of her. At the thought that he might've lost her.

But his reaction was no longer surprising to him. Over the past few days and hours, he'd come to accept that Keira meant something to him. She'd taken over a place in his heart, filled a corner he once thought empty and bleak, and lit a flame of passion and intimacy in the darkness. He wasn't ready to call it love. Not yet. It'd take a while for his head to catch up with his heart and admit that. But the feeling was strong and tender, staunch and indefatigable. And it wasn't going anywhere.

Keira was one mixed-up woman, who'd need a lot of support over the coming months; years perhaps. To get over the death of her husband. She'd been married to him for ten years, and even though she refused to accept his death would have any impact on her—she said all she felt was relief he was no longer around—he knew better. She'd need to process it all. And she'd also need to process her abduction by Yoshio, as well as the effect his abuse, inflicted over the past few years, had had on her.

Dalton cast a glance at the door of his hospital room, where he could see the back of the policeman's head. There was a twenty-four-hour guard on his door, and neither of them was allowed to leave. But Dalton was sure they'd be able to sort this all out soon. It was now after midnight, and he was tired, but sleep wasn't on his agenda at the moment.

They'd driven straight to the hospital in Hilo. As they'd all tumbled out of the black sedan and into the Emergency Department, Dalton had called Captain Chin and told him what'd happened. Told him to come and get the trash out of the trunk of the car. Dalton wasn't even sure if the Yakuza leader was still alive, but he didn't give a damn. All hell had broken lose when the police arrived at the hospital. They'd tried to arrest Keira, because she was still on their wanted list. Until Dalton had pulled Joe Chin aside, took his phone from his pocket and played back the recorded conversation with Yoshio at the lava's edge. The one where he admitted to murdering the call girl.

So, Joe Chin had agreed to Dalton's request that they not frog-march her down to the local station, but instead get her statement at the hospital. Then later, if they needed to interview her again after they'd all been patched up and had some sleep, she could go back into the station for more interviews.

He'd also asked Joe to go and check on Flora and his son, and the Captain had dispatched an officer straightaway. About an hour ago, Joe reported back to him that, while quietly furious, Flora was happy to learn she and Tavi could return home safely now. It was as if the last of the great weight had finally lifted from his shoulders.

"Penny for your thoughts," he said softly.

Keira started, almost as if she'd forgotten he was there.

"Oh, lots of things. And nothing, really. You know." She smiled, but it never made it to her eyes. "I'm worried about Sierra. And Reed. They've been gone a long time."

Joe Chin was taking both their statements downstairs in a room he'd appropriated from the hospital staff and turned into his makeshift interview room. They'd wanted to take Reed first, but Sierra insisted she go with him, even if it meant she had to wait in the corridor outside until it was her turn.

"They shouldn't be too much longer," he said, in what he hoped was a comforting voice. "Come sit up here." He patted the bed beside him.

"What about your arm?" He had lied when he'd told her it was just a graze back at the house. The bullet had entered his bicep, nicked the bone, and come out the other side. But it was as clean a wound as any, if you were going to get shot. They'd x-rayed him, then stitched it up, and now he was on a drip, being pumped full of antibiotics and pain meds. The hospital wanted to keep him in overnight, at the very least.

"It's all good, can't feel a thing right now." He tapped the sling that was supposed to keep his arm immobilized with his good hand.

She slid up the bed until she nestled in the crook of his good shoulder, and gave a heartfelt sigh as she snuggled in close. "This is nice," she conceded.

He pulled her in tighter to his body. "Yes, it is." He laid his chin on the top of her head, and they stayed like that for many silent minutes, enjoying each other's company and comfort.

"I was really scared, Dalton," she finally whispered. Her

voice was so small and lonely, he almost didn't hear her.

"So was I," he admitted. "I was terrified I wasn't going to get to you in time." Even though it was uncomfortable to use his injured arm, he put his fingers under her chin and gently tipped her head up, so he could see her eyes. "And I want you to know how much it destroyed me to watch you walk away from me. That was the hardest thing I've ever done, Keira. I'm so sorry."

"I wouldn't have expected anything else," she replied. "And I'm the one who is sorry. You should never have been put in that situation in the first place." Something flittered through her eyes, but was gone again in a second. "I can admit it now, a tiny part of me wanted you to choose me, wanted you to turn around and drive right out of there, to safety. But when I thought about it, really thought about it, I realized you wouldn't be the man I've come to know if you did. You had every right to put your son before me, and I respect you more for that. You're a dedicated father, who would give his life for his boy, and that means more to me than anything else. It proves your strength of character, your devotion, that you love your son unconditionally. And I like that. I like that you're that kind of man. I like it a lot."

He studied her for seconds on end, wondering which part he should answer first. Finally, he said, "Thank you, I appreciate it." He lifted a finger and stroked it down her cheek, ignoring the twinge in his arm. "I did wonder if handing you over to Yoshio would wreck any chance we might've had to…" He stopped, unsure of how to go on. He had no idea where this thing between them might be headed. All they really had was one night together, and a few intense days spent in each other's company. But he knew he wanted more. How to phrase it, though? In the end he settled on, "… see where this might go."

Her chocolate eyes were fixed on his, and he noticed a few

tiny flecks of gold he hadn't seen before, almost as if her eyes were full of tiny fireflies, alight from within.

"No, it hasn't changed how I feel about you. If anything, it's made my feelings stronger. But…" She bit her lip. "So much has happened over the past few days I'm not really sure what those feelings mean. I do like your idea, though. About seeing where this *thing* leads us."

"Deal." He couldn't help himself; he dipped his head and let his lips meet hers. It was a gentle kiss, full of promise and potential. But soon she was pushing her body closer to his, her mouth clamoring for more. Heat rushed from his chest and pooled in his groin. One thing was for sure, they certainly had plenty of chemistry. His body reacted to hers immediately, and, as his hand roamed over the soft skin of her bare shoulder, he had to stop himself from slipping the strap down, from dipping his head lower, so he could taste her collarbone. Holy crap, he wanted to take her, right here in this hospital bed. He lightly kissed her Wonder Woman tattoo instead, letting his lips rest against her warm skin.

Dalton heard raised voices outside, and it finally brought him back to his senses. He smiled and brushed a thumb across her bottom lip.

"I think someone's coming," he said softly.

"Oh. Oh God." She pulled back and tried to rearrange her dress. "Is it Reed and Sierra back from their interviews?"

"I don't know—" Dalton was interrupted as the door opened, and he looked up in time to see Sam Mano stride through the door.

"That cop wasn't going to let me in," Sam said, by way of introduction. Dalton tensed. He wasn't sure how much Sam knew about the whole Cane thing. And whose side he might be on when the story came out. Keira must've felt him brace, because she moved away, dangling her feet over the edge of the bed, but not getting off completely, one hand laid protectively on his thigh.

"Well, we are sort of under house arrest at the moment," Dalton countered warily.

"Yes, I can see that. I had to show that cop my bounty certification before he'd agree to let me in." Sam nodded his head toward the door, and Dalton saw the cop on guard staring in at them suspiciously. Sam was one tough-looking dude, especially with those wicked scars on his face, so Dalton didn't really blame him.

"This is Keira," Dalton said, still trying to gauge Sam's mood. His boss's normally jovial face showed no sign of anger or antagonism. Showed no sign that he was about to launch himself at Dalton and beat him senseless for getting Cane mixed up in all this business. "Keira, this is Sam, my boss and Cane's father."

"Nice to meet you." Sam extended his hand and Keira took it, giving him a tentative smile.

"So, you're the woman of the moment, huh?"

"I guess so," she replied. Dalton had no way to convey the message, but he hoped she'd keep quiet about everything that'd happened, at least until he could sort out what Sam knew.

Sam pulled the only chair in the room up close to Dalton's bed and sat down, his genial smile disappearing, replaced by a serious gaze. "I'm here to apologize to you both."

Dalton opened his mouth to speak, but Sam held up his hand. "No, let me finish first, please."

Dalton nodded and Keira stared at him, eyes wide and curious.

"I want to apologize for my son. I thought I raised him with good morals, to be a loyal and trustworthy man. So, I still can't believe what I'm hearing from the rumor mill and the cops. That he sold you out. I'm so sorry, Dalton. If I ever get my hands on that boy…"

"You haven't seen him?"

"No." Sam's eyes were sad. "But I think he would know my stance. If he has any sense, he'll stay well away from me. If he doesn't want a beating, that is."

Dalton wanted to believe Sam. He'd always been genuine in everything he'd done and said. But then Dalton had also thought the same about Cane. People did out-of-character things when large amounts of money were involved. Greed arrived in all different forms and incarnations, turning a normally reasonable person into a selfish one. And people often justified their actions with a need—real or imagined—to vindicate themselves. Dalton was just so mad at himself for missing the signs with Cane.

"The police won't tell me anything. They say they're trying to locate him, and that's all they'll give me." Sam went on, his gaze drifting out the window. "Alani is frantic, as you may well imagine."

Dalton nodded. He truly felt sorry for Cane's wife. And his two young kids. Keira, who'd been sitting quietly on the bed the whole time, stirred. The mention of Cane's wife and kids must've given her cause for concern, because her brow furrowed lightly. But she followed Dalton's lead and held her tongue.

"I'm sorry I can't tell you more, Sam. All we know for sure is that he hit one of us over the head and escaped into the night." Dalton didn't add that by that stage the lava had been very close. But surely Cane wouldn't have been stupid enough to run towards the deadly eruption. Cane was very good at taking care of himself, he'd proven that time and time again when they'd been in the field together, hunting bail jumpers. No, Dalton was almost sure Cane had survived, had disappeared into the jungle and was probably trying to find a way off the island even now. He felt sorry for the man who'd once been his friend. He wondered what he'd been planning to do with that money. Two-hundred-thousand dollars was a lot of cash. And if Cane's plan had worked, both he and Keira would be dead by now, and Cane would be home free. No one would've suspected a thing. Cane would be able to spend up big on himself and his family. But Yoshio had changed the game by abducting Flora and Tavi. Cane would've known by that stage, Dalton would never let him get away with this, once he found out.

So yes, all things considered, Cane was better off fleeing the island. Because if Dalton ever found him…

A few satisfying images of exactly what he might to do to Cane if he caught him flashed through his mind. But then Keira's warm hand on his thigh brought him back to reality. Reminded him she was what mattered now.

"Anyway," Sam said brightly, "I wanted to come and see you myself, to apologize for my son's misdeeds and let you know that I hold no hard feelings."

Dalton grunted. All that'd gone down in the past few hours had been Cane's fault; not his. It was good Sam could acknowledge this.

"And to let you know that your job's still there, when you want to come back."

Dalton raised an eyebrow. He hadn't really thought past anything but getting out of this hospital, if the truth be known. Would he be going back to the bail bond company? It was a question he couldn't answer right now.

"Thanks, Sam. That's good to know."

Sam reached over and shook Dalton's hand. "I'll leave you to it," he said, and Dalton caught Sam's brief curious glance toward Keira, before he opened the door. "See you soon." Then the door closed behind him.

"Was he here just to see if you knew where Cane was?" Keira's astute question caught him off guard.

"I'm not sure," he answered truthfully. "But I'd like to

think not. Sam has always been upstanding and dependable. Everything by the letter of the law with him. I feel sorry for him," Dalton continued. "I mean, I'm repulsed by Cane and what he's done; what he was capable of. But Sam's his father, he must be feeling a whole lot more than that."

"Hmm," she murmured. "Probably betrayed and tortured, anxious for his son, but also furious at him at the same time."

"Yes, probably all of those and more," he replied.

"Are you going back to work for Sam? I mean when your arm is better and everything?" There was a tightness around her eyes that betrayed her feelings more than words could. She was worried about him. Worried about what would happen if Cane did ever reappear, how Sam might react.

"I haven't had a lot of time to give it any thought," Dalton admitted. "But there have been a few wild ideas going around in my head lately. Not just today, either. I've been thinking about this for a while. Even though Sam is a great guy, and even when I thought Cane was a good guy, too, I'd been contemplating branching out on my own."

Keira nodded, her eyes interested and discerning.

"I've been doing a degree to help me become a private detective. I've still got two more years to go. But I've also got a bit of money set aside. Plus, I get a nice little income from the antique shop, that'd be enough to keep me going for the next few years. Especially if I build the business up, like I've been planning for a while." Dalton stopped talking, suddenly thinking he needed to take Keira in and show her his shop, soon. With her artistic eye, he knew she'd appreciate the beauty and history of the furniture he sold. Then an idea suddenly hit him. Perhaps he could set aside a little corner of his shop for her to showcase her jewelry, if she wanted to move away from the shop John had set up for her, that was. It was an interesting idea, but he wouldn't mention it now, it was way too soon. But the idea was already growing on him.

"So, my answer to your question is, I don't know yet. But don't be surprised if I quit the bail jumping business sooner rather than later."

She smiled, one of her gorgeous smiles that showed off her beautiful white teeth and made his heart trip in his chest.

"Come back here," he said, tugging on the back of her dress. She complied, snuggling up under his arm once more.

He'd just started kissing her delectable lips again, when more voices started up outside the door, and Sierra and Reed walked in.

Sierra stopped short when she caught sight of the two of them on the bed together.

"Oh…umm, sorry." She seemed flustered for a second.

Until Reed said, "Good to see you're both feeling better." He had a large grin on his face, and then he winked at Dalton, who grimaced back at him.

Keira disentangled herself from Dalton's arms and went over to her sister, giving her a big hug. "I'm glad you're finally back. I've been worried about you."

"So I see," Sierra replied, but her sarcasm wasn't lost on anyone.

"Tell me what happened?" Keira appealed. "What did the police say?"

Keira came back to stand at Dalton's bedside and Sierra came with her, while Reed took the chair Sam had so recently vacated.

"That Captain of yours took a fair bit of convincing," Sierra started. "I'm glad we told him who we were when we first arrived on this island, otherwise I'm not sure he'd have believed our tale."

"Yes, well, I think handing over the Yakuza gang leader might've sweetened him up a little," said Reed with a grin.

"Do you think he believes us? Believes me?" asked Keira.

"I think he's coming around," Sierra said, laying a

comforting hand on her sister's shoulder.

Much to Dalton's surprise, Keira gave a little hiccupping gulp, and then there were tears shining in her eyes. "I can't tell you how much it means to me. That you're here. That you came to help me."

It looked like Sierra was as surprised by Keira's sudden emotion as he was. She raised her eyebrows and turned towards Keira. "Of course I came, you big dummy. That's what family is for. Come here," she said, pulling her big sister into another hug.

It wasn't long before both of them were sniffling in unison and Reed cast a look over the top of the women's heads that was full of affectionate amusement.

"Anyway, you might have to repay the favor soon," Sierra said, swiping at her eyes.

"What do you mean?" Keira asked, taking the tissue Dalton offered her from his nightstand and blowing her nose.

"I mean I still haven't heard from Logan. Have you?"

Keira straightened and pursed her lips. "No, I haven't, not for months and months, but that's not usual for Logan. Plus, I admit I've been avoiding both of you, and mum, for a while now." She had the grace to look sheepish as she said this.

"Well, I've been trying to track him down and he seems to have disappeared off the face of the Earth. It was one of the many reasons we came to see you. Mainly to make sure you were okay, but also to see if you wanted to come on a trip to the Caribbean with us."

"Wow," Keira mouthed. "I mean, sure. Of course, if you think he's really in trouble."

"I don't know what to think. But then again, I wasn't expecting you to be caught up with the Japanese Mafia when we came here, either." Sierra frowned at her sister.

"Fair enough," Keira said, with only half a smile.

"But that's in the future sometime," Reed butted in,

coming over and draping his arm around Sierra's shoulders. "Right now, we're going back to our hotel for a shower and a hot meal. I'm sure the Captain will have plenty more questions for us tomorrow. And then, it's time for bed," he finished, dropping his head and letting his lips graze Sierra's ear. She smiled up at him, a smile so full of adoration and warmth, Dalton had to look away. It was an intimate moment, and it reminded him what he'd been missing out on for so long. What he could perhaps have with Keira. If he let it grow.

CHAPTER TWENTY-THREE

The colors of the sunset reminded Keira of a flock of wheeling *galahs*. The Aussie parrots were known for their raucous sense of humor, and their gorgeous pink-and-gray coloring. The sky was losing the last of its pigment, the ragged mountains fading to dark gray, while the few puffball clouds were blushing a beautiful rosy hue.

"I could watch this every night for the rest of my life and never get tired of it," she sighed. Then she took a sip from her glass of chilled chardonnay and gave another, even more heartfelt sigh. "Pure bliss. I love Hawaii."

"I'm glad you appreciate my view," Dalton replied. But when she glanced over, he wasn't looking at the sunset, he was watching her over the top of his own wine glass with those dark and dangerous eyes. They were sitting on the lanai in the beautiful, comfy, cane chairs she'd admired on that very first day when Dalton had found her hiding in his shed. Spike stirred under the small table, glanced up at her with one eye, and then promptly went back to sleep.

Dalton still liked to wear all black, but his choice of clothing had grown on her. She liked how sexy and mysterious he looked in his bicep-hugging T-shirt and thigh-hugging jeans. She ran her admiring gaze over his broad shoulders and down the chiseled pecs the shirt did nothing to hide.

"Yes, I do appreciate the view." She gave him a slow, sexy smile. And took another sip of her wine, waiting.

"Keep that up, and we might have to appreciate the view from the inside of the bedroom." His voice took on a husky tone, one that set the hairs all over her body to tingling. But there were other things on her mind, things that needed to be decided, sorted out first. They couldn't keep living like this forever, however nice the arrangement was. Her life was on hold right now, and she needed to make some resolutions.

She'd been staying at Dalton's for the past two weeks. Back at the hospital, on the night they'd spent huddled together on his thin bed, he'd offered her a room in his house, a place to stay until she got back on her feet. No strings attached, he'd said. And she'd accepted his offer, but they both knew she wouldn't be sleeping in the spare room. Fran said there was always a room for her if she wanted to come back—actually, Fran would've been ecstatic to have her roomie back—and Keira thought fleetingly perhaps she should, it might be like old times all over again. But she wanted to be near Dalton, his pull was almost a physical force. In his arms was where she felt safest. And so, she'd given in to her heart.

She had to start the conversation somewhere, so she said, "Sierra texted me earlier. They landed safely in Adelaide. They'll stay with Mum tonight, and head back to Kangaroo Island tomorrow."

Sierra and Reed had finally left yesterday. Flown home to report to their mother. Sierra hadn't been looking forward to that part, and said it was most unfair Keira was leaving her to do it on her own. But both of them knew she needed more time on the Big Island to sort herself out. And anyway, Keira had phoned her mum nearly every day for the past two weeks, to satisfy her guilt and make up for all the many months she hadn't spoken to her.

"It was nice to have them here," Dalton said in his syrupy voice. "But it's also nice to have the place to ourselves again." Dalton had selflessly offered his spare room to Sierra and Reed, so they could stay on for another two weeks and not have to pay exorbitant hotel prices, and to put Sierra's mind at ease that Keira really was okay.

"Yes, my sister can be a little...shall we say...intense, sometimes." Keira laughed. She loved her sister, but she hadn't become a journalist for no reason. She was good at delving into people's secrets. "But it's nice that you and Reed seemed to get on."

"Yeah, he's a great guy. And a good man for your sister. She picked a fine one, there." Dalton raised his glass a little higher in a salute to Reed. The two men had become friends over the past weeks, finding a love of early-morning walks with Spike—Dalton was still taking it easy until his arm healed properly, so running had been curtailed—and an appreciation of all types of beer. They'd tasted every brand they could get their hands on. Many of their walks had been over to Dalton's Aunty Lei's house, to reassure her he really was all right, and to bring back some of her delicious homemade *liliko'i* butter. Dalton reported back to Keira that Aunty had given Reed her seal of approval, which made Keira laugh, but also more than a little thankful to the wise, old woman.

"My mind is still processing all that Sierra and Reed went through with that child abductor. I can't believe they both almost died." Keira placed the glass down carefully and tried to stop the worried frown forming on her forehead. Sierra had been in terrible danger, and she hadn't even known. Her guilt over being such a bad sister had grown tenfold when Sierra confided the tale a few nights after their run in with Yoshio. Her little sister had been going through hell, and she didn't have an inkling; had been wallowing in a mire of her own self-pity, instead.

"What doesn't kill you, makes you stronger. And I think that really applies to those two. Their ordeal brought them closer together," Dalton said, crossing one booted foot over his knee and leaning farther back in the chair. "And stop torturing yourself. You couldn't have known what was going on, and even if you had, what could you have done about it?"

"I know," she said, screwing her face up in mock self-disgust. They'd had this conversation many times over the past few weeks, and Keira knew it was time to let it go. "But you're right, Reed is good for Sierra. I can't wait for their wedding." The loved-up couple had already set the date for four months' time. No point in waiting, Sierra had said, they were both adults and they both knew what they wanted. It'd be autumn in Australia and the weather wouldn't be too hot, it'd be bright and perfect. It'd mean Keira would have to go home, and even though she didn't feel ready yet, it might be a good thing.

The past few weeks had been a rollercoaster of emotions. Keira had been so sure she wouldn't mourn John's death. That she was glad to be rid of him. But her subconscious had other plans, and she often found herself sobbing for no particular reason, at the drop of a hat. It took both Sierra nagging her and Dalton gently prodding her, before she finally agreed to go and see a counsellor, to help her sort through her raging emotions. The counsellor quietly warned her this wouldn't be an easy process. She said marriages were complicated things at the best of times, there were good times and bad in every single one. And even Keira knew her emotions were all tangled up in her relationship with John; it was going to take time and patience to untangle all those hooks and barbs he'd buried deep into her psyche. The best part about counseling, however, was the way she'd helped

Keira to begin the process of forgiving herself. And perhaps even forgiving John, but that might take a while longer than even the counsellor imagined. She wasn't feeling very magnanimous right now.

John's sister had phoned her the other night. She screamed at Keira down the line, hurling all kinds of accusations and excuses, not able to believe all the horrible things they were saying about John. Keira had let her rant and rage, listened to how devastated his mother was about his death and how she didn't think she could go on without her only son. Keira was truly sorry for their loss; they'd been blindsided by his death, and it wasn't their fault he was a reprobate. They were going to hold a memorial for John on O'ahu, and Keira was most definitely *not* invited. Which didn't bother her nearly as much as it should.

"It looks like you might be going on a trip to the Caribbean before the wedding, though," Dalton said thoughtfully, bringing Keira back to the present.

Keira only nodded. Nothing had been organized yet, but Sierra was keen to start searching for their younger brother, sooner rather than later. They both knew Keira needed more time to recover from her ordeal, but she didn't doubt Sierra would start to subtly put the pressure on, perhaps even begin booking some flights. Sierra had already been using her investigative skills to try and track him down. She had a few leads, but none of them had yet uncovered their wayward brother.

Keira sighed. Logan had always been the wildest one of the family. Being the only boy, she guessed it came with the territory, especially because he was a lot younger than both his sisters. On the surface, it might appear that Logan was a lot more like Keira than Sierra, as they both shared a need to see the world that'd driven them away from their home, while Sierra stayed. But as kids, all three of them had been highly curious, and now Keira could see that Sierra's curiosity had emerged as something different, that was all, turning her into a journalist rather than a questing gypsy. It'd be good to see Logan again. She could hardly believe it'd been nearly four years since she'd last seen him in the flesh, when they'd all met up in Adelaide at a family gathering.

"At least Stacy got the scoop she was looking for," Dalton said, breaking into Keira's musing.

"Yes, I think if you could say there was a winner out of all of this, then Stacy would be it," Keira agreed. Stacy had contacted Sierra the day after the shootout. She and Sierra had spent days working on a joint project, and had been able to negotiate a major journalistic coup, where both the newspapers they worked for agreed to run simultaneous articles on the truth about the Yakuza in Hawaii, and how the capture of one of the kingpins of the syndicate had broken the back of a money laundering operation.

"And hopefully Yoshio is the big loser," Dalton said darkly.

"Well, your buddy Captain Chin seems to think that if he's got anything to do with it, Yoshio will be going to jail for a very long time."

When the police had arrived at Yoshio's house in Nanawale Estate, the lava had surprisingly spared the property, even though it'd swallowed up five other houses farther down the road. All the evidence from Keira and Dalton's escapades had been left untouched, which helped to corroborate their story. The two dead guards were taken away, but there was still no sign of Cane. The police managed to track down, Amida, one of Yoshio's guards they'd allowed to escape, as he tried to hop a plane off the island. And with an offer of indemnity on the table, he'd finally opened up, being quite enlightening into the inner workings of Yoshio's corrupt dealings.

She and Dalton sat in silence for a few minutes, both

thinking about Yoshio and the effect he'd had on their lives. Dusk faded to night, the dark settling around them like a soft blanket. Sounds of night insects seemed to get louder as the sun disappeared, and Keira listened to their happy chirruping, feeling somehow soothed by the sound. A light from inside filtered through the window, throwing its soft rays on to the table and sparkling off the rims of their glasses. In some ways, Keira should be grateful to Yoshio. He had brought her and Dalton together, after all. But he'd also left terrible scars on her, mental scars that'd take time to heal. But when she was with Dalton, the memories of Yoshio's abuse faded. Making love with Dalton was nothing like the thing Yoshio, or even John, had liked to call sex. He was gentle and giving, coaxing her to discover herself again, making her want things she never thought possible.

It wasn't just the emotional support Dalton was offering. A few days ago, he'd finally taken her in to see his little antique shop in town. And she'd instantly fallen in love with the eclectic style of the shop, the mixture of rare, old, Victorian-era pieces, interspaced with some equally rare, but so totally different, old Hawaiian pieces. He'd left her to poke around the store on her own while he went to talk to his sales lady. But just as they were about to leave, Dalton had dropped a bombshell, by quietly suggesting he'd been meaning to set up a small jewelry display in one corner of the shop, to help entice the tourists in. And he'd love to show off her jewelry, if she wanted to. Keira was still thinking about it. Partly because it'd take a while for her to get her business back up and running. She'd lost everything, all her tools, supplies, all her stock of semi-precious stones and silver, in the lava flow. But maybe it was a good thing she was making a clean start. And also, partly because a bit of her didn't want to be so reliant on Dalton. She was reminded of how John had *helped* her to get her jewelry business off the ground, by plowing his money into it. Saying it was the least he could do. But with John, there'd been strings attached to that money. And she'd found out the hard way how he expected her to pay him back.

But Dalton was different. He would never hold anything over her. There were no strings attached to Dalton's affection. So maybe she would say yes to his proposition. Tomorrow. She'd tell him tomorrow. Tonight, she had other things on her mind.

Keira slipped her sandal off one foot, and lifted her toes so they rubbed gently up against his inner thigh.

"So…"

"So…?" he countered.

"I was wondering…" She rubbed her foot higher, gently back and forth, back and forth.

"Yes." The light coming through the window was just enough for her to make out Dalton's face, see his square cheekbones and stubble-roughened chin. And enough for her to see his eyes darken with desire.

Her foot worked its way higher, until it was resting in his crotch and she could feel the growing bulge beneath his zipper.

"I quite liked your suggestion. The one where we admired the view of the ceiling in your bedroom." She gave him that slow, sexy smile again. Only this time she really meant it. "And now that we finally have the house to ourselves…"

It didn't take long. He was out of his chair and around to scoop her up into his arms in the blink of an eye. She gave a girly squeal of delight.

Spike scrambled up and began to wag his tail, excited that something was finally happening.

"Out of my way," Dalton growled at the dog, who gave the doggy equivalent of a frown.

But Keira didn't have time to feel sorry for him as she

clung to Dalton's neck, breathing in his scent, that smoky aroma with a hint of his cologne and a good dose of manliness.

He carried her inside, and in two strides was down the corridor, maneuvering her in through the door to his bedroom, and then nearly tripped over the metal box at the end of the bed. It was the box of George's books. Reed had helped Dalton trek up to the hut and retrieve them a few days ago. The red journal was in there, as well. Dalton hadn't read it, yet, but told her he was working up to it. Keira had given it to him a few nights after the shooting, and had been suitably surprised when, instead of throwing it out of the nearest window as she'd predicted, he gently took it from her hand and said perhaps it was time he found out the whole truth about his father. At least then, he could make a balanced judgement on his character. It looked like they were both going to be doing some soul-searching in the near future.

Negotiating his way around the box, Dalton placed her on the end of his large bed and then stood back and began to undo his jeans.

"In a bit of a hurry, are we cowboy?" she teased.

"In a hurry to get naked and lie next to you, yes. But we've got all night to take things slow, if that's what you want." His words nearly melted her soul, and she was tugging at the hem of her T-shirt, pulling it over her head in one swift move. Then she wriggled out of her cut-off jeans, not taking her eyes off him as he also pulled his shirt over his head, revealing all that warm, butterscotch skin and rippling muscles she couldn't get enough of. The white bandage around his bicep was a reminder of how close they'd both come to not being here, not experiencing this moment. Her own bandaged arm was on the mend, as well. But Keira pushed the thought away; now was not the time for wallowing in guilt or regret. Then Dalton was lowering himself onto the bed, covering her naked body with his. Keira shivered as his hardened stomach slid over the top of hers, brushing against her belly ring, his chest gently sweeping her nipples as he settled over her.

"Ah, that's better," he sighed. "I've been thinking about this all day. Of being here with you." He balanced above her, resting his weight on both elbows, and stared down into her eyes, his face becoming suddenly serious.

She held her breath as she savored his long, lean body melding into hers. She didn't say it, but she'd been thinking the exact same thing. This was the most perfect place to be, feeling his body, warm and alive entwined with hers. She reached up to touch her lips to his, but he pulled back, that earnest little frown still wrinkling his brow. She stilled, bracing for something…exactly what, she wasn't sure, but her heart hitched in her chest.

"Stay with me, Keira. Here, I mean. Stay here in my house with me. We're good together."

Okay, that was a little unexpected. But truth be known, she'd been thinking along the same lines, perhaps even subconsciously hoping he might suggest it. But should she do it? She still wasn't sure she could name what it was she felt for Dalton. Would it be fair on him? On them?

She drew in a deep breath, unsure of how to answer, but he continued to speak, almost as if he needed to get the words out fast.

"I'm not asking you for a commitment, I know it's too early for that yet. But you do something to me, Keira. You're the proof that I need. The proof I can indeed fall in love." He pursed his lips and frowned again. What was he saying? "It's been so long, I thought perhaps I was incapable of it."

It took her a few seconds to process his words. "Are you saying what I think you're saying?"

"What? That I might be falling in love with you?"

"Mmhmm," she replied, not trusting herself to speak. That

was exactly what she meant. But she needed him to say the words. Only because it'd help her deal with the idea better. Was it true? Did she want it to be true? The counsellor might tell her it was all too soon, that it was happening too fast. But Keira had known right from the very first time she'd set eyes on him, Dalton was an exceptional man. And he did exceptional things to her heart. And body.

His dark eyes never left her face, never wavered. "The answer is yes, Keira. But only if you're ready to hear it. Otherwise, I'll keep those words to myself. Until you *are* ready."

Keira considered him. Considered his strong arms wrapped around her body. Considered the way he looked at her, with no expectation, no condemnation. Considered the way he'd put his whole life on hold in the blink of an eye to help her, even when he didn't know who she was. She adored everything about Dalton. Respected what he stood for; that he loved his son unconditionally.

"I think I am ready," she said finally. He stared down at her, a leisurely grin spreading on his face. "So..." she said slowly.

"So what?"

"Are you going to say it?"

"I'm falling in love with you, Keira."

Her whole body shuddered at his words. Whether it was with fear or exultation, she couldn't decide; the two emotions were so entwined. He'd said the words she'd feared, but also the words she so desperately wanted. And her whole world hadn't come tumbling down. Instead, her heart fluttered like a hundred butterflies were trying to beat their way out. It felt so right.

But there were still obstacles in their way, things that worried her. "What about Tavi and Flora?"

"What about them?" He said, cocking his head to one side

to contemplate her.

"I wouldn't want to get in the way. To change things."

"You've met Tavi, he loves you already."

Which was true. Flora had brought the little boy out to Dalton's farmhouse the day after they were released from hospital. He'd been asking to see his father. Had been worried about him. Even though he was little and didn't really understand that he and Flora had been held as hostages by the *bad men*, he still fretted after Dalton. Had run in to his arms, yelling, *Daddy, Daddy*, leaping at Dalton so he had to catch him mid-air, wincing at the strain on his injured arm. It was so sweet and yet so heartbreaking, Keira had found tears welling in her eyes. Of course, Dalton had done the right thing, rescuing his son. It was the only path to take.

Keira had never been really good with children, but after Tavi finished hugging Dalton, and put him back on the ground, the little boy made his way over to her, his face very serious. "Pretty lady," he said, and reached his arms in the air to be lifted up. "The bad men hurt you?" he'd asked. She could hardly believe it, but he must've remembered her from the night they did the hostage swap. That he could perceive she'd been in danger, that he'd been worried about her, made her hug him even tighter.

"No, honey, I'm fine," she said.

They'd met three times since then, and each time, she'd fallen a little bit more in love with the cute toddler.

"And Flora...well, she's still not all that happy with me, but she'll come around. We both knew we'd each find someone else, eventually. We can still make this work. Nothing will change, we can still have Tavi come and stay on weekends."

He made it sound so easy.

Was it that easy?

For so long, Keira had learned to keep her true feelings

hidden. Keep them silent. Not let anyone into the true heart of herself. Ashamed of how she allowed herself to be used by John. And by those other men. Especially Yoshio. But in her short time with Dalton, she was learning it was safe to let her emotions out. His warmth and caring, his sensitivity towards her wants and needs, the way he made her feel like she was special. Worthwhile. Valuable. Significant. But it wasn't just in their lovemaking that he made her feel good. It was in the everyday, small things that seemed insignificant at the time, but when Keira added them all up, they were the things that showed Dalton's true intentions towards her. Like the way he held the door open for her to walk through first. The way he tenderly wiped the trickle of ice-cream that'd run down her chin away with his thumb. The way he let her drive his new, stick-shift truck, without any comment on how many times she crunched the gears. The way he hugged his son, like nothing else mattered in the entire world; and then how he beckoned for her to join them in an intimate, giggling, cuddle. But most of all, it was in the way he stood back and let her make her own decisions. Trusting she knew what was best for her. Not controlling, but supporting her resolution.

Tiny cracks in the shield she'd erected around her soul were getting bigger every day. And soon those cracks would become so wide, the whole barrier would come tumbling down, leaving her heart naked and exposed. And she knew when that happened, she'd finally let Dalton in. Let him see the real her.

It wouldn't be easy, she decided. It would be damn hard. But he was worth it. She was worth it. No more keeping silent. From now on she was going to speak her feelings.

"Yes, I will stay with you," she said finally, and his arms tightened a little around her. "Because I think I might be falling in love with you, too."

He dropped his head and nuzzled her neck, not saying

anything for such a long time that Keira became worried. At last, he lifted his head and met her gaze. His dark eyes were intense and shone with a depth of passion she'd never encountered before. "That's good. You don't know how glad I am to hear that."

"But it won't be effortless," she said, part of her still wanting to protect herself; protect him. "I'm not the easiest person in the world to live with."

"Oh, believe me, I know," Dalton drawled. "You come with a bucketload of baggage, I realize that." The gentle tone with which he said this took the sting out of his words. "And this might surprise you, but I'm not the easiest person to live with, either." Dalton moved his body sideways, leaning on his good arm and leaving his injured one draped over her belly.

"I think I'll manage," she said, giving him a playful nip on the shoulder. "Spike and I can always move down to the machinery shed, if you become unbearable."

"You know what, I think my dog would turn traitor if it came to it. I think he loves you more than me." Dalton grinned. They both knew that wasn't true. Spike would always be Dalton's dog, but he was developing a soft spot for Keira, and would often lie at her feet when they were sitting at the table, or stay protectively by her side if they went for a stroll around the farm.

Dalton's hand ran lightly up the side of her torso, then his fingers fanned around the swell of her breast and she forgot all about Spike as she sucked in a sharp breath. He stroked over her nipple, once, twice, and her whole body suddenly came alive. His lips came down to meet hers, but there was an urgency in the demanding way he covered her mouth, and his stroking became more determined. And she knew with all her heart, this was the man for her. The man she'd always been destined to find. As her heart soared, she felt lighter than air and knew that his love would free her. She would never be bound by silence again.

If you liked Bound by Silence and want to hear more about Kiera, Dalton, Sierra and Reed, then you might like

Bound by Truth

Bound by the Stars

The books in this series can be read as stand-alone novels, but are enhanced if you read them together.

Connect with the Author

I really hope you enjoyed reading Bound by Silence. For more action romance info, upcoming release dates, and access to free books join the exclusive Suzanne Cass reader club. As an added bonus, you'll get a copy of my FREE STORY.

Solar Flare

http://www.suzannecass.com/contact/

Or you can stay in touch via my website
www.suzannecass.com

Facebook: www.facebook.com/suzannecassauthor/
Instagram: www.instagram.com/suzanne.cass/
Pintrest: www.pinterest.com.au/suzanne_cass/
Twitter: twitter.com/SusieCass1

Also by Suzanne Cass
NEW
Stormcloud Station Series
(A Stargazer Spinoff Series)
Small Town Romantic Suspense
Clear Skies
Starlit Skies
Crystal Skies

Stargazer Ranch Romance Series
Small Town Romantic Suspense
Combustion: Prequel Novella
Wildfire
Firelight
Snowbound: A Christmas Novella
Snowfall
Cloudburst

Island Bound Series
Mystery Romance (on an Island)
Books can be read as stand-alone
Bound by Truth
Bound by Silence
Bound by the Stars

Colors of the Earth Series
Small Town Romantic Suspense
Books can be read as stand-alone
Shadows in the Dust
Shadows in Deep Blue
Shadows of Red Earth

Romantic Suspense
Single Title
Island Redemption

Glass Clouds
Chasing Bullets

Love in the Mountains Novella Series
Small Town Short Romance
Novellas can be read as stand-alone
Rain on a Tin Roof
Lost and Found
Rescue his Heart

Please Leave a Review
The greatest gift you could ever give an author is to leave a review. You will be helping other people to discover this book and making a difference to me as an Independently Published Author. If you liked this book and want other people to read it to, please leave a review.

About the Author

Suzanne Cass is an Australian author who writes rural romance and romantic suspense abounding with passion and danger.

Her debut novel, Island Redemption, won the Romance Writers of Australia Emerald Award in 2016. Suzanne was also a finalist in the 2019 Romance Writers of Australia RUBY award.

She had always had a fascination with the tough resilience of people who live in our amazing red-dirt outback country. When not writing about the characters that inhabit her head, Suzanne can be found roaming the Perth beaches with her border collie, or encouraging from the sidelines as her two sons play sport.

Visit her website www.suzannecass.com or subscribe to her newsletter via: www.suzannecass.com/contact

Acknowledgements

This is the second book in an exciting new series, where each story is set on a new and intriguing island, all in different corners of the world, linked by three siblings, who follow their own journeys. I wanted this to be a global series, and what better way to do it. Bound by Silence is set on the Big Island of Hawaii. This island is on my bucket list of places to visit and I *will* get there one day. It's so dramatic and vibrant; the impossible blue of the ocean against the backdrop of verdant, green-jungle-clad mountains. Add the drama and danger of a lava eruption with a traitorous husband and you have a spicy mixture for this romantic suspense. Keira and Dalton are two strangers thrown together by fate, who must each face a heart-rending choice.

This book took a whole lot of research and planning. I learned a lot about lava flows, volcanic eruptions, the history of Hawaii and its people.

I need to thank my author tribe, and in particular Jillian and Rose. Without you gals there would be no finished manuscript. Thank you.

There is a team of people who I also couldn't do without, other beta readers (special thanks to Rebecca) and my ARC team, who are essential to an Indie Author like me. Big thanks to my editor, Tanya Saari.

To my two beautiful boys (who are soon to be gorgeous men). My husband, Gary is the support I need on the long days when I doubt myself as a writer. And my border collie, Dune, who accompanies me on all my author walks, where many of my plot twists and character quirks are dreamed up.

I am so very grateful to all the readers who have bought and enjoyed my books and who will continue to do so. Writing for you is what keeps me focused and motivated.